PENGUIN BOOKS

Napkins and Other Distractions

Writing as M.A. Wardell, LAMBDA Literary Award nominee Matt writes spicy queer rom-coms. His goal is to tell adult gay love stories with a diverse representation of flawed and damaged characters who find healing through love. Matt loves rom-coms and has always wished for better representation, so he's writing the stories he wishes existed. The queer men in his stories are flawed and messy. Helping them find their HEA is his passion. Matt lives near the ocean with his husband and cats. When he isn't writing, he's snuggling those cats, reading all the rom-coms, walking to unravel plot points, and taking long hot baths.

Also by M.A. Wardell

Teacher of the Year
Mistletoe and Mishigas
Husband of the Year

Napkins and Other Distractions

Teachers in Love: Book 3

M.A. WARDELL

PENGUIN BOOKS

PENGUIN BOOKS

UK | USA | Canada | Ireland | Australia
India | New Zealand | South Africa

Penguin Books is part of the Penguin Random House group of companies whose addresses can be found at global.penguinrandomhouse.com

Penguin Random House UK,
One Embassy Gardens, 8 Viaduct Gardens, London SW11 7BW

penguin.co.uk

First self-published by M.A. Wardell 2024
First published in the United States of America by Hachette Book Group 2025
First published in Great Britain by Penguin Books 2025

001

Copyright © M.A. Wardell, 2024

The moral right of the author has been asserted

Penguin Random House values and supports copyright.
Copyright fuels creativity, encourages diverse voices, promotes freedom of expression and supports a vibrant culture. Thank you for purchasing an authorized edition of this book and for respecting intellectual property laws by not reproducing, scanning or distributing any part of it by any means without permission. You are supporting authors and enabling Penguin Random House to continue to publish books for everyone.
No part of this book may be used or reproduced in any manner for the purpose of training artificial intelligence technologies or systems. In accordance with Article 4(3) of the DSM Directive 2019/790, Penguin Random House expressly reserves this work from the text and data mining exception

Opening and closing illustrations by Ian Leone
Interior illustrations by Mayhara Ferraz
LEGO and the LEGO logo are trademarks of the LEGO Group
Set in 12.5/14.75pt Garamond MT Std
Typeset by Six Red Marbles UK, Thetford, Norfolk
Printed and bound in Great Britain by Clays Ltd, Elcograf S.p.A.

The authorized representative in the EEA is Penguin Random House Ireland,
Morrison Chambers, 32 Nassau Street, Dublin D02 YH68

A CIP catalogue record for this book is available from the British Library

ISBN: 978-1-405-97936-8

Penguin Random House is committed to a sustainable future
for our business, our readers and our planet. This book is made from
Forest Stewardship Council® certified paper.

To my readers over forty . . . get yours.
To my readers under forty . . . the best is yet to come.

Author's Note and Content Guidance

Dear Reader,

First, thank you. For believing in my books, my characters, and the value of own voices stories. Writing Vincent and Kent's story filled me with joy, and I hope you enjoy reading about these two older, flawed, but loveable men. Their romance trajectory may look different from the ones in my first two books, but it's just as valid. These men captured my heart, and I hope you feel the same.

Napkins and Other Distractions is an open-door romance intended for mature audiences. The characters in the story are consenting adults, and there is explicit, on-page sexual content, explicit language, and adult situations.

While Vincent and Kent's love story is low angst, there are also serious issues. Here are the content warnings if you need them.

Vincent has clinical OCD (Obsessive Compulsive Disorder), which includes the subtypes of contamination/mysophobia, relationship, order/symmetry, and intrusive thoughts. There is a scene with blood (a minor scrape).

My hope is people with OCD feel seen and represented, and others will gain understanding and empathy. Through my research/interviews, one thing I've learned is OCD is not a one-size-fits-all disorder. This is Vincent's story, but everyone experiences OCD differently.

As always, if these are triggers for you, please take care of yourself.

All my best,

M. A. Wardell

I

Vincent

The pristine napkins stacked neatly on the table emit a fresh linen scent. Clean and pressed. I adjust the top one, and the soft cloth soothes my fingers as I ensure it's lined up with the one below. With each gentle nudge, the pile inches closer to perfection. Staring at the edges, my brain turns. Are they exact? Could I assemble them more precisely? My head tilts down, the familiar tunnel emerging, but thankfully, I'm interrupted.

'Vincent?'

The welcome distraction comes from a white man I'm assuming is my date. Make that hoping. I'd guess him to be about six feet, with silver hair and a beard to match. Way better looking in person than his profile pic, he's giving me Santa's-younger-brother vibes, and maybe he's my early Christmas present. He's wearing a light blue button-down shirt, and half of the front flaps loose from his khaki pants. I've heard about this trend: the French tuck. You can paint it any way you like. It's unkempt. There's something on the front of his pants. They almost look . . . frayed. But the smile on his full face, all cheeks, and maybe a dimple hiding under that scruff instantly warms my heart. His deep brown eyes shine behind red glasses, and a small smile forms on my face. One of his shoelaces dangles undone; it might be knotted, and I suddenly realize my date is more than frazzled.

'Kent?'

'Yes, it's me. Kent. I'm him. Me. Kent Lester, I mean. Gosh, I'm so sorry I'm late,' he says, shimmying out of his long dark coat and slinging it over the chair. He misses his target, and it thuds onto the dirty floor, the buttons clacking sharply against the wood.

I stand and put my hand out for a shake, and Kent takes it and pulls me into the biggest, warmest bear hug. The faint smell of a campfire wraps me in coziness as his arms gather my inch-shorter-than-his frame. The closeness tingles my skin, and I breathe in his toastiness, attempting to use my senses to shoo the uncomfortableness away.

'There you are,' he whispers into my ear. His breath dances onto my neck, sending a shiver up my spine. 'I'm a hugger.'

I am most definitely not. Especially with strangers, but it's fine. I'm fine. Everything's fine. I came last week for a dry run with Marvin Block, cute kindergarten teacher, reigning Teacher of the Year (his words, not mine), and current close friend. We first met at this very table almost a year ago. It was a classic Vincent-one-and-done date setup by SWISH.

When I first read SWISH was *'a groundbreaking queer dating app that promotes inclusivity by enabling users to chat and meet people who are looking for anything from casual friendships to serious relationships,*' I took the bait. While Marvin may not have been 'the one,' he kept his promise to stay in touch and we've developed a genuine friendship. In that regard, SWISH delivered on its promise. I've even been back to The Purple Giraffe with Marvin and his fiancé, Olan. Between the first time and now – many other unsuccessful dates, the two times I've come alone, and last week's dry run – I've been here exactly twelve times. Which makes tonight's date lucky . . . oh fuck.

'I hope that's okay,' Kent says, pulling out of the embrace, but still clutching my elbows.

'Sure, yeah, I love a friendly hug,' I fib. My skin prickles under my shirt, where his fingers still make contact. I find his eyes and they sparkle with kindness. A simple glance and he's somehow settling me. With a deep exhale, I offer a small smile and attempt to appear like a person this man might find acceptable to date. At least once. Dinner. Tonight.

After the last few SWISH matches crashed and burned, Marvin suggested we have a 'mock date' here so he could offer some tips to tweak my game. It's not my fault Jason (date five) never stopped talking, even with a full mouth. Crumbs shot across the table at me like a personal meteor shower. And then there was Mark (date eight), who took one look at my bald head and asked if I'd ever considered a hair transplant. When I didn't answer, he asked if I wanted the number of his toupee guy.

Marvin offered suggestions on managing my OCD, starting conversations, and body language, and I'm ready to implement them all. Stay open. Listen to your heart. Be brave. Take a leap for love. That, plus his encouragement to talk with my doctor about changing my medication, and I've been doing much better. Marvin is a sweetheart. He wants me to be happy.

As I take refuge in my chair, Kent, never breaking eye contact, attempts to sit, but slips on his coat, still sprawled on the floor, and almost falls off his seat.

'Are you okay?' I quickly move to assist.

'Fine. Sorry,' he stammers, catching himself on the table, 'I'm a bit disoriented, is all.'

'Take a breath. There's nothing to be anxious about,' I offer – Marvin's advice to me now attempts to soothe my date as I neatly fold and hang his coat on the back of his chair.

'Oh, I'm not nervous about, about, you. Us. This.' Kent motions erratically to the table and the small votive flickers in fear. 'It's Sweetums. My cat. He gets medication, and, well, have you ever tried to pill a cat?'

'I have not.'

'It's a bit like trying to cram a bowling ball into your pocket,' he says and lets out a loud guffaw that startles the people at the next table. 'Anyway, that's why I'm late. And, well, a bit of a mess.'

'You're fine. I was only here a few minutes.'

Kent's eyes fall on mine, and his smile returns. The whiskers in his beard prickle, but there's nothing dodgy about him.

'Thank you. Honestly, sometimes I wonder who's in charge, me or the damn cat.'

'Is he sick?' I ask, attempting to calm Kent and get our date moving along.

'Oh no. It's for his nerves.'

'You have a nervous cat?'

'Apparently. Technically, it's his tummy that's nervous, and the medicine helps.' He indicates the splotch and scratches on his pants. 'Me cramming it down his throat every other day, not so much.'

'Well, you're here now. And looking exactly like your profile pic on SWISH, I might add. I can't say that about most guys.'

'Really? I mean' – Kent runs his hands through his thick wavy hair – 'Thank you. I mean you, you . . .' He cocks his head.

'Shaved.'

'Yes, that's it.' He nods approvingly, and his lips turn up. His smile, sweet and kind, and the first hint of his teeth make my stomach flip.

'I tried the mustache and goatee for a minute,' I say, rubbing my naked chin, 'but it was hard to keep tidy. I probably should take a new profile photo.'

'No. You look, well . . .' Kent tilts his glass to take a sip of water and somehow misses his mouth. 'Cheese and rice!'

Water pours down the front of his shirt, and I'm not sure I've ever seen a more discombobulated human.

He takes a deep breath, pats his shirt with his napkin, and, with a lower voice, whispers, 'Can I be honest with you about something?'

The hairs on my neck tingle, and I need to remember to shave lower next time. We've just met, and he's already confessing.

'Of course, please.'

'My cat is only half of it.' He pulls his lips in and continues, 'I literally just installed the app. You're my first match.' A small giggle escapes his lips. 'And my first date. Since I divorced my wife. Seven years ago.'

I open my mouth, but nothing comes out.

'I'm bi. I mean, I was bi the entire time we were married. She knew. Knows. Corrine, that's my wife. Ex-wife. She's totally supportive. We're friends. Exes. But the split was amicable.'

Not that I'm keeping score, but so far, Kent is late, frazzled, rumpled, divorced, wet, has a cat with a nervous stomach, and I'm his first match on the app. This is his first date since his divorce. Seven years ago. From a woman. My fingers fondle the napkins, pushing the corners closer, tighter.

'Oh, well, that's nice,' I fumble out, tugging a loose thread on the bottom napkin. 'You're still friends with your ex. Not that you're bi.'

Kent's eyes go wide.

'I mean, that's great too. I mean for me, right?' My shoulders creep up into a feeble shrug.

Kent's friendly smile returns, and my fingers pause. The man may have a laundry list of cons, but Marvin's words replay in my head. 'Vincent, romance isn't about tallying points.'

As if on cue, knowing the awkwardness was about to explode like a suddenly active four-thousand-year-old volcano, our server Val approaches.

Portland, Maine, has more restaurants per capita than any other US city besides San Francisco, but I'm always going to end up at The Purple Giraffe. Yes, they have a clean report from the health inspector, but also, familiarity. Control. Val.

Even when I'm unable to snag my usual table, Val claims me. Since we first met, she's cut her hair, the high ponytail gone, replaced by a sharp bob that frames her pale skin. When I was here with Herbert (date four) she told me the fresh cut was part of her trying to embrace her thirties.

After my disastrous date with Marvin, I returned the next week solo. The food – a fusion of Mexican and Korean, a unique explosion of flavors in my mouth – beckoned. And I had a plan. If I kept coming back, I might become more comfortable and be able to relinquish some of my usual date rituals.

During that first return dinner, Val and I chatted. I explained and over-apologized for my OCD, and to my surprise, she was quite understanding. She always keeps a close eye on me and brings extra napkins without asking.

'How are we tonight, gentlemen?' Val asks, her familiar voice a welcome salve.

'Good, we're good,' I say, willing it into reality.

'Have you decided on drinks?'

We haven't discussed drinks. Or food.

'Kent, do you like wine?'

'Very much.' He folds his damp napkin in his lap. Maybe there's hope for us after all.

'Merlot?'

He nods, and his sweet smile, perhaps even a little goofy, prompts me.

'How about a bottle?' I say, pointing to the wine list.

Val dips her chin and raises her left eyebrow.

'Absolutely. I'll be right back with it.'

I move my hands to my lap, the promise of wine and

a small connection lulling my fingers to relax. Marvin's words replay in my head. Be in the moment. Don't dismiss outright. Sitting across from me, even in his tangled state, something about Kent intrigues me. He's clearly older, but the SWISH age ranges only told me he's 'over 40,' which technically, even though only by a few months, so am I.

Finally settled, Kent scans the restaurant. 'This place is nice.'

'Yeah, I love it. The food is fantastic.' I dab the napkin on my lap. 'Thanks for agreeing to meet here.'

'Oh please, I'd meet you anywhere,' Kent says, and his smile, soft, kind, and full of empathy, sparks something in my stomach.

'So, you're divorced. And you haven't dated in . . . seven years?' I ask.

'Honestly, no. I haven't had the courage. Corrine and I were college sweethearts, and well, I'm so out of practice. With apps and all, it's not quite the same. Back then, you went to a club. A bar. Or met at a party. You gave out your landline number, went home, and waited impatiently for your answering machine to blink.' He grabs his phone and lifts it. 'None of this nonsense. My family takes a lot of my time. And my job can be consuming, and now, well, things at work are . . .' Kent's eyes drop to his lap and his voice trails off as he bites his lower lip.

Kent's mention of work turns my thoughts to tomorrow. A fresh start for me – a new school implementation. After the last disaster, I need this one to be successful. Hopscotch, the software company I work for, gathers and analyzes data more effectively for schools. If it's rolled out correctly. This time I won't fuck it up. My OCD won't derail things. This time will be better. It has to be. My job depends on it. Bringing up work on these first dates is a convenient option, but it can be a minefield. Perhaps Kent shares this perspective.

'Kent, may I propose we don't discuss our jobs?' I suggest. 'Just for tonight.'

His eyes find mine again. Tiny lines crinkle around the edges as he grins at my offer. My heart beats a little faster. When he's not tripping, falling, or spilling, Kent's face has a warmth that's doing it for me.

'Really? You know, that sounds amazing – no shop talk. Let's get to know each other without those boring details,' he says.

'Deal.'

'Deal.'

Val returns with a tray carrying two wineglasses and a bottle. She pours the wine. I taste it, give her a single nod, and my shoulders drop as I sip. The weight of work, the stress, and the worry disappear down my throat along with the full-bodied, smooth liquid. Kent's radiating kindness, which is incredibly sexy, overshadows his scattered nature and messiness. Something about the wine and this man across from me has my head swimming, and I'm optimistic this night won't be a total disaster.

2

Kent

Did Sweetums take his pill with the enthusiasm of a lion crammed into a tiny cat carrier? Yup. Did he gag, hack, and spit up all over me? Twice. Was I worried about being late? Of course. Did I arrive discombobulated? Obviously. But that head. That bald, shiny, perfect work surface of a noggin shakes me to my core.

Vincent's photo did not do him justice. Sure, he lost the facial hair, but he doesn't need it. I can see more of his face this way. His beautiful punim. His creamy skin. Perfection. The photo was sweet. Cute. Approaching handsome. In person? Vincent is scorching hot. As my daughter would say, all the flame and chili pepper emojis.

Theo, the prickly but sweet custodian at school, assures me I'm a catch. He says anyone would be lucky to date me. For him, a certified grump, it's a massive compliment or a complete load of crap. Ruth, the PE teacher and my work wife (Corrine's words, not mine), told me guys might consider me a 'daddy.' My daughter, Gillian, is twenty-six and hasn't called me Daddy since she was in pigtails. 'Dad' suffices just lovely now. Sweetums is my kitty baby, although sometimes our relationship borders more on warden and prisoner. Theo and Ruth are the only queer people I'm close with, and I'm beyond grateful for their counsel. Seeing Vincent in person, something springs alive I haven't felt in a long time. Something primal, deep, and it knocks me off center.

Agreeing not to talk about work is the blessing I need to get through this evening without melting into a puddle of despair. My life revolves around Lear Elementary. The kids. The staff. With our test scores nose-diving, the board mandated new software to collect and report on student data. The district is spending a fortune on the rollout, and I've got until spring break to see the implementation through. That will give us the rest of the school year to show growth with the new system. I see through Hopscotch's innocent name; this is anything but good news.

'To no talk of work,' I say, lifting my glass. Vincent smiles, and his eyes sparkle. Maybe it's the prospect of being on a proper date with a man for the first time in, well, ever, but I really hope Vincent doesn't think I'm a complete dolt.

'None,' he replies, crashing his glass against mine. The force of the impact shoots an eruption of wine onto my shirt.

Vincent's eyes open wide, and he immediately sets his glass down and grabs a napkin.

'Kent, I'm so sorry.' And he's up, over, dabbing at my shirt.

'It's fine. Honestly, it was only a matter of time before I made a mess. You're simply helping me hurry things along.'

I move my hand over his, and when my fingers brush his knuckles, a warmth sparks in my hand and travels up my arm. It's been less than twenty minutes, and we've made skin-to-skin contact. Add that to the hug, and this is more intimacy than I've had in over seven years. My center simmers, and I shake my head, attempting to shoo the dizziness away.

He doesn't stop, his determination clear as he vigorously tries to remove the stubborn spot, but even I know that red wine stains are no match for a cloth napkin.

'Vincent, it's okay. Really,' I say and gently remove his hand, but keep ahold of his fingers. 'I'm good.'

He moves back to his seat, breaking our contact and biting his lower lip. And for the first time, I notice the way his eyelashes frame his eyes. Maybe it's the lack of hair on his head, but they're long and curl up, almost touching his eyebrows when he blinks. How soft would they be between my fingers? Crap. I'm staring at Vincent's exquisite eyelashes.

'Tell me something you love,' I say, scrambling to redirect myself.

Vincent's eyes stare at the ceiling, searching. '*Rumours.*'

'Gossip? About celebrities? Ummm, I remember when Demi Moore and Bruce Willis split. That's where my knowledge of celebrity news runs out.'

'No, the album,' he says with a laugh. 'By Fleetwood Mac. I love it.'

Nodding, I try to remember which songs are on that

specific album. The CD might be in a crowded bin under my bed with other vestiges from college.

'A solid choice. And what do you do . . . for fun? Not work,' I clarify.

'Hmmm.' His eyes find the ceiling again, apparently his tell for deep thought. 'Well, I love LEGO.'

'Really? That's brilliant.'

'Something about the organizing, counting, building, following directions . . . it calms me.'

'I can see that,' I say. 'I haven't built a set in years. My granddaughter is more into . . . dramatics.'

'You should do one sometime,' he says, and my face immediately scrunches.

'I'm not the most . . . graceful. I'd lose a piece. Knock it over. Ruin it somehow.'

Vincent's entire body seems to tense at the mention of a missing piece. Or maybe it's me.

'Listen, I need to tell you something,' he says.

'Shoot.' I wink and hope I don't appear an ass.

Vincent takes two quick breaths before speaking.

'I have OCD. Messes . . . They're one of my triggers. Crumbs. Dirt. Chaos in general.'

My ribs grow tight, and I'm suddenly short of breath. The dizziness comes marching back, dragging along some lightheadedness for flavor. If you looked up 'mess' in the dictionary, there'd be photos of me in various states of disarray. Slipping with a tray of food in the cafeteria. Tripping on my own feet and falling on my ass during the third-grade science fair. Stumbling over the wires on the stage at the holiday concert.

'But that's not it. Sometimes I get stuck. It's hard to

explain.' Vincent nudges the napkin sitting next to his plate. 'But with certain tasks, it's like falling into a pit and not being able to climb out until the job is done.'

'You like to finish what you start,' I say, offering a smile.

'Yeah, you could say that.' Pushing his shoulders back, Vincent takes a deep breath. 'And while I'm confessing, contrary to my profile, I'm not really allergic to cats. Or dogs. Animals just scare me. Technically, the germs scare me. Generally speaking, animals are filthy,' Vincent says, glancing in his lap, and somehow this moment of vulnerability makes him even sexier.

'Oh, well, that explains the wine on my shirt.' I take my napkin, tuck it into my collar, and fan the fabric to cover the offending spot. 'There, all gone.' I smile. 'Out of sight, out of mind.'

'Thank you,' he says, 'I just want to be honest because, well, it's been an issue. For other men.'

'Vincent, I don't know much about OCD, but you seem sweet, and nobody's perfect. Look at me.' I motion toward my oversized napkin bib. 'And, I'm not other men. And, well, your SWISH photo didn't do you justice,' I say, and Vincent's ears tinge pink. His lack of hair allows me to notice the gentle flush of his skin around his ears, enhancing his handsomeness.

'Oh. Um, thanks. You too, I mean, you look better than your photo.'

'Thank you. My daughter took it and promised it was the best option. She tried to convince me to color my beard first, but this is me.' My fingers run through my soft scruff. 'I try to take care of myself, but you know, once you round fifty, everything gets so much harder to, well . . .' I pause and pat my stomach. 'Take care of.'

'I bet. I mean, I can imagine. I just turned forty in September, but I can already feel gravity becoming an adversary,' he says. 'And the beard. Don't change a thing.'

A smile blossoms on my face. He likes the gray.

'Ah, forty, you're a baby. Forty is fabulous. I started discovering my true self when I hit forty. But fifty, fifty is the new thirty, or that's what I'm told. I'm fifty-two, by the way.'

I search Vincent's face, hoping to catch a glimpse of his true thoughts on our age difference, but he only lifts the corners of his mouth as if I've just told him he's won a luxury Hawaiian vacation.

'If fifty is the new thirty, then forty is the new twenty. Which makes you a real daddy,' he says playfully, twiddling his fingers on the napkin still resting on the table.

'I've been told.' I smile through the nerves in my tummy. 'Nobody's called me that in a very long time.'

'Well, take it from me, it's hot,' he says. Vincent raises his eyebrows, and my wineglass slips, but I catch it before adding to the mess already paying rent on my shirt.

Val comes and takes our order. Vincent gets a bulgogi taco salad, and, feeling adventurous, I order the Seoul Burrito. When the food arrives, Vincent plays a game with his napkin. He's doing some kind of origami. There's folding, unfolding, refolding, moving, dabbing, and then he repeats the whole thing. When he catches me staring, he smiles.

'I'm aiming for a clean spot each time I wipe, and well, I wipe often,' he says with a chuckle. 'You should've seen me before. Piles and piles of napkins.' Vincent motions to an imaginary tall pile on the table. 'A friend taught me this trick. Now, I get by with only one or two.'

Vincent's candidness is a breath of fresh air. Transparency, especially about anything considered difficult to discuss, isn't easy. He's winning points for being so straightforward.

'Hey, that's smart. And you know, I'm thrilled you're comfortable being honest about it.' My lips arrange into a smile at his openness.

'What I've learned,' he says, carefully digging into his bulgogi taco salad, 'it's just better for me to be frank from the get-go. Like this.' He nods toward his food. 'I don't like my food to touch on a plate. But a salad. In a bowl. Everything mixed and touching? Perfectly fine. So, when I'm out with a handsome man . . .' He blinks, and fuck, those eyelashes may be the death of me. 'I stick to salads. My OCD can be annoying as hell, mostly to me, but it doesn't define me.'

'Of course not.'

Vincent takes a small bite, chews, and, before he even swallows, wipes what appears to be a clean mouth. He does his little folding ritual and starts over. There's something endearing about the methodical way he moves, and I have the urge to find out more about him.

'What about you?' he asks. 'What red flags are hiding under that wine-stained shirt?'

'Which one would you like to hear about first?' Another smile spreads across my face. 'It's been over seven years since I've been with someone. I haven't been with a man since high school, and that was only once,' I say, omitting the gory details.

'And don't forget your cat,' he offers.

I laugh, and my eyes focus on Vincent's plump lips. Does all the wiping make them any less soft? Would he ever let me find out?

'Yes, Sweetums can be a handful. But he's not all bad. I promise.' I take a sip of wine, careful to make sure my lips make contact with the glass. 'And neither am I.'

'Definitely not.' His hazel eyes lock with mine. Those fucking eyelashes. Vincent blinks, and they pull my focus like a magnet. There's a moment of silence. He seems to study me, and having him scrutinize me makes my skin tingle.

Val returns to clear our plates and asks, 'Can I interest you in the dessert menu?'

Without taking his eyes off me, Vincent replies, 'No, just the check, Val.'

He does this half-smile thing, and my pulse revs as my heart pounds in my chest.

'Well, okay then, I'll get the check,' she says, and Vincent's gaze falls to my lips.

'How about dessert back at my place?' he asks.

My eyes go wide and, en route to my lap, my hand smacks the handle of my fork, sending it sailing across the room until it crashes against the wall with a loud clang. On its journey, it fortunately misses the other guests and only serves to humiliate me.

A spinning breathlessness overtakes me. Back to his place? We just met. This was not on my bingo card for my first date in ... forever. With his gentle smile and non-threatening demeanor, Vincent wouldn't hurt a fly. But that look in his eyes – a sparkling simmer intrigues me. What is he after? Catching my gaze, he raises his right eyebrow.

'Um, sure.'

My head whirls and I grab my wallet from my pocket. What have I gotten myself into?

3

Vincent

I have never done this before. A blind date, one-night stand. Hookup. Whatever it's called. It's one of the reasons I like SWISH. The men are typically looking for more than a roll in the hay, but something about Kent . . . That beard. That silver hair. Those kind eyes. The soft dad bod I sense underneath his crumpled clothes. It's been four years since anyone but my right hand has touched my cock. Marvin said to listen to my heart, but he didn't mention my dick. Take a risk. Stay open. With Kent, all my cylinders are firing. I decide to go for it. Him.

Kent follows me home and parks in my condo's guest spot. As we walk up the path, the sound of our footsteps echoes through the quiet night air. I offered him dessert but don't have anything sweet. He has to know I didn't invite him back to make hot fudge sundaes. Approaching the entry, I turn and shoot him a grin. Somehow, this sends him tripping over my doormat.

'I'm fine. Sorry,' he says, catching himself on the doorframe.

Nervous tension bubbles, but I'm not turning back. Marvin texted me on the ride home, and I told him the date was going extremely well. That man loves to text. I'll give him the details in the morning. When there's something to divulge.

Removing my shoes at the door, I glance at Kent, and without a word, he pops his off and carefully places them next to mine. Shoes are a start, but right now, I'm determined to separate Kent from his clothes.

'I'm sorry again about your shirt. If you give it to me, I can use a stain stick on it. Get the wine right out,' I say.

'Are you trying to get me to strip?'

I am. This isn't me. No one has ever been to my place for a date. Ever. But something about Kent's sweetness. His face. That wavy hair. I don't want to make a fool of myself, but the mood doesn't strike often. And I can't remember it ever striking like this. Sparks. Flames. The iron isn't hot. It's scorching. It wouldn't be wise to waste it. There's no backing out now.

'Maybe.' I close the door, and when it clicks, my palms find Kent's chest, thrusting him against the wall. His glasses wobble with the impact and land askew on his face.

With the under-the-counter lights in the kitchen providing a modicum of illumination, we lock eyes. Kent pushes my buttons. His woodsy smell. I'm not an outdoorsy person, but I'd love to be smothered in this campfire. I grasp Kent's shirt, but his eyes widen so I hastily let go, not wanting him to think I'm assaulting him.

'Is this okay?' I reach to fix his glasses.

He nods, but his searching eyes give me pause.

'I really want to kiss you.'

My eyes land on his soft lips, surrounded by that shaggy but trimmed beard. The thought of kissing his mouth sends a wave of heat to my core.

'Me?' he asks.

'No, I was hoping we could drive to your place, and I could kiss your cat.' He laughs. A low, deep throttle and his Adam's apple bobs up and down. It's rare for me to be this close to someone without wanting to flee. 'Yes, you.' My nose almost touches his. 'You're very sexy.'

'Oh. Um, okay. Sure.'

And because almost everything about Kent butters my biscuit, I lean in, my nose brushing his. But then it hits me like a landslide – our mouths. We just ate. Both of us. Even all the wiping in the world won't stop the odors. The textures. The germs. Familiar uncertainty looms. My stomach turns in tight coils, and fuck, I was so into this.

'Can I ask a small favor?' I ask, attempting a quick rescue.

'Um, sure,' he says. 'You kind of have me up against the wall.'

'Would you mind' – I glance down – 'brushing your teeth?'

'You want me to drive home, brush my teeth, and come back?'

'Gosh, no, I have a toothbrush. Toothbrushes. I buy them in bulk.'

A new brush every week because they're a breeding ground for germs. And they're amazing for cleaning grout and getting into tight corners.

'I'll brush, too. Please,' I beg and begin unbuttoning his

stained shirt. A white V-neck allows a little of his chest hair to poke through, and for fuck's sake, it's silver too. The sight of it sends my cock lurching in my briefs.

'I need us to clean our mouths.' I brush his bottom lip with my index finger. It's soft and warm. 'Now.'

'Vincent, listen,' he says, reaching for my chin and lifting my head so our eyes lock. 'My lips are vibrating because I want to kiss you so badly. Let's get brushing.'

My head and heart tussle over the mood and my fears, but desire crackles at his comment. He's so damn empathetic. He really doesn't seem to mind.

'Come,' I say, taking his hand. My thumb grazes the velvety hair on his knuckles, igniting a wave of desire within me.

In the bathroom, I hand Kent a brand-new, still-in-the-package blue toothbrush. He pops it open, and I put a dab of toothpaste on it for him before applying some to my own. We stand beside each other, brushing, facing the mirror, at my double vanity that's never had a purpose before tonight. Kent scoots closer and knocks his hip against mine. When I look at his reflection, an encouraging foamy grin greets me.

'My mouth is going to be so fucking clean,' he mumbles through the toothpaste.

His words send another jolt of electricity straight to my cock. My weekly service scoured the bathroom yesterday, and I scrub surfaces every other day in between. It's spotless. I can almost smell the bleach under the minty-ness in my mouth, and when I spit and rinse, Kent, taking his cue, does the same. I quickly wash my hands with soap, and Kent follows suit, copying every step so we're equally sanitized.

Before he finishes drying his hands and mouth on the guest towel, I clutch his open shirt and begin tugging.

'Can we take this off?' I pull gently at it, avoiding the stain. 'Please?'

'So polite. Of course,' he says and peels it off. He stands in only his white V-neck. His stomach protrudes enough to lift the hem of the shirt, and his soft belly, covered in salt-and-pepper hair, peeks through. My erection now aches against my pants. Kent holds the wadded-up garment, glancing around to find a place for it.

'I can get that wine out for you.' I take the shirt and throw it into the hamper in the corner. The remote on the vanity beckons, and I reach over and click play. Simple strums fade in, Lindsey Buckingham's tenor begins, joined by the perfectly matched harmonies of the ladies, and 'Second Hand News' pours out of the ceiling-mounted speakers, filling the bathroom with music.

'*Rumours*,' Kent says.

'Now,' I say, rubbing my hands on his chest, sneaking up toward the exposed skin and hair, letting my clean fingers get lost in his silver forest. 'May I?'

Our lips are inches apart, and his breath tickles my nose. Fresh and pristine. Fuck yes.

'Are you ready for a kiss?'

Kent answers by brushing his lips on mine. His beard is softer than I thought, and I pull him closer, wanting to feel his body. All of him. He's bigger than me, taller. Softer. Yup, there's a sexy dad bod underneath his T-shirt, and my cock, at full attention now, rubs against his. I hope he's not alarmed. He wraps his arms around me, drawing us even closer.

His hands land on my waist, and there it is.

Kent's stiffness rivals mine, and the scared, worried me seems to take a temporary vacation. He could've taken one look at me, my rituals and triggers, my needs and insecurities, and said, 'No, thank you.' But he didn't. He's here. Deepening the kiss and slowly grinding into me.

Kent's tongue slowly parts my lips, but he's tentative. His kindness might be the sexiest thing about him.

Pulling back, he pauses the kiss. 'Vincent, this all working for you?'

'C'mere.'

Now I part his lips, my tongue jutting in, and he lets me enter. Soft moans escape his mouth, and kissing Kent here in my bathroom, the sensation of both our dicks pining for each other makes my head spin. His hands are above my ass, and a soft moan escapes my lips from the thrusting and friction. I'm fairly certain there's precum in my briefs, and the seething heat takes over as my cock slides against the wetness.

'Kent?'

'Uh-huh.' He's back at my mouth. His hands have migrated to my neck, and his fingers explore the back of my head.

'I don't usually do this.'

'Me neither. Never, actually.'

'Okay, I just didn't want you to think –'

'Vincent, you know what I think?' He nibbles my upper lip and runs his palm over my smooth head. When his fingers land on my ears, he rubs the lobes. 'I think you're beautiful.'

The electric guitar solo joins the song just in time to

fade out, and the drum kick and synths of 'Dreams' wash over us, saturating the room with musical perfection. My hands move under his shirt, and his body, velvety, but unexpectedly firm, makes my fingers tingle. Soft fur covers his entire chest and belly. Jackpot. My fingers locate his nipples and softly massage. 'Dessert,' I say.

'You're hungry?'

'We were supposed to come back here for dessert.'

'I'm fine, I promise.' Kent dips back in for a kiss that takes my breath away. My mood. Something about Kent unglues me and right now coming untethered intoxicates me.

'Kent, may I please suck your cock?'

Apparently, my rational thinking has taken a momentary leave of absence.

'Um, what?' Kent stumbles back against the vanity. He catches himself on the edge, and with a tilted head, his eyebrows have gathered for an important meeting.

'I'm not always in the mood or ready, but right now, with you, I'm so fucking turned on,' I explain, pointing to my tented pants, 'and your dick is . . .' I gently cup his groin. He's firm, thick, and rock hard. 'May I suck it? Please?'

'Vincent, you don't have to . . .'

'I want to.' I lick my lips, coating them in minty saliva. 'Like, really want to.'

I massage him through his khakis, thankful the fabric is thin and soft.

'I showered before our date,' he blurts. 'Before the cat pill fiasco, not after, but still, I'm only a few hours from sparkly clean. If you wanted me to jump in here, say the word, do you have guest towels?'

I unbutton his khakis, grab the waist of both his pants and his boxers, and push them to the ground in one fell swoop. Kent's beefy cock pops up, and he wobbles for a moment. He steadies himself on the sink, and before I have a change of heart, I lower myself to my knees and take him in my hand. It's been a while since I've held someone else's dick, and Kent's is a beauty. Long, thick, and cut, the pink tip taunts me.

'You okay?' I ask.

'Um, yeah. Definitely.'

He's looking down at me, watching me stare at his beautiful cock.

'Could you . . . talk to me?'

The music. The harmonies. The crispness. It's almost enough.

He's been babbling until now, and his voice will seal the deal.

'Talk to you?'

'Yeah. Tell me what you like, what I'm doing well. If you could tell me, I'm' – if I'm doing this, there's no reason not to ask for exactly what I want – 'good. A good boy.'

Ten years ago. In the sauna. A quick blow job. I barely remember him, but I'd seen him shower-scrubbing like there was no tomorrow. While he was using me, fucking my face, he called me a 'good boy,' and bliss washed over me. I felt safe. Cherished. Comforted. I've only had a couple of hookups since. Nobody's called me that, and I haven't had the guts to ask. But with Kent, I'm at ease. And why not? I won't see him after tonight.

He reaches for my face, cups my cheeks, and rubs my ears with his fingertips. The music swells as his cock stiffens. Lindsey Buckingham's sweet voice fills my head, singing about being secondhand.

'Vincent. I'll do whatever you want.' Kent bends over and kisses the top of my head. 'I'm happy to talk to you.' He stands, and the tip tempts me. 'Now, please suck my dick like a good boy.'

And with that, my entire body eases, and I take Kent's gorgeous cock in my mouth. Only the head first, and yup, he definitely showered recently. The mountain spring smell of his soap enters my nose, and the crispness, mixed with a tiny tinge of sweat, makes my dick expand in my pants.

'Vincent,' he whispers and tips my head up, his cock slowly sliding deeper into my mouth. 'Please let me know if anything doesn't feel good. Or if you want to stop.'

I move off him for a second. 'More talking.' That's all I've got. He's showing concern about my comfort, my needs, even as his thick dick stretches my lips. Hearing his deep voice while I suck Kent off might be all it takes to elicit my orgasm.

'Taste those balls,' he coos as I lap at them. 'Good boy. Nice long strokes. Get it nice and wet.'

I reach around and grab his ass. It's fuzzy – thank you, Jesus – and carefully guide him to thrust into my mouth. As Kent takes over, slowly picking up the pace, plunging deep down my throat, he grabs on to my head, rubbing and massaging the dome. I reach down and free my cock, palming it with my right hand while my left continues to assist my mouth in swallowing Kent's delicious dick. 'Vincent, you're such a sweet cocksucker. So good.' His fingers brush my forehead, and when I close my eyes, his thumbs sweep my eyelashes. 'You look so beautiful with my dick in your mouth.'

For someone who hasn't been with a man since high school, Kent's verbal game is on point. His words deliver a tingling pleasure through me. 'Mmmh,' I mutter, and then pull off, spit dripping from my lips and his tip to say, 'Your cock is fucking delicious. It's perfect.'

'You like sucking it?'

'I do.' I gobble him up again, doing my best to take as much of him down my throat as possible.

'Oh, damn,' he gasps. He rests back on the vanity. 'Legs. Tired. Fuck, Vincent, you suck so well. You take my cock like a good boy.'

His words splash over my entire body, and my dick throbs in my hand while Kent fills every space in my mouth, creating a shockwave of intense pleasure. Finally, I'm able to deepthroat him, the furry salt-and-pepper fuzz on his belly tickling my nose, and I'm done for. My balls tighten, and I know I'm about to make a massive mess. Right now, I don't care.

My small groans must tip him off because Kent asks, 'Are you close? Do you want to come while I'm in your mouth?'

I peer up at him, his cock filling my mouth, and nod.

'Be a good boy, and come for me, Vincent.'

I jerk myself faster, using both hands now, and Kent takes charge. He's fucking my face like a champ, and my orgasm rises, taking over, and I whimper as he slams his cock into my mouth. Moans sneak out of my lips as I shoot thick ropes all over his shins and onto the floor.

I lean back and rest on the tile, the cool surface shocking

my skin. My dick, still dripping, slowly softens and I'm suddenly hyperaware of my current situation. What have I done? Something about Kent overrode the intrusive thoughts. It was fucking glorious. Until now. The marked wave of shame washes over me. The heat of the moment over, I'm tempted to flee, but we're in my bathroom. My condo. Kent stands before me, still hard, and embarrassment surges through my veins. This isn't me. I don't do this. Kneeling on the floor. Where we've walked. I don't even know this man.

Kent bends down and cups my face. His lips brush the top of my head, and he says, 'Vincent, my friend, you are a master cock sucker.'

I force a 'ha' because I don't have a genuine laugh in me. 'Thanks.'

'Are you okay?' he asks, and the pounding in my chest grows louder.

Even now, he's concerned about me. My ears ring and I'm unable to answer.

'Do you want me to go?'

I don't want to be rude, but every atom in my body screams for him to leave.

'Why don't you finish,' I suggest, his cock staring at the ceiling.

'Vincent, I'm fine. I should get going anyway. I have a big day at work tomorrow.'

'No shop talk, remember?' I say, glancing at my watch and wondering how soon I can shower and be alone in my freshly bleached sheets. I have my own important day looming.

'Right.' Kent pulls his pants up. 'I had fun.'

'Yeah, me too,' I say. The mortification of what I just did shadows me like a cloud, and the need to scrub every inch of myself overtakes me. Did I make the wrong call, having Kent over?

'I'll just . . .' I stand and grab a washcloth from the vanity to clean up, and before I can do it, Kent takes it from my hand.

'Let me.'

He turns the water on, and once it's warm he wets the washcloth and wrings the excess out. With a slow, caring touch, he wipes me first. My dick, my hand, my feet. 'There you go, spick-and-span.' Only once I'm clean does he use the rag on himself and, finally, the floor. He's a complete gentleman, and I've gone and fucked it up.

'Well, I'll be going then,' he says, buttoning his pants. 'Do you want to exchange numbers?'

The messaging in SWISH is archaic at best and truly limited to initial communication to facilitate setting up a date. This is the point in the movie where we swap numbers and think about seeing each other again. Communicating. More kissing. More sucking.

'Kent, you're a great guy, but . . .'

He winces at 'but.'

'Oh,' he says, and I've done it. In the span of a few hours, I've ruined everything. Ruined him. I take four deep breaths, counting each exhale in my head.

'It's just,' I begin, unsure how to communicate my humiliation at coming on to him that way.

'No, it's okay. Thanks again.' He dips down and kisses my cheek. His beard, his lips, the tender way he makes contact, pours more disgrace on my shame sundae.

'Bye.' He grabs his stained shirt, dangling from the hamper, and he's gone.

Even with Fleetwood Mac blasting through the speakers, the energy evaporates from the room the moment Kent leaves. I close my eyes and count breaths. How did we go from talking about his cat and *Rumours* to me blowing him? The disgrace consumes me. I need to focus on the music. I need to find my center.

I'm frozen – the aggressive drums and crashing guitars of 'The Chain' echo against tile, glass, and mirrors. My eyes fall on my pants around my ankles. My knees wobble with weakness, and I'm deeply grateful and horribly disappointed I'll never see Kent Lester again.

4

Kent

'Wait, you went back to his apartment?' Ruth asks from her usual position, a half step in front of me.

Her braids swing back and forth, framing her sepia skin. The tiny beads click-clack, creating a symphony of sound in the silent, frosty morning. With the spring of the newly installed track beneath her, Ruth glides even faster than she would on pavement. In only a tracksuit zipped to the top, the December chill has set in, but Ruth runs hot – no heavy coats for her.

'I mean, he offered dessert.'

The cold air stings my throat as my body warms up. After the first lap, I'm ready to unzip my jacket and attempt not to be a sweaty mess for the day ahead. Ruth has to be the fittest person I know. Yes, she's almost my age, but thirty years ago she was on the women's Olympic speed-walking team. I'm trying to keep pace with a roadrunner.

'Dick for dessert?'

I trip on a pebble. Or stone. Or air.

'Ruth Parrish, watch your mouth. I literally just met him,' I say, shaking my head.

'So what? Two men. All that testosterone flowing through your bodies. Gay men hook up all the time.'

'But, I'm bi.'

'Okay, men. Generally speaking, men are horny. All the time. It sounds like you experienced insta-lust. And good for you. For getting some.'

Getting some. Oy.

'What?' she asks, glancing back. 'Am I wrong?'

'No.' Even in the brisk air, heat radiates from my face. 'He wanted me to . . . talk. And your ideas for . . . bedroom talk were a hit. Or I think they were. Surprisingly, I fell right into it.'

'You dirty dog.' Ruth pauses and looks me up and down. 'I like this side of you, Mr Lester.'

'It happened so quickly. He asked and I remembered our conversation and your . . . suggestions.'

'Auntie Ruth will never steer you in the wrong direction. You had a good time.' She pats my back. 'There's nothing wrong with that, Kent.'

'Yeah. It's just . . .' Walking into the restaurant and seeing Vincent's face. His sweet hazel eyes. The skin of his beautiful bald head. My heart whispered to me, 'You found him.'

'Just what?' Ruth slows her gait enough to tilt her head, sending her beads dancing.

'When I saw him . . . after I got my bearings, I felt something.'

'In your pants.'

'No. Maybe. I mean inside. Something about him. His energy. The chemistry. I knew.'

'Knew what?'

'There was a connection.' My hand finds my stomach. 'It was like when you take a sip of champagne, and the bubbles travel up your nose and everything's tingly.'

Ruth's arm wraps around my shoulder. With pursed lips, she squeezes, and a hint of her warmth breaches my coat.

'It doesn't matter.' Brisk air leaves my nostrils in a huff. 'It was a disaster.'

'The date? Dessert? The dick? What exactly was a disaster?'

My head shakes, the sting of leaving Vincent's apartment dejected still fresh.

'I thought we hit it off. At dinner. Back at his place. He was so sweet. So sexy. Completely bald.'

'Ahhhh. Mr Clean vibes. Regina shaved her head. Super sexy.' Ruth nods approvingly.

'Yes. Exactly that.' Glancing down at the top of Vincent's head, my dick sliding into his luscious lips. Oy.

'What happened?'

'He has OCD.'

'So? Everyone I know has ADHD or OCD.'

'No,' I say. 'I think it may be clinical.'

Ruth shakes her head. 'Red flag.'

Her hands shoot up like she's making a call in a game, and somehow, she's still ahead of me. My chest burns with the effort required to keep up.

'I'm a fifty-two-year-old divorced bisexual man whose only encounter with another man barely happened. Thirty-five years ago. I'm in no place to judge anyone's red flags.'

'Kenneth Lester, you are a complete jaddy, and the sooner you accept that, the happier you will be.'

'Jaddy?'

'A Jewish daddy. Jaddy. Sexy AF.' She kisses her fingers one at a time.

'I'm not sure it's okay for you to call your principal and immediate supervisor a "jaddy," but I'll overlook it.'

'You are so not my type, Kent.'

'But you just said I was a jaddy.'

'Exactly.'

Another glance, her deep brown eyes peering, emphasizing her remark with a stare. Ruth was the first person I came out to at school. Being married to a woman, everyone assumes you're straight. Nope. Bisexual the entire time. When I told her, Ruth shouted, 'Hot damn. Yes. More queers at Lear. Welcome to the club.' Besides Theo, the custodian, Ruth is my only real confidant at school.

'And the talking . . .' I pause, taking a deep inhale.

'What?' Ruth's eyes widen.

'It wasn't just the dirty talk. He wanted me to . . .' Even though I know we're completely alone, I give a quick glance behind us. '. . . call him a "good boy."'

Ruth stops walking, pulls her head back, and stares at me.

'Praise kink? On the first date? Damn. Go, Mr Lester.'

'Is that weird?' I ask. Did I go overboard? Say too much. Maybe that's why he asked me to leave so quickly.

'Hell no. It's fucking hot. People love it for several reasons. Some want to feel valued. Desired.'

I picture Vincent on his knees, looking up at me with

his rich hazel eyes, lashes fluttering, and I stumble on the track's rubber surface.

'Did you like it?' Ruth asks.

'I . . . think so? Honestly, I was so caught up in the moment. It kind of just happened. I was . . . filthy.' Even in the frigid air, my face flashes hot.

'Yeah, you were.' She pats my back and resumes walking, gently prodding me along.

'Well, I'm not seeing him again. He made that clear.'

'That's too bad. He sounds hot.' Ruth shrugs. 'You put yourself out there. I give you props for that,' she says.

'Yeah, being rejected on a first date . . . not exactly magnificent for my confidence.'

At the restaurant, Vincent was sweet. Charming. His willingness to share so much about himself so quickly had me swooning. Maybe I shouldn't have gone home with him.

'Don't give up. This guy may not have seen you're a total package beyond a "jaddy," but someone will.'

Corrine pushed me to sign up for SWISH – the irony. One benefit of divorcing because you've become more companions than anything else? Keeping my best friend.

We walk in silence for a few minutes, and I notice a pensive look on Ruth's face.

'What are you thinking about?' I ask.

Ruth's signature smile skates over her face.

'Okay, *who* are you thinking about?'

'Regina. Her shaved head.' Ruth takes a deep breath, clearly reminiscing.

'Call her,' I say.

'Mr Lester, that ship has sailed. It's out of port. Lost at sea.' I shrug and hook my arm in hers, attempting to keep pace.

'Are you ready for today?' she asks, changing the subject from completed to impending disaster.

'To learn entirely new software from someone who knows nothing about teaching or education? To convince the entire staff it's critical only to discover it doesn't work and/or something better comes along in a year? To do all this by spring break? Sure, why not.'

'That's the spirit.' She slows her pace and hooks her arm in mine.

'If I'm unable to demonstrate our kids are learning, I mean in the way the board approves of, well, my contract is annual. They'll have no problem finding a new principal.'

'I know you know this, but listen carefully,' she says, gripping me closer, the heat from our bodies warming us as our pace slows.

'I have the unique perspective of seeing every child in the school. And I hear the teachers in the staff room. The children and, dare I say, the teachers here, are happy. Kids are learning. They're thriving. No data, and certainly no fancy software, will change that.'

I know Ruth is right. But Dr Cutler and the school board care about one thing. Scores. For them, testing data is the barometer to judge a school's efficacy. Hopscotch is supposed to help teachers collect information more frequently and capture more successes. I know I'm a damn good leader, but a tiny voice taunts me. Maybe I don't actually know what I'm doing. What if this all reveals I'm a fraud? Having no choice, I do my best to press forward with optimism.

'I know. It will be fine,' I say. 'And maybe it will help instruction. Teachers having more frequent and accurate data might not be a bad thing.'

'There's my Pollyanna.' Ruth pats my belly affectionately.

We head toward the school – and even with her tiny, compact frame, as usual, Ruth buoys me.

'Mr Lester, Good Morning! Your mail is on your desk, and I bought snacks for the meeting.'

Helen greets me, her glasses slightly askew against her fair skin. We both tend to be disheveled, and I'm grateful she assures I'm not the only one falling apart at the seams. While Helen Hall may lean a tad chaotic on the outside, her brain and a bevy of sticky notes hold all the critical information for running the school. I may be the principal, but as our secretary, Helen is the heart of the school.

'Thanks, Helen. What time do we begin again?'

'Nine. You can do arrival and check-in but be back by 8:55.' She dips her chin and stares over her glasses. 'Please.'

'Yes, ma'am.'

I'm not exactly sure how old Helen is, and I'm not asking. She's definitely younger than me. And I will still call her ma'am every single time. She's in charge. Full stop.

Walking into the conference room, I spot bottles of water and a basket of snacks. Helen stopped at the store on her way in. She didn't have to do that. She never has to, but she always does.

I was told two people from Hopscotch would be

coming. Shreya Shaan, our school's STEM teacher, will join us. Her role is to work with Hopscotch's technology person to make all the back-end pieces work. But Shreya will also help me understand how to explain all this to the staff. In her midtwenties, Shreya has a verve and understanding of technology I attempted to grasp when flip phones were all the rage but soon lost. The children adore 'Miss Shaan' almost as much as I do, with her wildflower tattoos and nose ring a constant source of questions from them.

'Mr Lester,' Shreya says. There's a bounce to her step, and I don't know if it's the platform sneakers or simply the adrenaline that comes from being in your twenties.

'Miss Shaan, how are you this morning?'

'Well, I was up until four this morning checking code, so I'm running on a cocktail of coffee and energy drinks.'

That'll do it. She shakes her head and smiles, jutting her shoulders back. 'How are you?'

Besides being our school's STEM teacher, teaching basic programming, tech, and engineering skills to the entire school, Shreya spends her free time with a group of college friends creating a fantasy video game filled with dragons, elves, and magic.

'Is everyone in the world still alive?' I ask.

'Avandia? So far, yes. I mean the main characters. But Philiador is fuming, and it's never smart to piss off a dragon.' Shreya moves a stray piece of hair behind her ear and her thin gold bracelets twinkle against her skin.

Young people. I smile and nod, not knowing enough to engage more.

Realizing I'm out of my comfort zone, Shreya deftly

changes the subject. 'Anyway, I've read the documentation, and it's a fairly basic system. It's a massive, complicated spreadsheet. That's it. They've designed a slick front end allowing teachers to enter data in the simplest way.'

'Wait, all this for a spreadsheet?'

'I mean, technically, yes. But there are formulas, pivot tables, and flashy graphics. It's not your basic budget.' Shreya shakes her head a little, knowing I'm once again about to be underwater.

'Do you think . . .'

'Yeah, it could help,' she says, reading my mind. 'It's going to be way easier for teachers. Hopscotch's concept appears to hinge on simplicity combined with usability, leading to more data collected. More data usually favors higher averages and overall results.'

Higher averages. Hopscotch might actually help. Shreya knows technology, and I trust her. If she thinks it could boost our scores, the smartest decision is for me to trust the process. Dr Cutler's warning last week rings in my head.

'If the trend line doesn't swing up soon, we'll have to make some tough decisions.' Florence Cutler's voice echoes.

Usually, I'd have pushed for clarity. What tough decisions? But in this case, I'm afraid to find out. The thought of leaving the one place that still needs me makes my heart sink.

Florence Cutler, with her short, cropped gray hair, puts a friendly smile forward, and by no means is she unkind, but behind closed doors, her earnestness comes out. Most people don't understand the superintendent works for the board. If the board is unhappy, it falls on her. And Lear's diminishing test scores have the bonus of dragging down the district average. The board is not amused.

'Listen, Kent,' Shreya says, 'these tech guys can be a little . . . cocky. If you start to feel overwhelmed, shoot me a look; I'll be happy to jump in.'

Shreya's confidence and protectiveness impart a wide smile on my face.

'Thank you,' I say. 'I love having young people around.'

Interrupting our pregame chat, Helen pops her head in to announce, 'They're here.'

A tall, slender white man with blond hair clutches a briefcase. He's wearing a green dress shirt tucked into dark jeans. His face barely moves, and a seriousness permeates from his pores. I extend my hand, and he takes it.

'Geoff Cozen, lead architect,' he says.

'Kent Lester, principal.' We shake and I turn my attention to Shreya. 'This is Shreya Shaan, our school's tech integrator.' Shreya stands but doesn't move from her seat.

'Pleasure,' Geoff says.

'Indeed,' she replies, and I'm fairly certain she meant for him.

'My partner needed the bathroom. He'll be here in a moment,' Geoff says, taking one of the empty seats around the conference table.

Geoff opens his briefcase and takes out a binder and folders, so many folders. When I look at Shreya, she lifts her left eyebrow and smirks. My face warms as my lips turn up, knowing she's got my back.

'Sorry about that,' a voice calls, entering the conference room.

Breaking eye contact with Shreya, I turn my attention to the door. 'Your bathroom sinks weren't cooperating and . . .'

Vincent Manda, squirting his hands with sanitizer from a small personal-sized bottle, marches over to the empty seat next to Geoff. He's wearing a crisp white button-down shirt and khakis that appear to have had their crease bullied into them. The minute my eyes scan him, my heart trips in my chest. I never thought I'd hear from him again, let alone see him in the conference room at Lear.

Looking up from his hands, Vincent's gaze meets mine. Oy.

5

Vincent

'Crashed and burned? What do you mean?'

Marvin, my gay guide through the trials of queer courting, tries, as he has for the past year, to unravel the enigma of my disaster of a date. He's determined to understand why my first dates never warrant a follow-up.

'It all felt . . . right. Until it didn't.'

'Vincent, listen. I may know a thing or two about over-analyzing a situation.' Marvin's voice booms through the speakers in my car, and I take the last sip of my black coffee.

'Oh, really?'

My tumbler from home fits perfectly in the center console next to the cylinder of hypoallergenic wipes. After my last slug of caffeine, I grab one, clean my mouth, and contemplate stopping for a coffee refill. A quick glance at the clock informs me I don't have time. The word 'late' isn't part of my vocabulary.

'Hush. Now, back up. Start at the beginning. Tell me every detail.'

'Marvin, I'm almost at the school. You're getting the

CliffsNotes version,' I reply, checking the address on my phone.

'Fine, but embellish a little. I may be engaged, but I still crave the juice.'

'Dinner was great. I folded and refolded my napkins like you showed me. And it worked like a charm. Two napkins. For the entire meal.'

'Two? You're kidding?'

'I'm not. Val was impressed.'

'Fuck, that's amazing, Vincent. You should feel so proud,' he says, and I smile, wondering how I ever thought there might be something more than friendship between us. Marvin's cute, but there weren't any sparks. When he suggested we stay in touch, I was certain I'd never hear from him again, but almost a year later, he's become one of my dearest friends.

'Thank you. Yeah, I was really riding high from the win. And Kent was, well, my walls came crashing down.'

'And . . .'

'He came home with me after dinner. For dessert.'

The interior of my Subaru goes silent, and I tilt my ear toward the left speaker, waiting for his reply. Nothing.

'Marvin. You there? Did I lose you?' I pull my beanie up, hoping to hear better.

'Um, yeah, here. I'm not sure I heard you correctly. He came home with you? To your condo? You let him inside? With shoes?'

My eyes find the car's ceiling, knowing I need to spill it. I wince, and the words gush out quickly.

'Yes, he came over. Inside. He took his shoes off. I didn't even have to ask.'

'Wow.'

'I listened to you. Stayed open. Didn't tally objections.' Stopped at a red light, I check my face in the rearview mirror. 'I'm rarely into someone like that, so I went for it. We made out . . . and did other things. I asked him to brush his teeth, which he seemed happy to do. And well, when the moment ended, I felt overwhelmed with embarrassment, and I asked him to leave.'

'Wait, rewind. Define other things.'

'Really?'

'Really.'

My cheeks flush. I pop off my hat and take another quick glance in the mirror, and yup, my face, ears, and entire bare head tinge crimson. I want to tell Marvin. We're friends. But awkwardness and shame overshadow my will to share.

'Not on the phone.'

'Why not?'

'Someone might hear.'

'Who?'

'I don't know. They could be monitoring my line.' I take a quick peek around the car.

'Who?'

'The government. Or China.'

'You think the Chinese government wants to hear about your sexcapades with a hot daddy?'

'I'm here. I need to go,' I say, pulling my car into a parking spot marked 'visitor.'

'Vincent, what things? What did you do to him? Wait. What did he do to you?'

'Marvin, I'll see you Saturday.'

'Fine, but we're finishing this conversation, friend. Illona will go to bed by eight.'

'Goodbye, Marvin.'

I grab my bag and head inside, hoping I have enough time for a brisk scrub down in the bathroom.

My quick trip to the bathroom lasts closer to ten minutes. Talking with Marvin about last night, recalling the details I didn't share, I get stuck washing. The automatic faucets are on timers. Six seconds is not enough nor advised as sufficient hand washing by the Centers for Disease Control. Pulling my hands out and thrusting them back under, I count, and that never ends well. I've been on intervals of four lately. It changes sporadically, but the numbers are always even. Once I hit thirty-two, the soap vanishes, my hands wrinkle, and I reach a standstill.

Already late, I rush into the school's office, past the secretary, who shoots me a kind but curious look as I barge into the conference room.

'Sorry about that,' I say, catching Geoff's narrowed eyes. Of course, he was here on time. Of course, he's the first to meet them. Yes, I'm late. Yes, it was my OCD. Yes, he knows. As Project Leads, technically, Geoff and I are peers, but his father sits on Hopscotch's board, so in his mind, he runs the show.

Fumbling for an excuse, I blurt, 'Your bathroom sinks weren't cooperating and . . .'

Scanning the room for an empty seat, my heart drops through my stomach, out my ass, and straight to the floor. Kent. Our eyes meet, and the vision of him from last night flashes in my head. In my bathroom. Standing above me. Calling me a 'good boy' as he fucked my face while I shot my load everywhere. Dear Goddess Stevie, help me.

'This is my colleague, Vincent Manda,' Geoff says, filling the air with confidence and presumed authority.

'Shreya Shaan, STEM Teacher and Tech integrator.' A beautiful Indian woman nods, and if I weren't so distracted by Kent in the room, I might get lost in her sweet perfume. There's notes of jasmine and vanilla.

After polite greetings, he's there. Next to me. Smelling like campfire and sex, or maybe it's just my nose reminding me of his cock dripping with my spit?

'Kent Lester, principal.' Kent extends his hand. My eyes fall on his fingers. The dusting of hair on his knuckles.

Okay. We're playing strangers. At least for now. For Shreya and Geoff, and maybe even for me. This seems prudent. Last night was a blip – a stain on my record, like Kent's shirt, covered in wine, bleeding out.

'Nice to meet you,' I reply, my hand – still tacky from the sanitizer – in his. The warmth of his fingers around mine. He takes his other hand and sandwiches mine. His skin on mine. I'm not supposed to be aroused. Here. Now. But my body apparently has a visceral reaction to Kent Lester. I close my eyes and, for a moment, wish it was just us, alone, without all the noise surrounding us.

'Same.' Kent's warm smile peeks out, reminding me how patient and caring he was last night. Why would someone like Kent waste his time with me, anyway? He might have been tripping over his feet with a half-tucked shirt covered in merlot, but I'm the mess. Inside.

'So,' Geoff interrupts, clearly ready to start the meeting, 'Vincent and I work collaboratively. I'm the technical lead. My job is to work on the back end, ensure all the wires connect and talk correctly, and the devices play nicely.'

He nods at me. Shreya and Kent both turn their attention my way. Kent's wearing a navy cardigan over a peach polo. The collar of his shirt is half up, forcing the sweater to fall unevenly across his shoulders. There are three buttons on his shirt. I typically button the bottom two and leave the top one open. Kent left all three open. Perhaps on purpose, but my guess is he didn't give it a thought. My eyes spy the soft smoky hair peeking out, and a trapdoor in my stomach gives way. Geoff clears his throat, and oh, this is the part when I'm supposed to talk.

'Yes,' I say, blinking four times to focus. Kent's stare falls on my face as my eyes open and shut. 'And I'm the implementation analyst. I'll gather information from users – teachers, manage data transfer, and training. Basically, all the ways Hopscotch interfaces with, well, people.'

A satisfied look overtakes Geoff's face. Now that we're getting started and, for the most part, falling into our routine, he's content. The district has already bought the product. Our job is to come in, get it up and running, and ensure everyone's satisfied.

'I'll need access to your servers, any devices teachers might use, that type of thing,' Geoff says, giving

Shreya his attention. This young woman – with her purple sweater covered in florals, and tattooed bees swarming around her arm – does not appear to be someone to take shit from anyone. Perhaps Geoff has met his match.

'And I'll need . . .' I begin, and before I can finish, Kent says, 'Me.'

6

Kent

My damn lower back spasms, and I arch slightly, trying to stop it. The combination of colder-than-typical temps and, well, the excitement from last night causes my muscles to revolt. I try to ignore it, but it nags me like an itchy label in a new shirt. Shreya opens her laptop and Geoff grabs a bottle of water. They talk about things I'm not familiar with. Megabits and gigabytes and terabytes, oh my! With the four of us in the room, a loud humming of chatter gurgles. If Vincent and I are going to get anything done, this isn't the place. And we need to talk about last night.

'Let's go to my office,' I suggest, nodding toward the exit. The main office has five doors around the perimeter. A copy room, the nurse's office, a bathroom, the conference room, and my office. I stand to leave, and Vincent follows. If we're going to work together over the next six weeks, we need to sort out what happened. Him on his knees. Staring up at me. Sucking my dick. Calling him a 'good boy.' Oy. But the way it ended gutted me. My big heart gets invested too quickly. Clearly, not everyone prefers middle-aged Jewish guys who look like Santa's little brother.

I stand in the doorway, wait for Vincent to enter, and turn my attention toward Helen.

'Hold my calls, please.'

She nods, jots something down on a notepad, and returns to her computer.

Besides a desk, my office has a small round table with four chairs. I typically meet with children or parents here, saving the conference room for larger meetings. Low shelves line the window, and a family photo with Corrine, Gillian, Louis, and Lia sits beside one of Sweetums sprawled out on a bench. The sun cascades over his long, thick orange fur, and I swear he was posing for me when I snapped that photo.

Vincent enters, and I close the door behind him. When I turn around, he hasn't budged an inch. He's facing me, and breath from his nostrils blows against my beard.

'You didn't tell me . . .' I begin, but his index finger covers my lips.

'No shop talk. That was the deal. But well, clearly, now we need to chat,' he says. The harsh fluorescent lighting creates a glare on Vincent's head, and I squint when the light catches my eye.

'Sit.' I pull away from him and nod toward the table.

'Wait. Please.'

His lips find my neck – small pecks tickle across the tendons. He asked me to leave. Didn't want my number. Why is his mouth on my skin? I lean against the back of a chair. My fingers grip the fabric, attempting to keep myself upright. Blood surges to my groin, and I tilt my head slightly, giving him better access. My back twitches and I wince. We need to discuss the situation. Last night. This morning. All of it.

'I don't have a toothbrush. I mean, I could get one. The nurse has some.'

His lips crawl to my ear, and his hands paw at my back.

'We have some students who don't regularly brush at home, and she takes them each morning to practice dental hygiene.'

'Are you talking about clean mouths to turn me on?' he whispers into my ear, the heat sending chills up my spine. I move backward and stumble on my heel before Vincent grabs at my sweater and catches me, holding me close.

'No. No, I honestly, I'm rambling,' I say.

His mouth lands on my neck, and his warm, sweet breath enters my ear, constricting my chest.

'Why are you so fucking sexy?' he purrs.

'Me?'

'Keep your mouth closed. Okay?'

I nod. Vincent's lips dance across my face, my beard prickling at this touch, until his mouth lands on mine and he pauses. With his eyes closed, his long, brown eyelashes come into full view. I keep my gaze on him. I need to see this.

Carefully, he takes the tip of my bottom lip in his teeth. A hand lands on my pants and cups my package. He lets out a little moan.

'You had something buttery for breakfast.'

'A croissant,' I whisper with a smile. 'From this bakery a few blocks from my place. The couple is French. They visited Maine one summer and never left. France's loss is our city's gain. And my stomach's.'

'Shhh.'

Once again, his presence sends blood rushing to my cock, filling his hand through my pants. Vincent's mouth leaves mine, and he buries his face in my neck, clutching me.

'I'm sorry,' he says, removing his hand and collapsing into me. 'I didn't expect to see you. Here. And well, I kind of go haywire around you.' He covers his eyes with a hand. 'I thought if you kept your mouth closed . . .'

Having Vincent here. In my office. Close. My heart flips. I wrap my arms around him, gathering him up, trying to hold him tight enough to squash all his insecurities, at least for a moment.

'Let's sit,' I suggest.

Letting him go, I move to the chair closest to the window. Vincent follows, taking the one across from me. He settles into his seat and glances at the table – crumbs from my breakfast. The French make the flakiest croissants. The smell of butter assaults my nose when I'm almost a block away, and I imagine an entire stick baked into each delectable treat. Rushing to our meeting, I neglected the mess. I grab a tube of wipes from the shelf and quickly wipe down the table, catching the crumbs in my hand as the scent of lemon bleach fills the room.

'Maybe we should have talked about work.' I drop the crumbs from my palm into the trash can and grab some sanitizer from my desk.

'Yeah, maybe.'

'I don't want to put you on the spot,' I say, returning to

the chair. The aroma of alcohol from the sanitizer, still wet on my palms, mixes with the bleach from the wipe, and I'm not sure it could smell any cleaner. 'Maybe I'm out of practice, but I thought things were going well. Um, you asked to suck my . . .'

'I know. I was trying to take a risk. Be brave. I wasn't myself. I'm sorry. I shouldn't have done that,' Vincent says, and his hands move to cover his face. 'Been so abrupt about you leaving, I mean.'

I lean across the table, not making contact but bringing my hands closer.

'What happened? You seemed to be . . . enjoying yourself.'

'I was. Absolutely. Most definitely enjoying myself. I just, I mean, it's not usually how I behave. Most of my first dates don't make it past the check. I'm not really sure what happened.'

'Vincent, look at me. Please.'

He moves his hands to his lap, and our eyes meet. Framed by those alluring lashes, there are tiny amber flecks in those hazel depths.

'I know you've been on many more dates than I have,' I say, pushing my glasses up, 'but I'm guessing we both fall into the novice category.'

He chuckles and adds, 'That's one way to put it.'

When Vincent looks at me, his face softens, and I can glimpse the scared boy inside the grown man sitting across from me. The urge to connect. To encourage Vincent. A light floaty sensation overtakes my chest – there's a hopefulness percolating inside me.

'All this stuff.' I grab the container of wipes and hold

it up. 'The napkins. The wipes. You know they're just distractions. It doesn't matter. I mean to me.'

'Stop being so sweet. You're making this more difficult.'

I'm not trying to confuse him. We need to stop whatever this is. It's not professional. Sure, he's sexy. With those broad shoulders and shiny bald head, my dick was harder than it's been in a long time. No pill required. Corrine would get a kick out of that. Wanting me to talk to him, unsure of what to say but craving to understand what tickled his fancy. Not knowing what I was doing, but he clearly got off on the attention – being called a 'good boy.' Vincent seemed to enjoy it, and my cock throbbed at the praise–feedback loop. This isn't how first dates are supposed to go. Not mine, anyway. Have dinner. Make small talk. Shake hands. Maybe a hug. Go home.

Unlike other queer dating apps, SWISH caught my attention because Gillian assured me it's for more than hookups. I have a propensity to lead with my heart, and yet there I was, after my maiden voyage, back at his house with my dick in his mouth. Oy.

'Listen, we have to work together for at least the next six weeks,' I say, remembering why he's here. 'Why don't we forget about last night? It never happened.' I glance around my office. Helen tries to keep my mess in check, but small piles of books, folders, papers, and a few stray empty cans of seltzer give away my propensity toward sloppiness. As much as I'd love to get to know Vincent better, this isn't the time to become distracted. 'My job hinges on this software implementation going smoothly.'

A hint of a smile wanders onto Vincent's face. Would I love to revisit the scenario in his bathroom last night?

Obviously. But getting this software up and running comes first. The school's reputation and my job depend on it.

'Deal?'

Vincent nods four times, a blink accompanying each one, and replies, 'Deal.'

7

Vincent

Nod and blink.

Nod and blink.

Nod and blink.

Nod and blink.

Each time, my eyes close when my chin is closest to the floor, not on the upswing, never on the upswing. Kent doesn't seem to notice; if he does, he doesn't mind. Yet.

I'm not married to it, but I definitely have a type. A sweet face. Older. A soft, cozy, furry body. A scrumptious cock. Kent Lester. People often wonder why I'm into older men. They assume I must have daddy issues. Nope. I have a healthy relationship with my father, who seems more confused by my OCD than my sexuality. My parents are still married, going on forty-eight years together – and, from what I can tell, still happy. I simply prefer men who have some experience. Wisdom. Warmth. Patience. Give me something to grab on to and get lost in. My dick pulses, remembering Kent's silver chest hair poking out from the V-neck. Stop. Focus on the task at hand, Vincent. This isn't the time to get distracted.

Crash!

Pulling his hand back, Kent knocks into his coffee, sending it tumbling to the floor. Thankfully, he's guzzled most of it, and only small splashes paint the carpet, splattering like a Jackson Pollock.

'Oy, I'm such a clumsy crab.' Kent grabs the wipes from the shelf. Behind the tube he now holds, I notice a stockpile of them and my skin sizzles.

'Kent, it's okay,' I say. He crouches down and wipes the floor and then moves to the legs of the table and chairs.

'No, it's not. I'm the principal. I shouldn't be such a hot mess.'

Seeing him on the ground, swiftly wiping, doing his best to clean up, my throat tightens. I swallow hard. I'm not sure what I can do to help, but I worry my presence caused some of this.

'Kent, please, it's fine.'

I stand, wanting to help but not sure what to do. When I crouch, Kent pops up and knocks into my face with the back of his head. Hard. A burst of pain flashes, and my nose throbs and burns from the brunt of the force. I fall back into the chair, dizzy, and cover my face with my hands.

'Oh shit, your beautiful face. I'm so sorry, I didn't mean to, crap, I mean crap, sorry, I shouldn't curse at school,' he blathers, and he's over me, grabbing at my hands. Beautiful. He called me beautiful. Well, my face, anyway. Pulling back, I do my best to avoid his hands, but his compliment, mixed with the smells of the citrus and bleach from the wipes, soothes me, and I let him make contact.

'Let me look, please.'

His fingers clutch my chin, and he tilts my face up. Looking at the ceiling, I'm fairly certain he's staring straight up my nose.

Wonderful.

'Is it broken?' I mumble.

'No.'

'Bleeding?'

He gets closer, his eyes only an inch from my throbbing nose. Static from his beard tingles my chin.

'I don't see any. I should probably get the nurse – or at least an ice pack. We have tons. She hands them out like candy.'

His breath, a mix of coffee and mint, travels right up my aching nose, and – clean mouth or not – I'm under Kent Lester's spell. My fingers, suddenly with a mind of their own, grab his collar and pull him in for a kiss. His lips are tentative, but I wrap my arms around his torso, and he quickly softens into me, letting my tongue play in the whiskers around his mouth before entering it and sending a jolt of adrenaline to my core.

Kent Lester covers me. Between my nose, which still pounds with each beat of my heart but seems to settle, and the smell of cleaning products overtaking the room, I forget to worry about, well, everything. Kent's moved a hand to my face. He caresses my cheek, and then his fingers travel to my ear, taking the lobe and gently massaging it.

'You're so beautiful,' he murmurs.

Again. Beautiful. And this time not only my face, but

'you.' That has to mean all of me. My belly rumbles with a pang of desire. But a sharp exhale out of my nose, followed by a glob of snot, causes me to pull back.

'I need a tissue.' I turn away and pull my forearm up to shield my face. The reality is, I need a complete scrub down from the neck up.

He pushes himself up and heads to the box of tissues on his desk.

'Uhhh, I'm out. Crap. Don't move.'

Opening the door, he sticks his head out.

'Helen, do we have any extra tissue boxes?'

'We're out. I can grab some in the supply closet.'

'No, I'll go,' he says and turns toward me. 'I'll be back in five.'

Hearing Helen's voice and the chatter of other people in the office agitates the flickering desire in my belly.

'Wait, I'll come with you.' I follow Kent into the hallway, covering my nose with my elbow.

Kent unlocks the metal door with a key from Helen's desk.

'The light's here somewhere ... there,' he says, illuminating the space with a long flickering fluorescent bulb hanging from the ceiling. I hold the heavy door with my shoulder as he enters.

Shelves line the long and narrow room, covering them with random supplies. Boxes of pencils, crayons, paper, glue, and anything needed to run a school crowd the space. Kent scans the area and finally shouts, 'There we go!'

He moves toward the far end and reaches for a box. I follow, and the door slams behind me with a bang. Kent jumps, slips, and the crowded shelf rains tissue boxes down on him.

'Are you okay?' I mutter through my arm. I've got snot on my sleeve, and I'm grateful I keep extra clothes in my car. When will there be time to fetch them?

'Good, all good,' Kent says, bending down and retrieving a box, ripping off the top, and handing me a clean tissue. 'There you go.'

'Thank you.'

I blow and attempt to clean my nose, and Kent walks past me, turning the lock on the door. He takes another tissue from the box, pulls my face toward his, and wipes right under my nose, carefully cleaning it. 'There we go. Now you're good. No, better than good.'

Without hesitation, he kisses my nose. Right where the snot was a second ago. I take a deep breath, trying to discover the moment again.

'But I thought,' I say, 'we're supposed to be professional.'

'We are. I mean, supposed to be.' He's back at my lips, his soft beard capturing the wetness of the kiss and encouraging me to forget we should be working. 'Your lips. They're so damn perfect. How am I supposed to ignore them?' he asks.

My career may be on the line but still, the only thing I can think about is his mouth on mine. Fuck. Hopscotch can wait. For now.

I remove Kent's glasses, carefully placing them on a nearby shelf covered in boxes of pencils.

'Vincent, how are you so damn sweet *and* sexy?'

His mouth lands on mine, and I grab at his belt. His smell. Earth. Pine. Embers. He's fucking intoxicating.

It's hard to unbuckle without looking. My fingers pull and poke, and finally, his hands leave my face, and with his tongue twirling with mine, he undoes it himself. The swoosh of his pants falling to his ankles prompts me to reach and take hold of his thick cock. I stroke with my right hand while my left lifts his shirt enough so I can rub his furry belly. My heart thumps faster, and I'm not sure how this will play out, but I can't stop myself. We're in a supply closet. The door is locked. His pants are off. My dick stands at full attention in my khakis.

'No. It's my turn,' he whispers.

Taking my hand from his stomach and pulling me, Kent sits on a short stepladder in the closet's corner. Naked from the waist down, he doesn't seem to mind sitting on the metal. Interesting.

With my stomach at his eye level, he draws me closer. His fingers find the buttons, and he works at them. 'Now, be a good boy.' My pants open, but Kent only yanks them down mid-thigh. 'Tighty-whities,' he says.

A small wet spot gives away my excitement, and the tip almost escapes the waistband. I blow a deep breath out as my shoulders drop. 'Please,' I plead. His fingers peel back the fabric enough so the head of my cock can breathe, and his index finger touches the tip, pulling back a small bead of precum, forming a long band.

'There we go,' he soothes. 'Such a good boy.'

He takes the sticky liquid between his finger and thumb and rubs it gently before putting both fingers in his mouth. What in heaven and earth?

'You okay?' he asks, licking his lips, and I'm not sure how to answer. 'Okay' doesn't capture it. The door locked ... but the bustle of the school outside ... the fact that we should be working. What magic does this man have over me? 'Okay?' Euphoric would be a more accurate word choice, so I simply nod.

He leans in and, without removing my underwear, gently kisses the exposed tip of my cock. The tickling from his beard is undeniable as I shudder. I tilt my head back and attempt to breathe through it. Taking the first inch in his mouth, Kent slowly begins sucking and licking and then gently pulls my underwear down to free me.

'Bald?'

'Excuse me?' I ask.

'You shave everywhere?'

'Yeah, it's just cleaner that way, I don't like ...' and before I finish, he's taken my cock in his mouth, at least half of it, wrapped inside his warm mouth, and his whiskers titillate in a way I've never experienced before. I poke my fingers in his thick hair, grateful there's no product, and slowly massage his head.

He pulls off and says, 'I haven't done this –' A gasp, he sounds out of breath. '– in a very long time, so please tell me if I do anything wrong.'

'No, nothing wrong. Just keep talking and telling me ...'

'You're a good boy,' he finishes for me. My dick fills at the phrase. 'Letting me suck your cock in the middle of the day. Such a clean, good boy.'

He looks up at me, his eyes glistening, and opens wide, waiting for me. I plunge back into the warm dampness of his mouth, and he resumes. His whiskers tickle the sensitive skin of my cock, creating more pleasure. Once more, I give myself over to Kent Lester. Seated, Kent reaches down, and begins stroking himself, and after I rushed him out last night, I'm hopeful he'll come.

'Jerk yourself. Nice and slow,' I say, hoping he enjoys my voice as much as I do his. He slows down on himself, but the slurping speeds up. Soft groans escaping through his lips wrapped around my hard cock give me a hint he's enjoying this.

Still stroking himself, he pauses and looks up at me. There's desire written in his eyes. 'I'm close, Vincent.'

Without thinking, I lower myself to a squat, careful not to touch the floor, and we swap roles. I stroke myself faster to speed up my orgasm and savor his irresistible dick – my mouth instantly thrilled at the familiar sensation of him filling me up. As he thrusts into me, I grab his waist, letting myself fall completely under his charms. 'Keep sucking. You've got my cock rock hard.'

His words prod me to move faster, harder, making a sloppy mess of myself.

'You look amazing with your lips around my dick. Such a beautiful, good boy.'

There it is. Again. That word. Beautiful. Me? Spit, and lord knows what else, drips down my chin, and I couldn't care less. Who am I, and what happened to the real me?

'Vincent, I'm, I'm . . .' he warns, attempting to push me off, but I resist, burying my head further, the glorious fuzz on his belly shoved against my forehead.

'You want it?' Kent's breath quickens with small gasps.

I bob my head and moan as he fucks deep into me. I want to taste him. Swallow him. Maybe if I keep a part of him inside me, I'll feel this free forever.

Eruptions of warm pleasure jolt to the back of my

throat. The closeness, the heat, and the thick texture send shivers down my spine. He leans over and begins rubbing my back through my shirt. I swallow his salty seed quickly, knowing the warmth came from inside him. It's perfectly pasteurized.

'Fuck, Vincent, you take my cum like such a good boy,' he purrs, and my dick, throbbing in anticipation, takes it as a cue to unload. With Kent still in my mouth, I shoot all over the floor, avoiding my pants or shoes.

My legs wobble beneath me, and I topple backward and land on the closet floor, the cool tiles providing an unexpected shock to my bare ass. My heart races, and I don't even pull my pants up or care about being on the filthy floor. That's what Kent Lester has done to me – cracked me open.

Kent stands over me, lifts my face, and drags his thumb across my chin. 'Look at my cum dripping off your lips.' He licks it off before kissing me gently. 'You're going to be trouble, Mr Manda,' he says, and I'm fairly sure he's right.

8

Kent

Apparently, reckless behavior that could not only get me fired but also have me losing my principal's license was the name of the game before the holiday break. What in the world was I thinking? Doing that. In a supply closet. At school. Clearly, I was thinking with the wrong head. Can I get a therapist for my cock? Paging Doctor Dick. I need to stop this nonsense. Immediately. Retroactively if possible. Find a DeLorean, build a time machine, go back two weeks, and never go on that date with Vincent Manda.

Sitting across from me, where I crashed into his nose before break, leading to the 'closet incident,' Vincent taps away at his keyboard. I'm more determined than ever to put the kibosh on anything beyond friendship. I'm not looking for a scandal. No contact with Vincent for fourteen days helped. New year, new me. Time with the family. Hanukkah and Christmas with Lia. She loved her stuffed unicorn. I'm not sure she understands how silly the name Corny is for it, but her first choice (Horny) was understandably a screeching no from her mother.

After our shenanigans in the closet, Vincent and I agreed we needed to immediately stop this . . . well, whatever was brewing between us, and the long holiday break allowed time and space to reset. But having him this close again, his eyelashes fluttering, remembering the short time we shared . . . not just sexually, but there was a connection. At least for me. Something about Vincent Manda makes me want to tuck him into my pocket and care for him like a treasure.

Vincent scratches an itch. A tingling I didn't know existed – and the talking. I never knew it could be so damn hot. Maybe it's just the excitement of being with a man after all these years. And by years, I mean since high school.

Brian Hall, my tall lanky track teammate, had offered to help me with my chemistry homework. The formulas confused the hell out of me and Brian was a science whiz. Between practice and tutoring, we spent a lot of time together. A friendship blossomed and the chemicals we studied in my thick textbook weren't the only thing bonding. Feelings deepened. And that's when it hit me. I realized my heart's inability to take things slowly, as I swiftly recognized my crush on Brian. Then one afternoon, it must have been May or June because I remember the humidity, we were showering after a late practice. Alone in the stall, Brian soaped himself up, staring at me. My cock, unable to hide my excitement, gave me away. Quick grabs. Slick sucking noises and panting echoed in the empty locker room. Right when he was coming, Brian pressed his forehead to mine, and for a fleeting moment, I thought, maybe. Maybe something more was possible.

But immediately after, he acted like nothing happened. 'I don't like you like that, Kent. I'm not gay.'

Meeting Corrine freshman year at the University of Southern Maine allowed me to lock that experience in a box. It was easier. And I loved Corrine. I mean, I still do. Being bi was something I always felt but didn't have the words for – the observation of lips, shoulders, muscles, and necks. I felt a tingle of attraction with everyone, regardless of gender, but I never knew what to do with it.

The rawness of the shower incident had scared me. Passionate. Hard. Thick. All those sensations, combined with our budding friendship galloped back with Vincent and his fucking sexy bald head. I want to take my tongue and run it over every inch, but I'm certain he'd never approve. I'm caught off guard by the unexpected side of me that comes out when I'm with him. Just like after the shower incident with Brian, I'm rethinking my decision to pursue men. Falling for Corrine was easier, that's for sure, but it never erased my bisexuality.

'Dr Cutler provided us with your high-level data,' Vincent says, interrupting the spiraling in my noggin. I shake my head like Sweetums does when he's trying to brush off my numerous kisses, and attempt to center myself.

'And I'll work to extract the GradePlus data,' I say. As the building admin, I own the data and I've tabbed the thick manual with the extraction process which appears to be a few clicks.

'It would be helpful for me to see what it might look like in the classroom. How much can we push for more frequent data collection? The teacher's setup. Can you make that happen?'

'Sure, um, yeah, of course,' I say.

There's a knock on the open door, and I jerk and almost spill my water. The bottle teeters on the table's edge, but I catch it just before it decimates Vincent's laptop.

'Mr Lester, can we grab your garbage?'

It's Theo, with his mop of sandy blond curls, sounding happier than he has in, well, as long as I've known him. Apparently, dating the cute-as-a-button first-grade teacher will do that to you.

'Of course, Theo, and remember, Kent is fine when students aren't around.'

'I know, and . . .'

Brodie, a small first grader with jet-black hair pops into my office. Completely hidden by Theo's frame and without making eye contact or uttering a word, Brodie grabs the trash can and hands it to Theo, who promptly empties it before returning it to Brodie.

After the 'fire-alarm incident' last year, Brodie's plan to earn points to help Theo has worked like a charm. Something tells me that Sheldon and Theo's budding relationship helps them communicate about everything, including Brodie.

'Brodie, how are you today?'

Silence.

'You must've had a good morning to be helping Mr Berenson,' I say.

Theo taps Brodie on the shoulder and raises an eyebrow.

'Yes, sir,' Brodie says in a faint, raspy voice.

Vincent's eyes dart between his laptop and the conversation, and I realize I've forgotten my manners.

'Mr Berenson, Brodie, this is Vincent. He's helping me with some new software.'

Theo shoots me a look. I mentioned a date with Vincent to him weeks ago, but I'm not sure he remembers.

'Oh, Vincent. Yes, Kent's mentioned you.' He remembers.

'Really? What has he said about me?' Vincent asks.

'Thank you, boys.' I fumble, moving to close the door. 'But we have important work to do. Say hello to Mr Soleskin for me.'

A huge grin sweeps over Theo's face, and my heart warms, knowing the universe and our exploding classroom numbers brought these two together.

'He seems like a sweet guy,' Vincent says.

'Theo? He really is. Took him a while to come out of his shell, but he's got a heart of gold.'

'And the kid helping him?'

'Brodie. He earns points for staying safe in the classroom. Theo's his reward. Sheldon, that's Brodie's teacher, is Theo's boyfriend.'

'And the kids all know?'

'They do. They're ecstatic about it. You can't help but fall in love with Sheldon. Younger students want their teachers to be happy, and Theo makes Sheldon happy.'

Vincent purses his lips and nods, seemingly impressed by the level of acceptance here at Lear.

'I've worked hard to cultivate a school community where everyone is welcome and celebrated.'

'It really shows,' Vincent says, grabbing his travel pack of wipes and cleaning his hands, keyboard, and screen.

'I'm glad,' I say, pleased my diligence has paid off. 'How about you? Are you out at Hopscotch?'

'Oh yeah. Geoff couldn't care less. I don't think anyone at Hopscotch gives it a second thought.' Vincent folds the dirty wipe and tosses it into the empty trash can. 'Geoff's more concerned about my mishaps at work than my sexuality.'

Vincent's wiping ritual happens a few times a day, almost on the hour, and the growling in my stomach notifies me it's almost lunchtime.

'Hungry?' he asks. The right side of his mouth turns up, and the urge to lean over and nibble his lip needs to stop right now. Thank you very much.

'Yes, wanna break? I have a few emails to catch up on, but I can be ready in half an hour if that works for you,' I offer.

'Sounds good. I'm going to run and grab something. A buddy told me about this great Jewish deli –'

'Schmear and Far. The best bagels in existence. Apologies to New York City, but it's my favorite,' I say. 'They smoke their own lox, a few varieties, but the pastrami lox is something everyone needs to experience at least once.'

My mouth waters, thinking about the perfectly smoked fish, the edges peppered with spices that mix with the lox to create a sandwich anointed by God.

'Kent,' Vincent says, the smell of bagels and fish still swirling in my head. 'Would you like to come? Or I can grab you something?'

I grip my hands together, my mouth suddenly as dry as stale matzoh.

'Vincent, listen. What happened before break . . . um, twice. We need to cool our jets. I need this' – I point to his laptop, the folders, papers, all of it – 'to work. Without a solution to Lear's toppling scores, it's likely the board won't renew my contract.'

'Kent, I asked you if you wanted a sandwich, not to elope.'

A chuckle escapes my lips, and Vincent's hazel eyes scan me. His eyelashes dance with each blink, and the hunger in my stomach radiates outward.

'It's important to me, too. The project's success.'

'I'm sure it is,' I say, and screw it, I'm starving, and the frozen burrito in my bag cannot compete with a bagel and fixings from Schmear and Far.

'You know what? You're right. Clearly, the universe wants me to enjoy pastrami lox. Can we bring it back here so I can catch up on those emails?'

'Of course,' he says, his hand resting on my back, and why'd he have to go and touch me like that?

'Let's go.' I grab my coat and head for the office door.

In his passenger seat, I'm instantly taken aback at how neat Vincent's car is. It doesn't have the new car smell, but the pristine shine on everything makes me wonder how long he's had it. He pushes the ignition, and the dash comes to life with lights and beeps. The cab fills with guitar plucking from every direction. When the male voice interrupts, singing about being down a time or two, Vincent rushes to lower the volume.

'You really love Fleetwood Mac.'

'*Rumours*. Yes.'

'Pardon.'

'I mean, yes, I like the band,' he says, clicking his seatbelt, 'but for me, it's really all about this one album.'

'It's definitely a classic. I mean, I was a kid when it

came out, and I remember it fondly even then. But you're younger than me. You weren't even born. Why this album?'

'My parents loved the band and when I heard this record as a child, something stuck. The guitars. The harmonies. The layers. Everything just works together perfectly. Nothing is out of place.'

The napkins. The teeth brushing. Vincent's propensity toward order means we'd never work, anyway. But maybe, if I can temper my heart, we can be friends.

'Well, turn it up.'

'You don't mind?'

'I insist.'

I glance over, and he's smiling. He thumbs a button on his steering wheel, and the music crescendos, overtaking our voices, and Vincent's face relaxes. Once again, I want to reach over and grab him. His hand. His arm. His beautiful face. He's so damn sexy. But I don't. I sit and behave like a nice Jewish boy.

9

Vincent

Yesterday's gone. What happened with Kent is over. Put it out of my mind.

Working with him every day may prove harder than I thought. It's been almost three weeks since we agreed to pour cold water on our shenanigans. Friends only. Professionalism and all that jazz.

The guitar solo floods the walls of my car. All I want is to see Kent's smile. Something pops deep inside my core when his lips turn up, his entire silver beard moving with them. I need to look forward, not back. Maybe I'm confusing the intense attraction with real emotion? My thumb finds the volume rocker on the steering wheel and cranks the music, attempting to overtake thoughts of a sexy, slightly younger St Nick with a fuzzy chest and thick dick.

After a twenty-minute ferry ride, I find myself wrapped in my late January warmest jacket at the front door of Marvin and Olan. As their relationship flourishes, I'm reminded that we were destined to be friends. While he's completely adorable, Marvin's almost ten years younger than me, and Kent's shown me that being the younger one really melts my butter. Memories return. Running my hands up and down Kent's stomach, his delicious dick filling my lips. Words of praise flooding me with pleasure. I shake my head, push my erection down, and ring the doorbell.

'Vincent!' Olan Stone, Marvin's fiancé, opens the door. His tooth gap greets me smack in the middle of his Hollywood smile. Olan's deep ebony biceps stretch his T-shirt and how I ever thought I could compete with this guy is beyond me.

'Olan,' I begin, and spot small hands wrapped around his thigh, 'and Illona, how are you?'

Her cute face peeks around her dad's waist. A small smile cracks into a giant one, revealing her dimples, and it's no wonder Marvin's the happiest guy I know.

'Come in, it's frigid out. How was the ferry?'

'A little rocky, but I stayed inside,' I say, slowly untangling myself from my winter gear.

'Smart,' Marvin calls from the kitchen. He's pouring the seltzer he loves from a dark blue bottle. 'Lemon?'

'No thanks,' I reply with a grin. According to an article I read, citrus rinds can harbor a surprising amount of dirt and bacteria. Nobody needs salmonella doing backstrokes in your beverage.

Before I know it, I'm enveloped in a huge embrace. Marvin's arms wrap around me, squeezing, and I take a deep breath. I hug him back and allow the closeness to ground me. When I pull back, Illona stands near me, and I know she wants a hug, too. I've gotten better at picking her up. Marvin explained things to her, for sure, because she checks in way more than any child naturally would.

'Your turn,' I say, and she holds her arms up. As I lift her, the pressure of her legs wrapped around my waist settles in, her embrace filled with love and affection.

'How's this? Not too tight, right?' she asks.

'Nope. You're perfect,' I whisper into her ear. And she is – the sweetest angel.

I've never even thought about having children. I'd need a partner, right? I don't think I could handle it on my own. Who am I fooling? I don't think I could handle it with an army of nannies. Children are . . . a lot. And infants? Baby food. Diapers. And the snacks. A cacophony of crumbs. Bloody knees. Mud. That would be a big fat no.

But Illona is Olan's daughter. Marvin will be her stepfather soon. And she's so courteous. In small doses, I can handle this.

'I'll keep Gonzo away from you,' she says, and maybe I'd be okay with a child like her. 'I ate already. Mac and cheese with a little baked chicken. You're having baked chicken with just a little mac and cheese.'

As if summoned, Gonzo saunters in and rubs on my leg. The only thing worse than children – pets. Dogs. Cats. And don't get me started on hamsters. A literal rodent in the house. Hell no.

Illona jumps down, scoops the feline up, cuddles him like a baby, and says, 'Now we'll go play in my room and let Daddy and Marvin have adult time with Vincent.' She kisses his head, and phlegm crawls up my throat.

'One movie, sweetheart,' Olan says, patting her shoulder. 'Holler if you need anything.'

With a wave, she and the beast fly up the stairs. Without a word, Marvin turns the faucet on for me.

Having friends who make an effort to understand how my brain works has made a world of difference for me. No explaining. No apologizing. It's a game-changer.

Standing at the sink, scrubbing my hands from the contact and in preparation to eat, I sigh. The good kind. Olan threads his hands under Marvin's arms and hugs him from behind, resting his chin on Marvin's shoulder. I'm grateful they're comfortable showing affection in front of me. My lips part as I watch them. Someday. Maybe I'll be comfortable with so much closeness.

'Marvin tells me you're seeing someone?' Olan asks.

'Saw. Seen. Was seeing,' I say. 'It's complicated.'

'Wait, what happened?' Marvin moves away from Olan and grabs a pot and casserole dish from the stove. 'I thought you were super into him?'

'I am. Was,' I correct. 'But we're working together. It's not professional.'

'Um, hello. You're talking to the teacher who had a secret affair with the parent of one of his students.' Marvin uncovers the food, the savory aroma filling the room. 'Unprofessional is the goal. It's hot.'

Olan comes from behind, his clear favorite way to approach, and kisses Marvin's neck.

'I concur.'

'Well, I'm not trying to lose my job,' I say. 'After the snafu at the last school, I need this to go smoothly. Falling for the hot, gray-bearded principal isn't going to help.'

'Oh, he's a daddy?' Marvin asks.

I wince because, well, Kent Lester is the definition of

a daddy. The thought of him holding me close, his soft body embracing every inch of me, fills my mind.

'He's Jewish,' I say, attempting to change the subject.

'Oh, a jaddy?' Marvin says, his eyebrows dancing. 'Nicely done.'

'He's older. Yes, but he's, well, not that much older.'

'We all have preferences.' Olan pulls chairs out for Marvin and me. 'As long as nobody's getting hurt, there's nothing wrong with that.'

'And what happened at your last school, it won't happen –' Marvin says, but I interrupt.

'It might. I missed the meeting. They made the wrong decision. It was my fault,' I say, reminding myself how horribly the rollout at River Elementary went. Because of me. Wash. Scrub. Rinse. Repeat.

'Vincent.' Marvin places his hand on my forearm, my sweater shielding skin-to-skin contact. 'This is a new school. A new project. A new principal. A sweet, sexy one.'

'Yes. One that is all wrong for me.' I dish extra macaroni and cheese onto my plate. The cheese stretches from the serving spoon, and I pause to prevent any from getting on the table.

'You hate your job anyway. Maybe getting canned would be a blessing. Bang the principal and make it happen.'

'I don't hate it.' I grab my glass to quench my parched mouth.

'You don't love it,' Marvin replies.

'Who loves their job anyway?' I ask.

'I do.' Olan hands me an extra napkin.

'Me too,' Marvin says with a shrug.

'In any event, my bills aren't going to pay themselves. And "banging the principal" isn't going to help.'

'But you like him?' Olan moves the casserole dish closer. 'And he likes you? I'm not comprehending the issue.'

'Sweetie,' Marvin says, serving me four slices of chicken breast. I smile because he remembers even numbers are my preference. 'They're working together. This job needs to go off without a hitch for Vincent. Shtupping Kent isn't a good idea.'

'There's shtupping?' Olan asks.

'No shtupping,' I say. 'Maybe some shtupping-adjacent activities . . . but that was weeks ago. No more.'

'Shtupping adjacent?' Marvin asks with a tilt of his head.

'Before the holidays. Only twice.'

'Twice?' Marvin's voice squeaks and Olan lets out a small laugh. 'I thought it was just once?'

I force a smile, teeth showing, and shrug. 'It just . . . happened. Again. I didn't mean for it to happen the first time.' I turn to Olan, who nods with furrowed brows. 'And the second time' – I glance at Marvin – 'it was, well, him. It's just . . . physical. Was physical.' I shake my head. 'No need to conflate that with emotions. He does something to me. Did – past tense. We're just friends. Or trying to be.'

'In my experience, when things happen, and then, well, happen again, it means maybe you're bashert,' Olan says.

'Bashert,' Marvin repeats. 'Meant to be.'

'Look at me.' I nod to my fingers. With precision, I fold my napkin inside out and twist it around, scouring for a spot that's still pristine. 'Nobody wants this. There's nothing bashert about us.'

Marvin stands and moves toward a drawer in the kitchen. 'Let me get you another. We have plenty!'

'Thank you.' I don't protest. 'Now tell me about the wedding planning.'

'Planning a wedding is not for the faint of heart,' Olan says.

'Marriage isn't either,' I reply.

'Noted.' Marvin places a fresh napkin on my lap. 'But when it's true love, you persist.'

'I'm less concerned about the wedding and more interested in being married to this one,' Olan says, taking Marvin's hand as he returns to his seat.

Marvin grins. 'My mother would disagree.'

'Your mother isn't getting married,' Olan replies.

Watching these two, the weight in my chest reminds me I'm older than both of them. Will this ever happen for me? The countless SWISH dates at The Purple Giraffe would argue no. Do I even want it? Would anyone ever be able to handle my idiosyncrasies on such a permanent level? Kent's sweetness and patience never waned. But that foolishness is done. I tuck the edge of the extra napkin into my pants pocket, securing it tightly, hoping it doesn't fall to the floor.

Bright guitars tangle and tease before Lindsey's voice comes in, singing about the wrongness of loving you. When the ladies' voices crash into his, a wall of harmonies washes over me, and my bathroom's walls shake with the ferocity of the drums.

I step into the shower and the bleach scent soothes me. Warm water cascades over my body, and I adjust the temperature to make it hotter. The scalding spray hits my shoulders, and I brace myself against the wall, hoping to sanitize every atom. As I squeeze the bottle of liquid soap, its silky texture glides onto my hands. I begin with the top of my smooth head. Slowly scrubbing and scouring every inch, I move my way down.

Washing my chest, my fingers linger on my nipples. The attention brings them to life, and my thumbs prod and poke, and my groin simmers. Slippery bubbles help the sensation, and my right hand travels south while the left continues giving my pec attention.

When my fingers reach my cock, it's already swollen, blood racing south as thoughts of Kent swirl. His thick beard. His furry chest and stomach. His delectable, long dick sliding in and out of my mouth, stretching my lips in the best way possible. His hands on my head. Massaging my earlobes. Telling me to swallow him like a good boy.

Palming myself, I stroke slowly, the soap billowing between my fingers, my cock stiff and unyielding. Teasing the head, my thumb glides back and forth. The steam and fragrant orange and honey soap cocoon me in bliss. As my insides smolder, I glide my palm harder, faster, and pinch at my nipple, sending shivers of pleasure through my chest, straight to my core.

The music pours over the glass shower door, the guitar solo hinting at the imminent fadeout. I use both hands to create a tunnel and begin thrusting faster, fucking my hands to the rhythm of pounding drums. My hands wrapped around myself, I throw my head back, savoring each stroke and brushing the sensitive tip with my thumb until my knees shake.

I reach around with one hand and place my index finger near my hole. I have no interest in entering myself, but the right pressure, right near the base, yup, right there, and everything kicks into overdrive. Closing my eyes, I picture Kent's face, the saliva gathering at the corners of his mouth, grabbing his fuzzy ass, his fat cock plunging inside my mouth, filling me up. It all blankets me, and my orgasm crawls up. My toes tingle, my balls begin to tighten, and with a few more tugs, I shoot thick ropes into my hand. Water rushes over my face, and I blow out, pushing it away from my mouth. With each spasm, my hole clenches, and my mouth falls open, gasping as my fingers catch every drop.

I run my hands under the water as the guitars layer over each other, and the song trails off. Exhaling sharply, I stare at the mess I've spilled down the drain. Kent's face ripples in my head. What has this man done to me? I close my eyes and start counting breaths.

10

Kent

'This isn't for you.'

Corrine gives Sweetums her best attempt at a teacher's glare. We used to play this game of trying to stare each other down. As a human resources manager for a small local shipping company, she doesn't have much practice, but we always laughed about who could give our daughter the sternest stare-down.

'He just likes to watch.' I pet Sweetums's long, thick orange coat before settling in on a stool and rubbing the fluff at the end of his pointy ears.

'Just watch, my ass.' Corrine tips her chin. She's never bought my bullshit.

Sweetums, unswayed by my attempts to soothe him, swats at the waving ends of the scallions as Corrine chops. Now, I'm the proud recipient of her glare. I lug Sweetums off the counter and move to the sofa, turning so I'm still facing the kitchen island where Corrine does her magic.

Since our divorce and her subsequent marriage to Charlie, we still chat regularly. We don't see each other often, but after the last few weeks with Vincent, I needed a night with my best friend.

'Still no citrus,' she asks, a bowl and whisk in her hand. Her new diamond, bigger than the one I bought back in college, shines against her fair skin.

'Nope,' I answer. My cholesterol medication warns against grapefruit specifically, but being an overcautious Jew, I avoid all citrus.

She spoons more sugar into the bowl and begins whisking.

'The implementation is going well?' she asks. Corrine has always been my biggest champion. Even after our divorce, she still plays the role of my loudest cheerleader.

'I think so. We have weeks before we go live.'

'Right before spring break?' She pours the dressing onto the salad and tosses it with large wooden tongs.

'It's a blessing. We'll finish before the school board meeting. I can report out and then relax over break.'

'Why they have these board meetings right before vacations is beyond me.'

'It's their way of making me earn the break,' I say, knowing the stress will probably have me snuggling with Sweetums most of the time off.

'And so far, everything's going smoothly?' She places the salad on the table and joins me on the couch.

'Shreya is handling the technology parts I don't understand,' I say. Sweetums has flopped into my lap, chin up, and purrs like a motorboat while I scratch his chin.

'So, all of it?'

Now it's my turn to give Corrine my patented teacher

look. She catches my gaze, and we engage in a short stare-off until we both erupt in laughter.

'I know technology,' I say through the last few chuckles.

'Excuse me? I had to explain to you how to like something on Facebook. And why liking your own posts is redundant. You do not "know technology," friend.'

'This is why I keep young people around.'

'Three years qualifies me as a young person?'

'Younger than me.'

'And how old is Vincent?' The familiar lilt in her voice cues me to her prodding.

Corrine knew I was bisexual midway through our first date. We sat across from each other, knees knocking under the table, poking our ramen bowls with chopsticks, me wondering how to eat the giant bowl of salty yumminess without making a fool of myself. When a gorgeous specimen of a man sauntered by to grab his takeout, we both stared. She asked. I explained. If anything would become of us, and it certainly did, I knew I had to be honest from the start.

'Forty.'

Sweetums buries his face in my lap and lies belly up. At his massive size, I don't argue when he demands attention.

'So much younger. Does that make you his . . .'

'Don't say it. The whole "daddy" thing makes me cringe.'

'You didn't mind when Gillian called you that.'

'No, because I'm her father. And she doesn't call me "daddy" anymore. And clearly, it's not the same thing,' I say.

'Well, you are a total –'

'Corrine.'

I tilt my head, giving the most severe glare I can summon.

'Handsome older man. A catch. That's all I was going to say.' Her signature half-smile envelops her face as she brings the salad to the table.

'I don't know how I feel about the . . . gap.'

Standing to join her, I gently prod Sweetums, who jumps to the floor and heads to his chair at the table.

'Age is just a state of mind. You're both adults.'

'Or trying to be.' Sweetums jumps up to his chair.

'When I bought you a kitten, I didn't expect him to assert himself as king of the castle.'

'You were simply trying to distract me from your proposal news. Sweetums's impending reign over my monarchy wasn't even on your radar.'

With his size, Sweetums's enormous head reaches a few inches above the table – darting his gaze between Corrine and me, waiting to be served.

'I don't feed him at the table.'

'Kent, he looks hungry. And demanding.'

'He's always hungry. Just ignore him.'

Corrine pulls her plate a few inches away from my adorable fluffy feline.

I open the pizza box, and the steam escapes, filling the room with the delicious smell of extra cheese and a crispy crust. As I serve Corrine, Sweetums's paw darts out, making a game out of it, and she shouts, 'No!' My heart leaps in my chest, and I drop a piece right on her lap. *Splat!*

'Oh my gosh. Cori, I'm sorry,' I blather, heading for the roll of paper towels.

'I wouldn't consider it a successful visit if I didn't leave your house with something on my clothes.'

She sits calmly, waiting, and I'm reminded just how patient and understanding she has always been with me. We fell into a comfortable rhythm that included her understanding my propensity for clumsiness.

'Charlie's playing tonight?' I ask, handing her a wad of paper towels for her pants as I wipe up the table.

'It's almost February. He plays almost every night,' she says, wiping the sauce and cheese off her jeans like it was the most normal thing in the world.

Corrine's marriage, only a year after our divorce, surprised me. Our split was beyond amicable, but we both decided we needed space to figure out our next steps. Three months later, she met Charlie. Two months after that, they moved in together, and they were engaged soon after. Charlie's a wonderful guy. I know my girls are in good hands.

'Well, I'm happy he's busy enough with hockey that we occasionally get to have pizza,' I say, my mouth watering at the sight of the piping hot slices before me.

With pizza lodged in her mouth, Corrine gives me her sweet, crinkly-eyed smile. The one that caught my attention freshman year at USM and has kept me on my toes for years. Her smile lets me know she accepts me. Loves me. Even when I drop hot pizza in her lap.

'And then I put the scores in this notebook where I try to gather the remnants of student observations and work and attempt to formulate them into information for conferences and report cards.'

Sheldon Soleskin, first-grade teacher and a shining star since his transfer to Lear right after Thanksgiving, stands almost a half-foot shorter than Vincent as he walks him through his current data collection process. I give them space, attempting to survey the class and ensure I'm available to intervene while Sheldon gives Vincent his attention.

'And this is how most of the teachers do it?' Vincent asks.

'Oh, no. Everyone has their own method. Becky uses sticky notes – a different color for each child. Jolene uses index cards. Also, a different color. But for each subject, not the child. Becky uses a board, and Jolene uses rings to organize them.'

Vincent scratches his head. How often does he shave to keep it so smooth?

'And that's just first grade.'

Vincent's fingers fly across his laptop, and he nods slowly while biting his lower lip. My eyes focus on his upper teeth hanging over the bottom of his mouth. A small dot of saliva forms, and what might it be like, slurping it up? After we both brush our teeth, of course. I didn't mind the oral hygiene at his house, and Vincent was all for kissing in my office before the break sans brushing. That mouth. Those eyelashes. That bald head.

'Mr Lester, I'm done!'

Kylie stands at my feet, waving her math paper like a flag. As her assignment rattles, I'm unable to see it clearly, and I'm not sure what to do with it. I'm here to watch the class so Vincent and Sheldon can chat, but before I can reply, Sheldon calls over from his desk.

'Kylie, remember, our finished papers go in the "done" bin, and then you can . . .'

'Make a math choice,' Kylie shouts.

I smile at her and walk around the classroom, seeing if anyone needs me. They don't. Sheldon's class runs like a well-oiled machine.

'I think I have what I need,' Vincent says, walking toward me. With his open laptop balancing on his forearm, he types with his free hand.

'Are you sure?' I ask. 'I'm happy to stay and watch the class longer.'

'Nope. All good. I need to aggregate the requirements.'

'Go ahead, I'll be along shortly,' I say. Vincent thanks Sheldon with a nod and heads back to my office. He's set up shop on my table while Geoff and Shreya spread out in the conference room. Occasionally, he joins them, but mostly, he opts to work alone. He vacates the space when I need my office, and it hasn't been an issue. I've grown accustomed to having him around.

'Mr Manda seems lovely.' Sheldon sidles up to me as I return to roaming the room.

'He's a nice man. Yes. We're friends.'

Sheldon's eyebrows, so light they're barely visible against his porcelain skin, race to the top of his forehead. Clearly, Theo's been talking about us.

'That's all,' I say.

Sheldon's eyes go wide, and he gives a cheeky half-smile. 'Sure thing, Mr Lester.'

'Have a good afternoon, Mr Soleskin.' I tilt my head, offer a grin, and head for the door.

*

'Is it bad?'

Hunched over his laptop, Vincent's furrowed brow makes his handsome face appear even more snack-worthy. After I left Sheldon's, I stopped in a few other classrooms on my way back.

Checking in on teachers, ensuring nobody needed a bathroom break. I remember what it was like being trapped for hours, needing to pee. It also might be wise to give Vincent some space . . . for both of us.

'No, nothing bad, just me.'

'You?'

'Geoff wants this data streamlined and formatted. I have to go through each line and remove commas, add spaces, that sort of thing. It's just . . . tedious.'

Vincent's lips form a circle, and he lets out a massive sigh. 'Can I do anything to help? I can re-do the extract.' I sit opposite him, ready to assist.

'Nope, I just need to finish.'

His eyes dart up, another deep inhale, and then, 'But thank you.'

Glancing at my watch, I see it's almost time for dismissal.

'Okay. I'll be back in twenty minutes.'

He doesn't move his eyes from his screen but gently nods.

As I walk into the equipment closet off the cafégymatorium, Ruth relaxes, feet up, fiddling on her phone, waiting to head out.

'Can you do my car duty today?'

'Of course, boss.' Ruth relinquishes her phone to the desk.

'Everything okay?'

Vincent's glazed eyes and frequent sighs tread water in my head. 'It's Vincent. Something's up.'

Ruth grabs the jacket of her tracksuit and walks toward the exit. 'I got you. You take care of your man.' He's not my man. But I don't correct her.

When I return, Vincent's precisely as I left him – hunched over, gazing diligently at his screen, while his fingers tap, attempting to keep up with his brain.

'Vincent, I'm just going to sit here and reply to some emails. If you need anything . . . well, I'm here.'

Nothing. A swirl of worry churns in my stomach as I see the tight pinch on his face. There's something he's not telling me. With students, I often have to ask questions and wait. Let them calm down. Settle in. And then the talking comes. But Vincent doesn't want to talk. With a set jaw, he's glued his gaze on his screen.

When my emails have been read, replied to, sorted, and filed, he's still at it. It's been almost two hours, and I'm expected at Gillian's for dinner tonight. I have dinner at her house on the first Friday of the month. 'Poppy time' with my granddaughter is a highlight for me.

'Vincent, it's after five. Are you almost ready to stop?' A terse shake of his head.

I stand, peering over his shoulder to assess what he's doing. A spreadsheet is open, rows and rows of numbers. It looks to be in the thousands. Vincent's fingers scroll as he taps, deletes, taps, deletes. It suddenly dawns on me he hasn't moved since he returned from Sheldon's class. That was hours ago.

'Vincent, are you hungry? Don't you need the bathroom?' Again, he shakes his head.

I take the seat across from him and watch. Still trying to figure out what to do.

'I'm supposed to have dinner at my daughter's tonight.'

Vincent's fingers tap, tap, tap, and small beads of sweat form on his brow. I stare at one as it infiltrates his eyelashes. My fingers fumble in my pocket until I find my phone and dial Gillian's number.

'Where are you? Louis smoked brisket, and Lia has a play for you.'

'Really?'

My mouth waters, thinking about the salty, smoky meat melting in my mouth.

'I'm not sure I'm going to make it.'

'Why not? It's almost six. On a Friday. You're allowed to leave school, Dad.'

'Something's come up.' Vincent uses his sleeve to wipe his brow.

'You're coming. Lia can stay up until eight. Eight-thirty. It's Friday. Come when you can.'

'Okay. I'll see you soon.' Vincent's eyes haven't wavered, and I'm unsure if he's even heard my conversation. 'Hopefully.'

Something has taken over, and Vincent's determination to finish the task won't untangle its clutch from his psyche. I'm not leaving him in my office alone on a Friday night. I grab my computer and begin working on the school newsletter. That will be one less thing for me to do next week. Helen will be thrilled.

We sit across from each other, typing. I place a bottle of water next to his laptop, but he doesn't touch it. By six-thirty, we're the only people left in the building.

'Vincent, you must be starving,' I say, my stomach growling.

'My daughter is expecting me. Do you like brisket?' His fingers strike the keyboard in a crescendo of sound.

'I need to lock the school. Set the alarm. We have to stop soon.'

'Four more minutes.'

It's the first time I've heard his voice since we returned from Sheldon's class, and the tension in my shoulders releases at his familiar timbre.

'Okay.'

I pack up for the weekend. Typically, things begin to slow down in February. I'm not intending to do much this weekend after the work I just banked. My laptop and planner make it into the messenger bag Corrine bought me for my fiftieth birthday. It's navy-blue, with white trim, and nothing I would ever buy for myself.

There's a good chance nothing will leave my bag.

'Done.'

The perspiration on Vincent's brow now drips, and he's sweated through his shirt. He's completely soaked.

'Vincent, you're, you're . . .' The hair on the nape of my neck lifts, thinking about telling him about his current state.

'I'm sorry,' he mutters. His voice is soft and apprehensive.

'Don't apologize.' I place my hand on his back, alarmed by the dampness. 'What happened? Are you okay?'

'I had to finish.'

'Is Geoff waiting on it? He left hours ago.'

'You don't understand. I had to finish. Now.'

I rub my chin, my fingers getting lost in the whiskers, as a fluttering flies in my stomach.

'I got . . . stuck.' Vincent's eyes lower and I take a seat. 'It's this constant mental rumination. Checking. My brain can't think of anything else besides the task.'

'You were focused.'

'You could say that.' Vincent braces himself on the table and sweat flecks his shirt. He can't be comfortable. 'I feel like a fool. And I need to pee. And eat. I'm starving.'

'Go pee. You're coming with me to Gillian's. She has food. A feast.'

'But . . .' Vincent's chin drops to his chest.

'You're in luck. I happen to keep backups.' I open a drawer and reveal clean, folded shirts. I hand him an olive Henley and say, 'Go to the bathroom. Freshen up. I'll text my daughter.'

'Thank you.'

He takes the shirt. Our fingers brush and my heart skips a beat. I close my eyes as he heads for the bathroom. As I contemplate his circumstances, a wave of empathy tightens my chest, igniting a strong desire to offer support. Right now, my son-in-law's brisket is all I've got, and it's been known to be magical.

11

Vincent

'Finally! Fifteen minutes before bedtime.'

A tall, slender woman with fair skin and strawberry-blonde hair opens the door, shouts at Kent, and immediately marches back inside. I'm not sure she even noticed me.

The urge to bolt home, take a shower, and curl up in bed for the entire weekend was overwhelming after what occurred at school. But Kent Lester, with his kind, soft eyes, wanting to watch over me, take care of me, and the promise of 'the world's most magnificent brisket' swayed me. Besides everything else, the man generously offered me a clean shirt.

I spent fifteen minutes in the school's bathroom scrubbing and washing, practically bathing in the sink like a muddy bird in a puddle. But when I emerged, he was there. Standing by the bathroom exit, bag slung over his shoulder, waiting patiently. For me.

He put his hand on my shoulder and led me to his car.

'I'll drive you back.'

Somehow, he knew I was in no condition to drive. He offered to play *Rumours*, but I declined, preferring silence to center myself.

Inhaling courage, I'm ready for an evening with Kent's family. 'Good evening to you, too, Gillian!' Kent shouts into the house. He nods toward the entrance, and I follow him, happy to take refuge from the frigid February wind. 'My daughter, Gillian. The house can be a little chaotic.'

'How's school? Are they off your back yet with that stupid software?' Gillian shouts from the kitchen.

'Mommy, you said a bad word!'

A little girl with the same strawberry-blonde hair as her mother and amber eyes brighter than the moon appears. She's wearing green flannel pajamas and slippers with a cartoon bunny's head on them.

'Stupid isn't a bad word, sweetie.'

'Well, it's not nice,' the girl says, facing us. 'Who are you?'

'Lia, this is my friend Vincent,' Kent lifts her up, kissing her cheek as she holds on to his neck. 'He's helping me with a big project at school.'

'The stupid one?' Lia says, parroting her mother.

'Vincent, it's nice to meet you.' Kent's daughter reappears with a dishrag over her shoulder. She kisses Kent's cheek and his face beams from all the familial affection.

'We're pushing bedtime waiting for Poppy, and well, things are spiraling,' she says.

'I'm sorry, we had to finish something,' Kent says. His hand moves to the small of my back, and instead of moving away, I lean into it, grateful for the support.

'Dad, please. She's been begging for you all night.'

Gillian pats her daughter's head. Their identical hair and features make them look like a matching set – one maxi, one mini. 'Go. Fifteen minutes, and then it's bedtime.'

'Lia,' Kent whispers, 'my shaina maidel.'

He puts Lia down, extends his hand, and she clasps on, dragging him into the other room.

'My dad and his pretty girl. Vincent, may I take your coat? Come. Eat. There's food. So much food.'

I follow Gillian into a kitchen with tall ceilings and beautiful white cabinets. A large island, covered in plates, silverware, and a fresh, crisp stack of napkins, serves as the centerpiece. The smell of meat, rich and smoky, intensifies, and a white man, slightly shorter than Gillian, stands over the stove, turning and poking at what I'm guessing is the life-changing brisket.

'Louis, this is Dad's friend, Vincent.'

'Vincent,' Louis says, slipping his fingers out of the oven mitt and offering me his hand.

'You look like a Vinnie,' he says, and I spy the sink a few feet away. I'll be able to wash before eating, but a trip to the bathroom for a proper scrub down may be in order.

I take Louis's hand, and his tough skin is damp against mine. It's probably from the heat of the oven mitt, and I swallow hard and plaster a smile on my face.

'No, just Vincent.' I've never had nor wanted a cute nickname. 'Sorry to intrude.' I quickly wipe my hand on the seat of my pants.

'Please. This beauty,' Louis says, back to poking the meat, 'would feed a small army. We're happy to have you. Any friend of Kent's is welcome.'

'Can I get you a drink?' Gillian asks, and – spying the

glasses and open bottle of wine on the counter – I decide a beverage might help take the edge off.

'Sure, I'd love some.' I nod toward the wine.

'After my day, I might need my own bottle.' Gillian grabs more wine from a small rack under the cabinets.

'Oh, I'm sorry,' I say, taking a glass.

'It's fine. I work in the front office of a chiropractor with two other women. Both older. Both there longer. And both a pain in my ass.'

'Sounds . . . interesting,' I say.

'I keep waiting for a call to come bail her out of jail.' Louis takes the lid off the brisket and steam fills the kitchen.

'It could happen.' Gillian pours herself a glass, filling it to the brim.

'Help yourself,' she says.

As I pour myself a half glass, a smile spreads across my face. I concentrate, using my breath to help me decipher the midway point in the unfamiliar stemware. New people. New place. There's no need to get tipsy.

'Why don't you go sit and relax?' Gillian nods toward the sounds coming from the next room.

'We need five minutes. Lia ate and had her bath, and it's almost bedtime,' Louis says, using tongs and a massive fork to transfer the brisket to a cutting board.

Following the noise, I find Kent in what appears to be the den, sitting on an oversized leather couch, Lia in front of him. A bright blonde wig covers her head, falling over her eyes, and she periodically brushes it aside. Her arms reach and her face scrunches. I've stumbled onto her performance. Kent pats the seat next to him, and I sit quietly, trying my best not to interrupt the show.

'This bed is too soft!' Lia shouts while a trio of stuffed bears sit on the floor.

'This bed is too hard!'

'This bed is just right.' She lies on the carpet and pretends to sleep. After a minute, I turn to Kent, who simply shrugs.

'Poppy, you're the bears,' she whisper-yells, eyes still closed. 'You come in, find me, and ask, "Who's this sleeping in my bed?" Okay?'

'Oh, right. How could I forget?' Kent moves to the floor, lowering himself carefully.

'Who's this sleeping in my bed?' His inflection mimics his granddaughter's, but he lowers his voice, and the growly tone sends a jolt of heat to my core.

'Oh my! Bears!' Lia screams. She jumps up and bolts toward the kitchen.

There's silence as I sit and watch. Unsure what to do, I eye Kent for a clue. He groans as he pushes himself up and returns next to me. When he claps profusely, I join in. Before I know what's happening, Lia returns from her dramatic exit, climbs into Kent's lap, and buries her head in his chest.

'Poppy,' she says, kissing his neck. 'Did you like it?'

'Yes, so much. You're a wonderful Goldilocks.'

'What about you?' she asks, turning toward me. Her eyes open wide like giant saucers, staring. Before I answer, Lia climbs over and settles into my lap.

The soap on her skin from the aforementioned bath travels up my nose. Her face, inches from mine, searches for a clue about my opinion of her performance, and how does she have no sense of personal space? Parched, I struggle to swallow and wish I hadn't left my wine in the kitchen. She can't weigh over forty pounds, but her knees dig into my thighs, and my skin tingles. As she stares at me, her little face inches away, the warmth from her skin reaches mine.

Her breath smells like brisket, cheese, and spearmint. Why is she on my lap?

'Poppy usually tucks me in when he's here,' she says, her cheesy, meaty, minty breath snagging my senses.

'Yes, let's go upstairs. Your parents are waiting for Vincent and me to eat.'

When Kent stands and puts his hand out, Lia leaps off to grab it.

'There's a bathroom right there,' Kent says, nodding toward a door in the hallway between the kitchen and den.

Closing the door behind me, I take four deep breaths. Slowly, through my nose and out of my mouth, I attempt to center myself. Between getting stuck on the spreadsheet and being pounced on by Lia, I'm tempted to strip naked and give myself a sponge bath in the sink. Knowing that might take some time and appear . . . foolish, I roll up the sleeves of the shirt Kent gave me and turn the hot water on. The liquid soap – peppermint, most likely leftover from the holidays – quickly fills the bathroom with a sweet, fresh, sharp aroma, and I scour my forearms, slowly working down to my wrists, palms, and finally, my fingers.

Rinse, soap, lather, scrub. Rinse, soap, lather, scrub. My eyes focus on the water. The soap. The bubbles. The drain collects the germs and carries them away. I'm not sure how long until we eat, but I need to wash again – one more time.

'Vincent?'

The door opens a sliver, and Kent's voice enters the space. 'Just a second.'

The door clicks, and he's next to me. Watching. Staring. At me. Stuck in another loop. This time in his daughter's bathroom, scrubbing my hands until they're raw.

'Vincent, what can I do to help?'

I'm not sure what to say: the water, the soap, the germs. Rinse, soap, lather, scrub.

'Vincent, can you look at me?'

'I just need two minutes.'

'Two?'

'Has to be even.'

His hand lands on my shoulder, the pressure enough of a distraction. Leaving my hands under the water, I turn and face him.

'There you are,' he says – those eyes. There's no judgment. No disappointment. Lines gather around them as he gives a half-smile.

'Can you tell me the songs on *Rumours*?'

'*Rumours*? Why?'

'I'm curious.'

'All of them?'

'Yes. In order.' He gently squeezes my shoulder. 'Please.'

'Well, first is "Second Hand News." Then "Dreams," "Never Going Back Again," "Don't Stop," then . . .' My head scrambles. I try to replay the end of 'Don't Stop' in my head. '"Go Your Own Way" and "Songbird." That's the first side. On vinyl. Or cassette. CDs lose the punch of sides which is a travesty if you ask me.'

Kent's palm glides over my head as his lips wind into a smile. 'I thought you might know.'

'But what about the second side?' I ask, biting my bottom lip.

'Maybe another time.'

'But why did you want to know?'

His eyes double in size, and he nods toward the sink. I've stopped.

'How did you . . . ?'

'Let's eat.' With a wink, he passes me a hand towel, and opens the door. Calm. Cool. Collected. When he needs to be, Kent is like a Jedi Master of emotions. Maybe he can teach me a few tricks. I swallow past the lump in my throat and follow Kent Lester to the table.

12

Kent

'You may find this hard to believe, but Dad was actually clumsier when I was little,' Gillian says, and my stomach tingles. Bringing Vincent here means she will spill every embarrassing story.

'Really?' Vincent asks as Louis dishes out brisket, piles of it, to each of us.

'Four slices for Vincent,' I instruct. Louis nods, counting out pieces with the silver serving fork and I shoot Vincent a quick wink.

The table brims with mashed potatoes, coleslaw, salad, fresh corn, and wine. Bottles and corks litter empty spaces, and the dining room fills with the clinking of forks and knives. With a napkin plastered on his lap, a sly smile sneaks across Vincent's face. 'Please tell me more.'

Gillian's eyes light up with a magical sparkle, signaling her imminent delight in mortifying me. 'Dad didn't get his glasses until . . . How old were you?'

'You were five.' I adjust my glasses. 'So, thirty.'

'Wait, why didn't you get glasses until then?' Vincent asks.

'I honestly didn't think my vision was that bad,' I say. 'But it steadily got worse as I got older.'

'And he fought the progressives,' Gillian says.

'Listen, needing glasses for distance and reading is admitting I'm –'

'Distinguished,' Vincent interrupts me. Our eyes meet, his eyelashes flutter and my breath catches.

'He almost killed me,' Gillian says. 'A few times.'

Vincent prods the food on his plate – segregating items. It's the first food he's had since, well, I'm not sure when, and I'm relieved to know his body's getting nourishment.

'Okay, that's a tad dramatic,' I say.

'Is it?' Gillian asks.

'This guy?' Vincent nods toward me. 'He seems pretty harmless to me.'

'Harmless?' Gillian laughs so hard, she almost chokes.

'Sweetie.' Louis pats her back. 'Slow down.'

Gillian gulps wine. 'Dad was pushing me in a stroller. To this day, we still don't know exactly how, but he didn't see a row of bright orange cones alerting him to the Grand-Canyon-sized pothole in the road.'

'I've heard this story a thousand times, and the hole gets larger each time,' Louis says through a mouthful of food.

'Baby Gillian in the hole,' I say. 'The squad had to come and rescue her. The Worst Father in the World award. Child protective services. Yada, yada, yada.'

'Wait, where was your mother?' Vincent asks.

'She was hopelessly stuck in the eighties,' Gillian says.

'So probably rollerblading in leg warmers while listening to crappy music.'

'Hey!' I shout. 'That's the music of my childhood. "Don't You Forget About Me" might be the best song ever written. Apologies to Fleetwood Mac.' I smile at Vincent.

'Are they always like this?' Vincent asks Louis.

'Always.' Louis leans over and grabs Gillian's hand. He kisses her knuckles, and once again, I'm grateful my daughter has such a loving husband.

Closing my eyes momentarily, I take a breath and smile. A gentle warmth washes over my hand, bringing a sense of comfort. It's Vincent. His fingers take mine, and a soft smile greets me when I look at him.

'But yes, they've always been this way,' Louis says.

'Before the glasses, Dad couldn't see. He was constantly tripping over things,' Gillian says, the verve back in her voice.

I dip my head.

'Including his own feet,' Gillian adds.

'Anyway,' I interject, 'I got my glasses when you were five, and things got better.'

'Marginally,' Gillian adds.

We finish eating while my daughter and her husband continue to tease and embarrass me, and my heart swells, knowing it comes from a place of love. When the brisket has a small dent in it (Louis swears it will 'feed us for a week'), and the table's cleared, Vincent's yawning cues me it's time for us to go. He's had a long, rough day, and I should get him home.

'Thank you for the lovely evening,' Vincent says at the

front door, wrapped in his long caramel-colored wool coat. 'And the brisket,' he says, turning to Louis. 'It really is life changing.'

'You're welcome anytime.' Gillian opens her arms, and Vincent hugs her.

'Call me this weekend,' she says, kissing and squeezing me tight. With her head nestled in my neck, she whispers, 'He's hot.'

My stomach flutters because she knows. And she's right. Vincent and I head out, the full moon casting a glow that lights our path to my car.

We drive quietly along, and while Vincent seems more himself, calmer than at school or in the bathroom, I'm still not convinced he should be alone.

'After I take you back to your car, would you mind if I just followed you home?' I ask.

Vincent stares out the passenger window into the darkness. He's quiet. Thinking. Finally, he replies. 'I had a lovely evening, Kent. And thank you. But remember, we're keeping this' – his hands move between us – 'strictly friends.'

My head knows this. My heart isn't sure.

'I know. I just want to make sure you get home safely.'

'You're a sweet guy, Kent. Do you know that?'

'I've been told.'

Back at Vincent's, sitting in the driver's seat as I gaze at the front walkway leading to his building, I am transported back to that first night. I do my best to squash the memories. His bathroom. Music blaring. Standing over him.

Stopped in his condo's small parking lot, I wave to him from my car and put the car in reverse to head home. Before I back out completely, Vincent's voice pierces the silence.

'Kent!'

I roll down my window and put the car into park.

'Did you want to come in?' he asks, and before I can answer, he adds, 'To talk.'

Vincent's condo appears different with the lights on. That first night, a blur of lips and mouths and motion, and what I remember most is . . . the bathroom. Oy.

His living room and kitchen combo room exude a stylishness that could easily grace the pages of a home-furnishings catalog. All sleek lines and sharp edges, everything appears to be earth tones and black. Simple. Clean. Neat. Just like him.

There's a dining-room table in the living room covered in . . . LEGO. Giant structures jut up from the surface, and small white bowls line the table's perimeter. I can't quite make out what he's up to, but clearly, it's monumental.

'Can I get you anything?' he asks, lingering near the island.

'I'm good.'

He takes a can of seltzer from the stainless-steel fridge and runs the top under the tap. A dab of liquid soap, and he's scrubbing the lid of the can. My throat aches, imagining what it must be like, walking through the world this way. That lingering urge to protect him – shield him from, well, himself – surfaces. But Vincent appears unfazed.

'Your daughter is a hoot,' he says, sitting on the caramel sofa that matches the jacket he removed when we entered.

'Yeah, she definitely would agree with you.'

'I love how close you are. I don't have . . . well, anyone. No kids. No siblings.'

He's an only child. This line of conversation intrigues me. I join him on the couch, leaving a respectful space between us. Facing him, I say, 'So, just you. What about your folks?'

'Married still. They live in Vermont now. My dad always wanted goats, and goats kind of need a farm.' He pulls his legs up and grabs a throw pillow. 'I don't visit much. Have you ever been around goats? They literally eat trash. Goats might be the filthiest animals in existence.'

'Noted.'

'You and your daughter. And your granddaughter. That's special.'

'Yeah, she's always been a daddy's girl . . . various almost-murdering incidents aside, we love each other. A lot.'

'I can tell.'

My lips ease into a smile, and warmth spreads through me as I think of my family. 'And Lia. I adore her to bits. Once a month, I take her on a Saturday. Sometimes we go to a movie. Or take an adventure somewhere new. Or stay at my place, and I read picture books all day. We make pillow and blanket forts.'

Vincent smiles, stretches his socked feet out, and pulls them back. I pat my lap. 'Here.'

'You don't mind?'

A laugh escapes my lips, and I grab his feet and carefully place them on my thighs. I slowly massage his toes and the pads of his soles. Dark navy wool, toasty and soft, makes it a bit of a challenge, but I'm able to press my thumb in and get some nice friction.

'It doesn't bother you?' he asks.

'Your feet?' I hold one up.

'Yeah.'

'Not at all. Why would they?'

'Feet are . . .' He scrunches his face. 'Gross.'

'Vincent Manda, feet are just another part of the body, and bodies are beautiful.'

I tug at the sock on his left foot. 'May I?'

He nods, and I slip the sock off. Not surprisingly, Vincent's toes are immaculate and pedicured. I'm not sure I've seen such beautiful feet before. His toes are perfect, almost the same length, with the big toe slightly longer than the others. There's not a trace of hair on Vincent's ankle or foot.

'Do you have hair anywhere on your body?' I run my hand up his shin.

He chuckles. 'Not really. A little, but along with OCD, I have mysophobia – a fear of germs.' He runs his hand over his head. 'Shaving is more streamlined. Clean. I love it.'

'Plus, it's fucking sexy,' I blurt out. Oops.

Vincent's head dips, but he doesn't move his feet away from my massaging hands.

'Thanks. Not everyone thinks so.'

'Those people are idiots,' I say, gently tugging his other sock off. 'No offense.'

Vincent grins and tilts his head back, seemingly lost in having his feet rubbed. His Adam's apple pokes out, the supple skin of his neck taunting me. Right now, I'm grateful his feet are on my thighs, not my groin.

'So, earlier today, at school,' I say, squeezing the arch of his foot, 'and at Gillian's . . . does that happen often?'

'It can.' His head still rests on the top of the sofa cushion. 'I can go days, even weeks, with nothing and then have multiple incidents in a day.' His foot relaxes under my care. 'Like today.'

A slight sting blossoms in the back of my throat, and sweat dots the top of my hairline. Was this partly my fault?

'I'm sorry,' I say.

Vincent's head pulls up, and my fingers pause their work.

'Kent, please don't take this as a hit to your ego, but this' – he points to himself – 'had nothing to do with you.'

I want to believe him.

'What *does* it have to do with?'

He returns his head back, closes his eyes, and his soft eyelashes curl toward the ceiling. I resume massaging his gorgeous feet. As I rub each toe, I'm amazed by the incredible softness of his feet. Something stirs inside me, but I reassure myself that it's just a friendly foot massage.

'People assume my parents didn't love me. Or there was some traumatic event. But that's not the case. My parents are wonderful – my father's infatuation with goats aside. It just kind of happens.'

My thumb runs down the underside of his foot. The arch of his foot has a supple texture, inviting me to trail my fingers over it. Vincent's voice becomes low and honeyed. My lips turn up, knowing my hands are having this effect on him.

'When I was little, maybe four or five, I remember standing in front of the toilet waiting to pee. I started counting the flowers on the wallpaper. Pink peonies. So many fucking peonies. When I finished, I moved on to the tiles on the floor. White octagons. I couldn't leave the bathroom until I'd counted them all. Twice. To check. If I lost track, I started over.'

'Did your parents know?'

'Not then, but they figured it out soon enough.' Vincent rolls his head back and forth on the cushion. 'It started with counting. Then, I went through a "symmetry" phase.'

'Symmetry?'

'Everything had to be even. Odd numbers were the bane of my existence. Still can be. If I counted something that wasn't an even number, I counted again, expecting a different result. The need for things to be even. Aligned. Arranged. That became . . . quite distracting, and my parents caught on quickly.'

A smile dawns on my lips, and a whir spins in my stomach. An intense longing to wrap my arms around Vincent and hold him close almost overcomes me.

'I still prefer even numbers. And by prefer, I mean require.'

A yawn overtakes his face, and glancing at my watch, I realize I've probably overstayed my welcome. I lost track of time and somehow became rooted to the sofa.

'I should go,' I say, reluctantly pulling my hands away from his bare feet, already missing the sensation of their warmth.

'I'm sorry, I'm talking your ear off,' he says, pulling his legs under him. The moment his toes disappear, my hands itch to grab them. Hold them. Feel them. Taste them.

'I'm a talker. And I enjoy talking to you,' I say. 'But it's late. I should go.'

'Do you want to stay?'

'But we're, we're, not, you're not, me, um . . .' I stammer. Even stationary, I manage to be clumsy, tripping over my words. I could stay on his couch. Friends do that.

'Just lie with me. I promise, no hanky-panky.'

'Did you just say "hanky-panky"?' I ask, my mouth spreading into a grin, because why is this sweet man also so fucking cute? And do friends cuddle?

'Come.' Vincent stands and offers his hand. As I look into his eyes, Vincent's fingers reaching for mine, a sense of peace flows over me and I reach out and put my hand in his.

13

Vincent

Kent follows me into the bathroom. The warmth of his hand in mine radiates up my arm, creating a new expansiveness in my chest. Holding hands was never something I did, not even with my parents when I was little. With the simple, innocent connection, my heartbeat becomes steady. Even. Calm.

Side by side, we wash our hands. Kent waits patiently for me to rinse, matching my every move in the mirror. Needing no reminder, he grabs a fresh toothbrush from the box and immediately starts brushing, vigorously scrubbing his teeth while wearing a goofy grin. Toothpaste foam drips onto his beard, but he quickly wipes it with his arm. He flicks both brows up and my stomach flutters. Even though we haven't known each other long, the familiarity of him in my bathroom, his presence, grounds me.

Kent spits into the sink. 'I don't have pajamas.'

'Wear your T-shirt and underwear,' I say, remembering his flimsy boxers. 'I'm going to shower.' I pull my shirt off and Kent's gaze flicks to my chest. 'I won't be long, I promise.'

Standing with my back to the scalding water, I do my best to focus. No counting. No loops. Kent waits in my bed. My fucking bed. Wearing a white V-neck and ratty boxers. Reaching to pump the liquid soap, I remind myself, two pumps. Big ones. But only two. The clean scent of orange, with the familiar tinge of honey sweetness, coats my chest. I shaved my entire body yesterday and the gel glides over my smooth skin. With the small amount of natural body hair I have, I only need to do it weekly.

Running my hands over my pecs, the firmness of my muscles and the sensitivity of my nipples send an electric wave of pleasure through me. I tilt my head back, the spray beating onto my neck, and my fingers drift back, lingering, the sensitive nerves in each nipple springing to life. The soap creates a slippery surface my chest can't deny. My cock, half hard, becomes difficult to ignore. There's no time now. Kent is waiting. In my bed. Kent is not the person to be thinking about right now.

I shake my head. One, two, three, four times, and turn around. While the shower rinses the soap, I quickly scrub my body, ignoring my chest.

Kent's folded clothes rest neatly arranged on the dresser. Wearing only my blue flannel pajama pants, I approach my bed. I can't remember the last time anyone was in my bedroom. The cleaning crew, of course, but not in my bed. With me. The last time was . . . never. The few encounters I've had always happened somewhere else. Quickly. At the gym. In the shower. That one desperate time in the hotel bar bathroom. They were freshly cleaned, with a private stall and a door to the floor. But my home? My bed? Sleeping with someone next to me. For an entire night. I take a deep breath and push those thoughts away. This is Kent. Sweet, patient Kent. We're friends. I'm safe.

'Good night,' I whisper, crawling into my bed.

The room is almost completely dark – the stove light from the kitchen casts the faintest glow down the short hallway, allowing me to make out Kent's silhouette. His whiskers poke up, and his lips protrude from the nest of hair on his face. Taunting me.

'Good night, Vincent.'

Propping myself up on my elbow, I lean over and give him a soft kiss on the cheek, his beard tickling my lips. 'Thank you.'

'For what?'

'For today.'

He pulls back, turns, and reaches up to cup my face. If my heart were made of ice, it would melt into a small, glistening puddle.

'Beautiful,' he murmurs.

And with that, I kiss his lips. Mouths closed. But the spearmint freshness still lingers. It's short and gentle, and the closeness removes all the tension and stress from my body. When I pull back, I pause, and before I return to my spot, Kent whispers, 'My good boy.'

I pat his chest, lingering for a second longer than I should, the thick fur beneath the fabric attracting my fingers like a magnet. Pulling away, I roll over.

We lie in stillness. The sound of his breathing, barely noticeable, hints he's still awake.

'Kent?'

'Yeah?'

'Would you hold me?'

Breathe in. Breathe out. A single arm surrounds me, slowly gliding over my bare chest like he's dipping a toe into unknown waters.

'Okay?'

I don't speak but scoot my entire body, plastering my back to him. Shutting my eyes and inhaling, Kent's heartbeat thumps, and the skin on my back gravitates to the chest hair escaping his V-neck as I clutch his arm and tug him close.

Overcome with the desire to taste his lips, I crane my neck, grasp his arm to hold him in place, and turn to kiss him. Kent's lips, soft and wet, brush mine, and his hand moves to the top of my head. Pausing, I whisper, 'Only kissing, okay?'

'Vincent, I haven't stopped thinking about kissing you.'

He presses his mouth to mine and leans over me, his weight providing deep pressure on my naked torso. He slowly crawls on top, never breaking the kiss, and I reach for his face. The softness of his beard between my fingers settles me, and then he turns from my mouth and gently kisses the palm of my hand.

'I'd be thrilled to do nothing but kiss you until the sun rises.'

I nip at his lips, and he mutters, 'So sweet.'

'Me?'

'You. Your lips. All of you.'

Nobody has ever called me sweet, and Kent's eyes are barely visible, but on top of me, the faint light from the alarm clock catches them, and there's a yearning there.

I let him take my finger in his mouth. And the moment it enters, and he begins gently sucking, my half-erect cock comes to life in my pajamas.

'Oh, hello,' he says, and wonderful, he's felt it too.

I slam my eyes closed and turn my head, covering my face with my arm.

'Vincent, it's okay. We're kissing.'

'It's a reflex,' I mumble through my forearm.

'We can kiss.' He gently removes my arm from my face and plants a soft kiss on my neck. 'And if you're hard, it's okay. It doesn't mean we have to do anything. I'm going to enjoy your lips.' He nibbles my bottom lip. 'Your mouth.' An index finger brushes over my mouth. 'Your tongue and teeth.'

'Really?' In my limited experience, this is not how it works. Erections mean sex.

'Really,' he says, his mouth on mine again. In a gentle, repetitive motion, he caresses my head as if coaxing out a shine.

'You really don't mind?'

'What?'

'Only doing this,' I say, touching his lips.

'Are you kidding? This is heaven.'

His evident pleasure from kissing puts the worries about my throbbing erection at ease.

Kent's whiskers tickle my chin. 'Can I ask you something?'

'Sure.'

'Where did "good boy" come from?'

'Someone said it once and . . . it did something to me.'

'Something?' he asks, nuzzling his beard on me.

'It makes me horny. Riled up. And . . . hornier.'

'Yeah, I kind of got that.' Kent palms my erection through my pajamas and I laugh. The closeness. The talking. The kissing. Fuck, what is he doing to me?

'I think maybe it means I'm doing it well. Pleasing you.'

'Yes. You most certainly are. My good boy.'

I reach up and slide my hands under his shirt, pausing on his stomach, fuzzy and soft, and ask, 'Okay?'

He nods quickly, and my fingers dance toward his chest – the hair I've only witnessed now in my grasp. The thought of hair growing on my body – taking over, crawling, and itching – sends shivers down my spine. On someone else? My fingers getting lost in each strand? Sign me up. When I find Kent's pecs, I take one in each hand and slowly squeeze, massaging, searching, until I find his nipples, hidden under the fur, and give them a little attention. Gently pinching, flicking, careful not to hurt him.

Kent's tongue explores my mouth, and now his cock, fat and firm, behind only thin boxers, pokes at mine, and I remind myself – only kissing, only kissing.

He pulls back, still close enough his sweet breath tickles my nose, and with both hands on my face, simply smiles.

'What?' I ask. 'Is something wrong?'

'Nope.' He dips down and kisses the tip of my nose. 'Being here like this,' he says, gently pushing his cock on mine. 'You're perfect.' Another peck on my nose. 'That's all.'

'Oh.'

Me? Perfect. Clearly, he's under a spell. It's probably

our hard dicks rubbing against each other. There's a naturalness to the closeness of lying here with him, like the rhythm of my heartbeat. Kent rests his head in the crook of my neck, and as his beard tickles my skin, I shudder and let out a little laugh. His head juts up, and he asks, 'Too much?'

I reach up and pull him back, exhaling deeply, centering myself, letting the pressure of his weight anchor me. I focus on his cock. Rigid. Thick. It's directly on mine, pushing on the tip, as my dick swells against him. Two grown men having an orgasm this way is nearly impossible, and it would be so easy to slip off his boxers – my pajamas. Only kissing. Only kissing.

With Kent's face buried near my chest, he slowly rolls off, staying right beside me.

'Vincent, my sweet, good boy.'

My cock, about to burst through my pajamas, indicates the closeness works for me. With Kent I'm protected. Safe. Cared for. Adored.

Kent turns on his side, facing me. His hand moves to my chest, and he snuggles up. His breathing slows. In bed with this man, being held, my dick eager but content waiting, my eyes grow heavy with exhaustion. I yearn for sleep but force myself to stay awake a little longer, listening to the soft hum of his slumber. Basking in the reality of him sleeping next to me beats any dream that awaits.

'Do you have any peanut butter?'

Seated at the lip of my kitchen island, Kent's wearing the same boxers I now realize have a ripped and tattered hem. His V-neck bears the telltale wrinkles of a night's sleep. Who am I kidding? Clothes probably wrinkle the minute Kent looks at them. His thick hair juts out in every direction, whatever grooming he does each morning to tame it not on display. He's sexy as fuck.

'No peanut butter.'

'Regular butter?'

'Um.' I open my fridge. Sparse doesn't begin to explain it. I went shopping two days ago. The few items I bought are displayed front and center. Variety is not a spice in my life.

'I don't cook much. I eat a lot of salads.'

'Vincent, kindergartners make PB&J sandwiches,' he says, standing behind me. 'It's not really considered a culinary masterpiece.'

'Let's see,' I stammer, and Kent puts his hands under my arms, pulling me back toward him. My fleece hoodie blocks skin-to-skin contact, and my ribs grow tight, wishing for his warmth on my chest.

'Seltzer. Bread. Veggies. Salad dressing.'

'You eat dry toast for breakfast?'

'Yeah.'

'Every morning?'

'Yup.'

'No butter? No jam?'

I shrug, the boringness of my palette washing over me in Kent's presence.

He grabs the bottle of fat-free ranch and heads back to his seat.

'Desperate times and all,' he says, pouring the dressing on his bread.

'You don't want me to toast it?'

'Nope. I'm good,' he mumbles, the dressing-slathered cold bread shoved in his mouth.

White creamy liquid drips from Kent's lips, pooling in his beard. I slide a plate in front of him, hopeful he'll use it. The man doesn't have a single napkin. I grab the roll of paper towels and place it before him.

'There,' I say, stepping back awaiting his next move.

He takes the smallest piece from the select-a-size roll, and places it on the counter. One napkin. Half a napkin, really.

I take my plate with a piece of dry toast and sit, leaving a stool between us. Kent and that amount of dressing on dry bread doesn't bode well for me. At least I have the roll of paper towels in reach.

'Tell me about that?' he asks, nodding to the dining-room table. My current build takes over the entire space. Identical white bowls pepper the perimeter. Each with bricks sorted by size and color. In the middle, the Eiffel Tower reaches toward the ceiling, surrounded by the rest of the under-construction city.

'Paris. The tower was my starting point, and I'm gradually constructing the surrounding areas.'

With half a piece of salad-dressing-covered bread, Kent walks over and circles my dining-room table, inspecting.

'Have you ever been?'

'To Paris? No. I'm not a big flier.' I shake my head. 'Too many germs.'

'Then how do you know?' He points to the tower's surrounding areas.

'There's this amazing thing,' I say, moving next to him,

'called the internet. It's filled with maps, photos, and all the information your brain desires.'

Kent smacks my behind and quips, 'Smart ass.' His palm connecting with my butt sends sleeping butterflies swarming in my stomach. 'Well, this is amazing. The kids at school would eat this up. Truly.'

Kent takes a brick from a bowl. A classic blue. Eight studs and three tubes. He fingers it while scanning the construction zone.

'I don't really like help,' I say. The muscles in my hand quiver and twitch, and I take the brick from him and place it back in the bowl, returning it home with the other blues.

'Sorry, I was just going to . . .' Kent stammers and trips, grabbing for the table on his way down. His fingers catch on a bowl of orange pieces, sending them cascading over him as he falls to the floor. Lightheadedness swirls, and I catch my breath before moving to help.

'I don't suppose you find this cute?' he asks, lying on his back, covered in random orange pieces.

'Here.' I offer my hand. Once he's up, we collect the scattered bricks. 'You don't think it's . . . strange?' I ask.

'Me falling? I'm fairly used to it by now.'

'No. All . . . this.' I motion to Paris.

'A grown man playing with toys?' He's beside me, taking my arm and squeezing. 'I think it's kind of hot.'

The touching. The kissing. The flirting. Maybe we're heading for a friends-with-benefits situation. Considering I can't get past a first date, I should probably count my blessings.

'Anyway,' I say, returning to the island and my toast, 'what are you up to today?'

'Brushing Sweetums. It's kind of our weekend thing. And it takes a while.' He shrugs. 'What about you?'

I shrug back. 'Laundry. Cleaning. The gym.'

'What gym do you go to? I've thought about joining, but honestly, at my age, I don't know if it's a habit I want to start,' he says, grabbing his stomach and giving it a little jiggle.

'None. I mean, the condo has a small gym in the basement. It's super basic, but it's here and free. Nobody uses it much, so it's usually spotless.'

'Gotcha.'

Kent finishes his dressing with a side of bread and puts the plate in the sink.

'Want me to wash it?'

'No, it's good, leave it. I'll take care of it,' I say, satisfied with the sanitize button on my dishwasher.

'You know, that was fun last night.' Kent turns the faucet on and scrubs his hands.

'Your daughter and son-in-law are fantastic. And Lia, I mean, I'm not the biggest fan of kids, but she's pretty spectacular.'

'My family is wonderful, but I meant us. In bed. The canoodling.'

'Oh.'

He wants to talk about us. Kissing. Cuddling. Grinding. I reach for my phone and start the music. The bass drum kicks. Hard. Guitar plucking joins in, and before long, the harmonies of the entire band join in. They sing about the wind blowing and the sun rising, and I close my eyes, anticipating what's about to come.

'You know, we don't have to be more than friends,'

Kent says, grabbing a paper towel to dry his hands. He slips on the bottom of the stool but catches himself on the island. 'But also, the kissing, and well, the rest, was a lot of fun. For me.'

'Me too,' I say, my knee bouncing.

'We could do it again. If you wanted,' he says, fidgeting. 'Not now, I mean another time.'

'I'd like that.' My mouth becomes as dry as the toast I've almost finished. Maybe he has the same idea about friends with benefits. I'm sure that's it. Regardless, if Kent and I are ever going to fool around more in any capacity, I need to be honest with him.

'The thing is, Kent, well, there's something I need to tell you.'

'Is this an ogre/human situation I need to know about?' he asks, a soft smile tugging at his face. 'How long do I have until your ogre form? Midnight? Does it involve you getting wet?'

I turn down the music as they sing about not being loved on a glorious, endless loop.

'I hope not. I mean, no, definitely not. It's just for me . . . sexually . . .' I wipe my mouth, letting the napkin hover. 'I'm a side.'

Kent doesn't say anything or move, and I'm pretty sure this will be the nail in the coffin of anything between us. Given our current professional proximity, it's probably for the best.

I turn toward Kent, and he's looking at me. Silent.

'I know it's unusual for most guys in the gay community,' I say.

'Actually, I'm bi.'

'I know, I'm just saying, for men. Who sleep with men. It can be unusual.'

'Vincent.' He moves to the seat beside me, wrapping his arm around my shoulders. When he pulls me closer, he slides off his stool and falls into me.

'Sorry, I'm fine. Hold on a sec,' he stammers, pulling himself onto his seat. With his balance momentarily restored, Kent leans over and whispers, 'I don't know what you mean.'

Rubbing the back of my neck, I take a deep breath. It's not the first time I've had to explain it, and it won't be the last.

'I'm not a top. I'm not a bottom.' My mouth pinches. 'I'm a side.'

Kent squints, and he dips his chin and shakes his head slightly.

'Tops are –' I begin.

'I know what tops and bottoms are, Vincent. But what's a side?' Two deep breaths.

'It means I don't want to top. Or bottom.'

'Oh!' he says. A loud, bellowing chuckle chases his exclamation. The solo bass guitar has its moment before the band's crescendo joins Kent's laughter.

'It never appealed to me, and the one time I forced myself to try, well . . . not an experience I'm looking to repeat.'

'Vincent, I would never pressure you' – he wraps his fingers around mine – 'to do anything.'

'What about you?' I ask, my stomach knotted.

'Well, I'm a . . .' He pauses, a serious look overtaking the smile. 'I don't really know.' He stands and kisses the back of my head. The whiskers on his beard tickle my naked skin. 'And you know what? I can think of lots of other ways to have fun.'

Kent was married to a woman for years. Maybe he thinks he doesn't care, but right now, as 'You Make Loving Fun' fills the kitchen, I bite my lip, breathe, and try to let that go. Christine sings about believing in miracles, and maybe she's right. Maybe it's time to believe.

14

Kent

'You slept together?'

New pastel blue, purple, and yellow beads at the end of Ruth's braids signal the looming spring. The trees surrounding the track also hint at the change of seasons with new buds. Ruth's determination to get my love life on track doesn't waver, but I'm still my usual half-step behind.

'Slept. As in sleeping. That's it.'

Ruth gives me her patented I'm-not-buying-your-fakakta-story look.

'Really, nothing happened.'

'Nothing?'

'Okay, we kissed. And cuddled.'

Her cheeks go soft, followed by her entire face. Ruth's eyelids stretch wide, and she slows her pace and hooks her arm in mine. 'Mr Lester, you spent all night canoodling with Mr Clean?'

Tugging her back, delight plastered on my face, I say, 'It was actually lovely.'

'You're preaching to the choir. Spooning is my love language.'

'Really? I wouldn't have taken you for a cuddler.'

'Look at me.' Ruth pauses, jutting her hip out. 'I'm all skin and bones. I love nothing more than burying myself in a curvy lady.'

We continue our brisk walk and a grin sneaks onto my face, thinking of Ruth losing herself in someone.

'He did say something interesting the next morning. Well, told me something.'

Ruth blurts out a blasting noise, mimicking the fire alarm. 'Incoming, red-flag alert!'

'Hush.' My arm releases hers, allowing us both to resume swinging them for extra cardio.

'He's a side.'

'Aside? Aside from what?'

'No, not aside, a –' I pause, holding one hand out with each word. '– side. Two words.'

'Oh, a *side*. Cool. My cousin Stewart is a side. It's way more common than people think.'

Of course, this is nothing new to Ruth. She volunteers at the queer community center in town, has dated more queer folks than I can count on all my fingers and toes, and is clearly a million times more hip than me. Not that it takes much.

She slows her pace and rubs my forearm as we stroll. 'People think sex equals penetration, but take it from me, that couldn't be further from the truth.'

'I told him I don't mind.'

'And do you?'

'I don't think so,' I say, scrubbing my face.

'I get big top energy from you. I'm talking sex, not the circus.'

I open my mouth to reply, but Ruth continues, 'Bottom? Verse? Wait, are you a side? That would be convenient.'

The moment the question leaves her lips, it dawns on me. I have no clue what I am.

'With Corrine, I mean, I guess a top?'

'That's with Corrine. But actually, you totally could've been a bottom with her.'

'Excuse me?' I reach for the base of my neck and stumble on the track.

'She could've pegged you.'

'Pegged me?'

Ruth's braids sway wildly as she shakes her head, clicking and clacking.

'Kent. Kent. Kent. You have much to learn from your Auntie Ruth.'

Tops. Bottoms. Verse. Sides. Pegging. What have I gotten myself into?

'What do you . . . want? When you're with Vincent.'

'I don't know. To look at him. Take care of him. Hold him.'

Ruth purses her lips. 'Kent Lester, that might be the sweetest thing I've ever heard. But sexually, when you imagine being with him, do you want to top him? Bottom for him? Both? Neither?'

My mouth goes drier than the Sahara, and I wish I'd brought my water bottle.

'I mean, I don't know. I've been happy with what we've done. More than happy. I never really thought about it much.'

'Much?' She pokes me in the side with her elbow. 'So some. This is a safe, judgment-free space,' she says, waving her hands in front of us.

'I mean, I guess, maybe both?'

'Both. That's verse. So, you'd like to fuck him and be fucked by him?'

Thoughts of Vincent's cock in my mouth. In my ass. Touching his ass. My cheeks flush red under my beard, and I blurt, 'Ruth, we're on school grounds.'

'Kent, it's six-thirty in the morning, and we're on the track. The only ears that might hear us are the birds.' She points to the trees dotting the track's edges.

'Did you know pigeons have the best hearing of any birds?'

Ruth cocks her head.

'What? You can learn a lot at the science fair.'

'Anyway.' Ruth shakes her head. 'Verse.'

'I mean, I guess so.' I rub the back of my neck. 'We're only friends. We're not doing anything. Not anymore. And he's a side! So, I don't think it matters.'

'Oh, it matters,' she says again, looping her hand around my arm. 'You guys are totally hooking up again. Mark my words.'

I let out a long exhale, unsure what any of this means for me. For us. Not that Vincent and I are an *us*.

'Sides don't like' – she lowers her voice to a whisper and nods to the birds – 'penetrative anal sex. With a dick.' Heat rushes to my face, and I close my eyes, knowing Ruth wants to help. 'Some enjoy a finger or rimming, that's a tongue. Many will do almost everything else. Oral. You've done that already.' She sticks her index finger in her mouth and pops it. 'Toy play. You could explore some light bondage. Maybe a harness,' she says, squeezing my shoulders. 'You could totally pull off a leather harness.'

My mind treads water, trying to stay afloat. 'Wait, rimming?'

'Kent Lester. Do we need to have another pizza and wine sleepover, so I explain the ins and outs of gay sex?'

'Maybe?'

'Here's what I'll tell you,' she says, patting my arm. 'Most people define traditional penetration as the standard for sex. But that's a heteronormative construct. As queer people, we get to buck that patriarchal bullshit. Sex acts are sex. Full stop.' I nod slowly, trying to take it all in.

'The important thing is communication. Ask him what he wants. Likes. Tell him what you want. And then do it.'

Maybe all this side business is a sign that the mishigas with Vincent was a foolish mistake. I enjoy his company . . . and the kissing. But maybe it's more complicated than I thought. Although what we've done so far has been some of the most amazing sex I've ever had. Do I really care about him being a side? Labels are for soup cans. Vincent's soft skin. His beautiful eyes focused on his laptop as he types away. In my office. Working together. The implementation. My job counts on this working and proving how amazing Lear staff and students truly are. I've been on my own for years now. Me and Sweetums. There's no reason to muck it up.

*

'What a good morning you've had, Brodie,' I say.

Standing at my door with Sheldon, Brodie can't conceal the bashful grin sketched on his face.

'Yup. He's been listening, staying safe,' Sheldon says. 'He got frustrated during phonics and went to his table spot independently.'

'Brodie, wow. You should feel proud.' I rest my hand on his shoulder.

'The cafeteria is a little loud today,' Sheldon says. 'I offered him headphones, but he didn't want them, and he asked if he could eat with Theo or you, and well, Mr Berenson is busy.' He pops an eyebrow, and I guess these boys are spending lunches together.

'Brodie, I would love for you to eat here,' I say. 'I'm just working with Mr Manda, but I'm getting hungry myself.'

I nod to the table where Vincent sits, tapping away on his laptop.

'Mr Manda, why don't we break and join Brodie for lunch? Sound good?'

Vincent's eyes finally land on us, and he's blinking profusely. I know children aren't his favorite, but this is only one child. Having lunch with Brodie is super chill. And I'm here.

Brodie approaches, carrying his dinosaur lunch bag, and without caring about personal space, pulls his chair inches from Vincent and starts unpacking his lunch.

'Sure,' Vincent says with a complete lack of enthusiasm. 'I just need to . . .' he stammers, folding his laptop, holding his hands up, and heading for the bathroom.

With my brown bag retrieved from the bottom of my

desk drawer, I join Brodie and offer him a squirt of hand sanitizer before using it myself.

'What's for lunch today?' I ask.

Brodie holds up a sandwich, and I push my glasses up and move closer to inspect its contents.

'Ah, cheese and . . . mayonnaise?' He nods and takes a huge bite. 'A classic. One of my favorites.'

Removing my sandwich from the bag, I show him. 'Peanut butter and jelly. You're not allergic?'

Brodie shakes his head, and we eat in silence. Since he started kindergarten, I've spent my fair share of time with Brodie, and one thing I know — above all else, he prefers silence. While he may not talk much, he's always watching, taking the world in, observing, analyzing, and reacting in his own unique way. Kindergarten, where there's more play and exploration, suited him better, and his transition to first grade has been . . . challenging.

'All set,' Vincent says, returning to his seat and taking his lunch box out. It's stainless steel and sparkles under the bright lights.

Brodie pauses his chewing and stares at Vincent.

'What's wrong?' Vincent asks.

Brodie nods toward Vincent's lunch box.

'I think he wants to know what you're having,' I say. Brodie nods slowly three times and smiles at Vincent.

'Oh, well, I have toast,' he says, removing a plastic container. 'A piece of rotisserie chicken from the grocery and a few nuts and raisins for dessert.'

Brodie's face scrunches up like he's just stumbled upon a foul, rotten egg.

'Nuts and raisins,' he says, and his first words in front of Vincent today come out in his usual raspy voice.

'I'll have you know, nuts have a ton of protein.' Vincent holds up a small container with his 'dessert' and offers it up for Brodie's inspection.

'I have a brownie,' I say, pulling the plastic-wrapped, storebought confection from my bag. It's topped with chocolate icing and mini chocolate chips.

Brodie holds up a small yellow bag of shortbread cookies coated in chocolate.

'Yum,' I say. 'Way better than . . . raisins.'

I shoot Vincent a half-smile and wink, and he replies, 'Oh, hush. Well, now I'm definitely not sharing.'

Brodie laughs at this, and I'm unsure if Vincent meant it to be a joke.

The three of us sit quietly with the occasional wrapper and chewing noises the only sound as we eat. Brodie and Vincent look at each other occasionally, but busy chewing, they mostly stare at their food until Vincent asks him, 'You like LEGO?'

Brodie's face, focused on his sandwich, lights up, and he nods his head quicker than I've ever witnessed.

'Me too. A lot, actually.'

'But you're a grown-up,' Brodie says with a full mouth.

'True. But grown-ups build with LEGO.' Vincent rips off a small piece of dry toast.

'You know,' I begin, 'some grown-ups have a job playing with LEGO. They create all the kits, think of new bricks and concepts. You'd be surprised how many adults spend a good chunk of their time with LEGO.'

Brodie's full mouth falls open, the contents of his

chewed cheese and mayo sandwich visible, and my gaze flits to Vincent, unsure how he'll take it. But he either doesn't notice or fails to react.

'Those people are living the dream. Paid to build,' Vincent says, his lips easing into a smile.

'Maybe we could do one together sometime,' Brodie offers.

'I don't think so.' Vincent quickly shakes his head. 'I prefer to build alone.'

Brodie shrugs off the rebuff and pops one of his cookies in his mouth.

'Finish up.' I nod toward Brodie's lunch. 'Mr Soleskin will be expecting you soon.'

When Vincent finishes, he begins the clean-up routine I've witnessed for a few weeks now. After disposing of his trash, he takes wipes from his bag and diligently scrubs down the exterior of every container, his lunchbox, and his section of the table. When the wiping reaches the perimeter of his area, Brodie quickly packs up his trash and bag and hugs everything to his chest. Vincent's gaze falls on the small boy, and he gives him a hasty smile, finally handing him a wipe. Brodie takes it and feverishly wipes at his area of the table.

'Mr Lester,' Brodie says, nodding toward my trash. I quickly swipe it up, and Brodie takes a wipe to my spot.

'Brodie, why don't I walk you back to class?' I extend my hand and Brodie swiftly takes it. With his tiny fingers enveloped in mine like a puppy snuggled in for a nap, we head for the door.

'I'll be right back,' I say.

Vincent takes a fresh wipe and meticulously cleans

every spot on the table. Maybe Brodie was too much for him. But they seemed to connect over their shared love of LEGO. Regardless of where this might be heading, I want to learn more about what makes Vincent tick. Brodie and I stroll down the hallway and a light quiver stirs in my stomach thinking about what waits upon my return.

15

Vincent

Wipe. Breathe. Wipe. Breathe.

Kent is one thing. His crumb creation ratio is relatively low. My gut tells me that it's higher when he's not around me, but as an adult, he has some ability to contain it. But Brodie? I'm unsure if more bread landed in his mouth or on the table. The floor is littered, but only the bottom of my feet will make contact, and I'll scour my shoes when I get home. After four wipes, Kent's office has a lingering scent reminiscent of a public pool, an ironically filthy place to put your almost naked body. The chlorine fools the brain into thinking it's fresh and ready for swimming. Never in a million years.

Walking back into his office, Kent holds his hands up. I cock my head, wondering what he's up to.

'Go ahead,' he says, twisting his hands in the air. 'Inspect if you like. I scrubbed so hard the hair on my knuckles vanished.'

'Hilarious.'

'Not trying to be funny, but I'll take it,' Kent says,

returning to his desk. 'Thanks for being patient. With Brodie.'

'He's a nice boy. What's his . . . why does he . . . ?'

'Brodie's in the process of being evaluated. It often happens with our younger students. We knew he had unique needs from his kindergarten screening – two years ago. It's taken that long to collect data and get the process started.'

'Evaluated? For what?'

'We won't really know until it's all completed. And unfortunately, that can take months. He has to be seen by many people – the district psychologist, school social worker, speech, occupational therapist, and physical therapist. It's a long list.'

'And then you'll know?' I ask, the lines on my forehead exposed.

'Hopefully. With what I've seen, I'm confident he'll qualify for services. That's my hope. Once we can identify his challenges, we can help him better.'

'He likes LEGO.' My mind wanders to my childhood. How tricky school was for me. Maybe if I'd had someone like Kent looking out for me, I would've gotten more assistance.

'And he's very sweet. Besides all the crumbs.' I motion to the floor.

'Did someone say crumbs?'

Theo, the custodian and apparently boyfriend of Sheldon, the first-grade teacher, appears at the door. Sandy curls frame his fair skin, bouncing as he moves toward us.

'Mr Berenson,' Kent says. 'Yes, by the table. Brodie was . . .'

'Enthusiastic,' I say.

'The kid loves to eat,' Theo says, holding a small cordless vacuum. He bends down and begins sucking away the offending crumbs. 'Doesn't talk much, likes to help.'

'You're two peas in a pod,' Kent says.

'There.' Theo maneuvers the vacuum in between the legs of the table and chairs. 'Crumb free.'

'Thank you, sir,' Kent says, patting Theo on the back. There's a gentle warmth and sense of ease between them.

'My pleasure.' Theo gives a small salute to Kent and then turns to me. 'Be careful with this one.' He nods toward Kent. 'He's one of the good guys.' And he's off.

'People seem to really like you here,' I say.

Kent shrugs, and his mouth transforms into a charming smile.

'I try. I know what it's like to be in the classroom.' He joins me at the table with his laptop. 'Many principals forget. I don't want to be one of them.'

'And Theo seems extra fond of you.'

'Theo's a special guy. Quiet but sweet. This thing between him and Sheldon seems to be helping him come out of his shell.' Kent's signature smile inches across his face.

'And you don't mind?'

'Them dating? Heck no. I encourage it. They're consenting adults. And professional. It's not like they're shtupping at school.'

We make eye contact. What we did. Here. In the supply closet.

Kent blinks hard, his body twitches, and, provoked by his erratic movement, his laptop falls to the carpet.

'Anyway, Theo's a great guy. He's Jewish, too. We're the only ones here at school.' He bends down, his head disappearing under the table to retrieve the runaway computer. 'We bond over talk of high holy days and family shenanigans.'

Bam! Kent's head smacks the underside of the table, and I wince at the sound.

'Oh my gosh, are you okay?' I kneel to check on him, keeping my hands off the carpet.

Crumpled on the floor, Kent rubs the back of his head, face down, groaning.

'Damnit all to hell!' he bellows.

'Should I get someone? The nurse?'

'No, I'm good.'

'Let me look.' Determined to keep my hands off the filthy floor, I rest the left one on Kent's thigh while I investigate with the other.

Kent's hair leans more salt than pepper. I try to conjure up a vision of him with a full head of dark hair, but promptly dismiss it. Carefully examining his scalp, I comb my fingers through, searching for any signs of injury.

'Here.' He reaches up, places his hand on mine, and moves it to the point of impact.

Rubbing his scalp, my fingers get lost in his thick, wavy hair as I assess the damage.

'You feel okay. Maybe the tiniest bump.' Pulling away, I say, 'I think you'll survive.'

Kent reaches for my hand and holds it in his. His eyes, darker and more intense than I've seen, search mine. Our gazes connect and, wrapped in his, the tips of my fingers become sensitive. The cuddling. The kissing. Kent holding me all night in my bed. His warm breath on my neck. My face flashes hot, and Kent's lips pull my focus.

'What's going on here?'

Geoff stands at the door, staring down at us with a quizzical look on his face.

'He hit his head,' I blurt.

'On the table.' Kent points up.

'We've got the system ready,' Geoff says as I detangle myself from Kent. 'The devices weren't syncing in the cloud.'

'I changed a firewall setting.' Shreya appears next to Geoff, staring at her tablet. 'We're good to go for testing tomorrow.'

'Awesome. We'll be ready,' Kent says, pushing himself to the chair.

'Kent, what in the world?' Shreya asks, finally noticing our predicament.

'I'm fine,' he says. 'Technology is trying to kill me, is all.' He holds up the offending laptop.

Shreya and Geoff shake their heads, turn, and leave for the conference room.

Standing over me, Kent continues to rub the back of his head. His shirt, which has become more untucked and crumpled, matches his now rumpled pants. The man is a complete mess. But something about the way he looks at me. Touches me. Perhaps we could at least be friends. Benefits to be determined. Maybe there's hope for something more. We need a hard reset. My body vibrates, almost like it could float out the window and over the entire school, and I blurt, 'Kent, let's have a do-over at The Purple Giraffe.'

'A do-over?'

'A first date do-over.'

'Wait, so you *are* dating him?' Marvin asks, the warmer-than-average early March day allowing his curly mop to break free from the confines of a sock cap. Meeting at East End Espresso has become part of our routine. The shop is only a few blocks from his school. It's small, with only a few tables inside, but today, with the warm early spring sun, we sit outside and chat.

'No. We're working together.' I clean the plastic lid on my coffee cup with a wipe from my bag.

'But you're going on a do-over first date?' Marvin asks, tilting his head as he places a stack of napkins in the center of our table. He always grabs too many, and my heart warms at his thoughtfulness.

'Only to have a clean slate.' I take a sip of my espresso tonic.

The bitterness and sweetness mix with the bubbles perfectly.

'A clean slate for what?'

'For working together. And being friends.' Marvin purses his lips.

'Vincent, I'm sorry, but this story you're selling . . . I'm not buying it.'

He wrinkles his nose and waits for a reply.

'Is he sexy as hell? Yes. Do his messy and awkward ways make me cringe? Yup. Can I stop thinking about his lips on mine? Nope. Would I appreciate a repeat of what happened after that horrible first date? Of course.'

'And in the supply closet,' Marvin says. 'What? I know the allure of scandalous sex in the school setting.'

He smirks, the straw of his iced coffee between his teeth. I probably shouldn't have told Marvin everything, especially about the blow job in the supply closet, but I had to talk to someone about it.

'That's not happening again. For a myriad of reasons.'

'Well, I think a first date do-over is . . . sweet. As usual, you have my full support.'

'Thank you. I appreciate that.' I fold my napkin for the third time.

'A second date. That's a big deal, Vincent.'

'No, a repeat first date,' I say, grabbing a new napkin from the pile. Unlike larger, more durable fabric ones, paper napkins can only withstand a few folds.

'Well, another date. With the same person. Do whatever gay math you want. My math skills top out at the kindergarten level.'

'Yes, another date. With Kent.'

Kent's warm smile. The way he sat with me while I finished making the corrections in the spreadsheet. Brushing his damn teeth for me. And that delicious long, thick cock.

'When was your last . . . second date?' he asks.

Marvin knows I've never had a boyfriend. Ever. I'm One-Date-Vincent. Because after seeing my OCD in action, there's never another. The sex is too hard. If the mood doesn't hit just right, it's not happening. And it's barely happened. I can count on one hand the number of sexual partners I've had – and not a single repeat customer. I'm like Space Mountain. One ride and you're done. I know more about sex from watching porn than from actual experiences. At forty, I've realized being alone isn't the end of the world. I'm not unhappy, but would I like more? Maybe. I'm not sure anyone could handle me on a permanent basis. I have my work. My builds. They say money can't buy happiness, but it can buy LEGO, and that's kind of the same thing.

'Technically . . . never.'

'Well, Kent will be your first . . . second.'

'First re-do.' I correct him.

'Whatever. It's monumental. Just remember to breathe. Fold your napkins, and for god's sake, good luck, and don't fuck it up.'

My stomach clenches, and I take four deep breaths, trying to center myself and not spiral. It's just Kent. We're already friends.

What could go wrong?

16

Kent

'Gentlemen.' The kind server from our first date greets us with a wide grin. Does the poor woman ever have a night off?

'Val,' Vincent says, his sexy smile illuminating the dimly lit room. He's wearing his standard uniform . . . a button-down shirt and slacks, all in solid, muted colors, and brown loafers. The small peek at Vincent's neck, where his shirt opens at the top, catches my eye, and yup, if it's not broken, don't fix it. Come to think of it, I've never seen him wear anything casual. Does he work out in business casual attire? The image of Vincent running on the treadmill in a tucked-in shirt and his dress shoes flashes in my head, and I chuckle.

Vincent and Val both turn toward my laughter.

'Oh, nothing, just um, hey, how are you?' I stammer, presenting my best smile as I attempt to keep the train on the tracks.

'Lovely,' Val says, 'and lovely to see you both again.' She nods at Vincent.

A newfound energy envelops the table, distinct from the memories of our first time here. We have some history now. That first night. The supply closet. Dinner at Gillian's. Cuddling and kissing in his bed. But we're being prudent. We're friends having dinner. And working together. To prove Lear staff and students are more than the data might show. To save my job. But Vincent asked for a date. A first date do-over.

He orders the same bottle of wine from our first night, and I peruse the menu.

'So,' Vincent says, 'you and your wife are still friends?'

'Oh yeah, we talk all the time. Our romance withered, not our friendship.'

His brow wrinkles, and the entire top of his shiny head attempts to join. Exes being close always causes some curiosity. 'People crave drama, but the fact is, Corrine and I simply didn't fan the flames of our relationship. We let the sizzle fizzle.'

Vincent sips his water, and his top lip peeks over the rim.

'She's remarried. To Charlie. That's her new husband. Happily married. I mean, as far as I know. We don't discuss their marriage in gory detail.'

'Makes sense. And Gillian is an only child?'

'She has a brother . . .' I say. Vincent's eyelashes flutter, and my stomach swirls like autumn leaves dancing. 'Sweetums.'

'Your cat.' A slight scrunching develops on Vincent's nose.

'He's a real baby. Maybe you'd like to meet him sometime?'

He blinks rapidly, and he pokes at the two napkins lined up on the table. His fingers grab the corner, tuck, push, and rub the edges.

The movement is slight, almost unnoticeable.

'I'm not the biggest animal person,' he says.

'Oh, Sweetums isn't an animal. He's my son.'

He snickers. His laugh is small. Barely there. People without pets often underestimate the companionship and love between a domesticated animal and its owner. Sweetums is my rock. And he weighs as much as a small boulder. He's always there for a cuddle. Corrine is remarried, Gillian has her family to care for, and my obligations to my school community end at five most days. Sweetums needs me. For food mostly, but still.

'That's actually sweet,' Vincent says, his lips curling. The light flickering from the candle casts a soft glow. His hazel eyes sparkle, and I remind myself we're here as friends. Or at least I think so.

'Gillian's grown. Heck, she has a family of her own. Sweetums keeps me company, especially on weekends. Lia and I have our standing date one Saturday each month. I get to be the fun one now. "Poppy time," she calls it. Plus, now I focus on loving other people's children.'

Vincent tilts his head slightly.

'At school. The kids. They're all mine.'

'And they seem to return the affection,' he says.

Val arrives with the wine and dribbles Vincent a taste. He sips, nods, and she pours for us both. The deep burgundy liquid splashes against our glasses, and I remind myself to be careful. Avoid spills.

'And what are we having tonight?' Val asks, pushing a strand of hair behind her ear. 'The usual?'

'Yup,' Vincent says and gives her a cool smile.

Scanning the menu, I order the Seoul Bowl with chicken. It seems like the least messy option.

'Lovely. I'll get that right into the kitchen for you,' she says, and once again, we're alone.

'Do you always have the same thing?' I ask.

Pursing his lips, Vincent looks up, searching for an answer, nods, and says, 'Yup. I pretty much do.'

He takes a sip of wine, and without thinking, I blurt, 'Well, maybe that will work in my favor for dessert.'

Vincent chokes on his merlot. Deep red liquid erupts from his lips, lands on his shirt, and splashes onto the napkin pile he's arranged. The fresh stain sprawls across his entire torso.

'Fuck, I'm so sorry,' I blather, grabbing a napkin from the bottom of his pile and standing to help. 'It was a joke. Or supposed to be. I didn't mean anything by it.'

'It's fine,' Vincent says, but his terse tone tells me it's certainly not. I dab at the wine as he stares with wide eyes, and I wonder if there's some incantation I can conjure to remove the stain immediately.

'Kent,' he says, but I'm too focused on removing the wine to answer. Holding my glass of water in one hand, I dip the napkin and attempt to clean Vincent's shirt.

'Kent. You're smoking.'

'No, never have. Nasty habit.'

'Your shirt. The candle.' He stands and pushes me off him, and yup, my shirt is indeed smoking. Right at my sternum. Heat builds near my chest, my eyes gape at the tiny billowing plume, and before I can speak, Vincent grabs the carafe of water and throws its entire contents at me.

'There.' He holds the empty carafe, assessing the damage.

'Not again,' I mumble.

'Again?'

'That's the third fire I've started at a restaurant. Maybe I should stop eating out.'

Now we're both on our feet – Vincent drenched in wine and me ready to rock a wet T-shirt contest. The giant lump in my throat prevents me from speaking.

Val appears, her tray piled with napkins, and assesses the scene. 'Maybe we need more.'

Vincent's gaze locks with mine and he asks, 'Can we get our meals to go, please?'

I'm reasonably certain this is the end of anything between us, including a friendship. Once again, my awkwardness throws a giant roadblock into something positive. Our first-date do-over was humming right along, and then I had to be ... me. Vincent picked me up, and the gesture seemed like a step in the right direction. But now, the thought of getting into his pristine car with a scorched, soaked shirt makes my stomach queasy.

'I'm so sorry,' I say, pulling out my mostly dry phone. 'I'm going to call a car.'

'I have towels. In the trunk.'

'Oh.' I bite my lower lip, the whiskers of my beard scratchy on my tongue. 'But, I thought ...'

'We have food.' Vincent holds up the takeout bag. 'And I have a hot shower. Big enough for both of us.'

'Oh.'

'My mood, Kent,' he says. His tongue brushes his top lip before swinging down to coat the bottom one with saliva. 'It's simmering.'

He turns and pushes me up against the side of the restaurant. My heart races to life as the brick rubs against my back. And he's suddenly upon me. Close. I watch his eyelashes dance, and then his closed lips tease mine.

'I haven't brushed,' I whisper.

'You didn't eat.'

Vincent kisses me. Soft for about two seconds, and then his tongue darts into my mouth. The taste of merlot swirls from his mouth and mixes with mine, and fuck, he's making my body hum. Hands wrap around my waist, and I wonder if sucking my gut in will diminish my love handles. Corrine always said, 'They're called love handles. They're meant for loving.' Right now, under the glow of the streetlight on a quiet Friday night, Vincent Manda seems to agree.

Breaking the kiss, he whispers, 'Let's go.'

He clasps my hand and tugs me toward his car. My head spins in the cool night. Under the moonlight, there's an urgency in the way he drags me, and once again, I'm asking what I've gotten myself into.

17

Vincent

'I'll take the towels,' I say, opening the door to my condo. Kent hands me the oversized beach towels I store in my trunk for emergencies. On the short drive here, the only sound in my car's cabin was 'You Make Loving Fun.' Christine's gorgeous alto crooning about the joy brought by someone's gestures. My mind races about what Kent might do. To me. To make me happy. Tonight.

In the restaurant, amid the chaos of wine and water, something strange occurred. I remained calm. The worst had happened. I was filthy. Smoke billowed from our table as the entire restaurant gawked. Kent's clothes clung to his body, saturated by my dousing. Even with his usual frazzled demeanor, Kent seemed unfazed. Even amid ruins, being with Kent, I felt safe. Relief washed over me, and that comfort ignited a blaze. If we're going to be friends, there will be benefits.

Holding the wadded, soiled towels in my right hand, I gently guide Kent into the bathroom. Quickly tossing them into the hamper, I catch Kent's gaze. He stands, mouth slightly open, and watches. Is he thinking about the last time he was here? When we kissed and cuddled. Does he want it to happen again? That was a measly appetizer. I'm craving a feast.

My hands are damp from the towels. A mixture of wine and water and my shirt, ruined beyond repair, sticks to my skin and takes extra effort to peel off. I unbutton my slacks and grab my erection, solid and throbbing, about to be free from the fabric. Kent doesn't break eye contact when I slide them down, and my cock springs up. What is it about this silver fox that makes my libido burn like a bonfire?

My open shower, large enough for two, with brown and gray tiles and a rain shower and wand, welcomes me as I turn the water on. There's no curtain or door . . . they're germ magnets. A minute of scalding hot, and then I'll lower the temperature – for him.

The water cascades over me, my bare head soothed first, and then slowly, my entire body becomes enveloped, warmed, cleansed.

Kent hasn't moved, but I sense him studying me. I take a few pumps of soap and begin my shower ritual. Moving out of the water, I lather bubbles in my palms and start at the top, washing my head, ears, and face before moving to my neck, arms, and chest. I linger a moment on my pecs, and Kent unbuttons his shirt, eyes still locked on me. Yes, please. I'm ready to be good.

Two fresh pumps for my cock, balls, and ass. When I slide my palms up and down my hard shaft, Kent lets out a soft, barely audible moan. His furry chest over that fucking dad bod, or I guess grandad bod, makes my dick pulse in my hands. He pushes his khakis off and stands in only his boxers. They're maroon and, from my vantage, appear to be in better shape than the ones I saw before. Maybe he bought new ones?

I reach around and separate my ass cheeks, meticulously washing and sanitizing every single bit of skin. For him.

My thighs are next, and while my hands grapple them, rubbing up and down, Kent takes a few steps closer. I try really hard not to stare, but I can see the head of his dick poking through the hole in the front of his boxers. He slides them off when I bend over to clean the lower half of my legs. And there it is. His plump, gorgeous cock grows thick and hard as he approaches. I've never been a size queen, but I've also never had a dick like Kent's. I want him gagging me while he holds my head and tells me I'm a good boy. Fuck.

Kent enters. Standing under the water, his gray mane instantly slicks back while he rinses off. The fur covering his torso glistens, beckoning my fingers to explore its velvety softness. I want to take him in my mouth immediately, but also, let's get this man clean first. With only my feet to finish, I brace myself on the wall to lift my foot for washing. Before I begin, Kent speaks for the first time since we arrived at my condo.

'Wait.'

I pause and search his face for a clue but come up empty. 'Let me. Please.'

Staying under the stream, Kent moves closer and kneels. More of him is touching the shower floor than I'd like, but I scoured it last night, and the cleaning crew came two days ago. And I'll scrub him myself soon.

On one knee, he takes my foot, still aloft, and slowly begins working the soap from my legs down. He rubs the top of my foot with all the lather, massaging bubbles between every toe. When I was a kid, I was extremely ticklish, especially my feet, but when Kent delivers the right amount of pressure, it's actually calming.

'Fuck,' he says. And even with my dick fully firm and pink from excitement, Kent Lester seems clearly focused on . . . my feet.

In this kneeling position, his cock is fully hard but still hangs because, well, I'm not an engineer, but gravity. Water drips off the tip, making it even more inviting. I salivate at the idea of how clean he's about to be.

After caressing and washing each toe, he moves my foot under the water, gently turning and twisting to rinse all the soap.

'Be a good boy, and hold on,' he says, nodding to my hand that's gripping the handle for balance. My cock shudders with his praise, and I do as I'm told as Kent slowly lifts my foot. I lean back and grab the metal as my center of balance shifts, with Kent bringing my foot toward his face. Bending down, my toes almost tickle his beard, and he looks at me and asks, 'May I?'

I'm not exactly sure what he wants, but with both our erections at full attention, all I can say is, 'Yes.'

With the water on his back, Kent slowly brushes his lips against my big toe. A kiss. Small. Teasing. His hands rub the tendons firmly, and after another peck where the nail begins, he takes my entire big toe in his mouth.

My shoulders tremble because this tickles more than I expected. With deep breaths, I move my hands from the handle to his head and steady myself in Kent's thick hair. The pressure on my footpads from his thumbs counters the sensation of my big toe completely in his warm, wet mouth. I teeter momentarily, and Kent pauses, lifting one hand to my waist. His fingers graze the tip of my hard cock, and it pulses at the brief contact.

'Heaven,' he says, taking my big toe and its neighbor in his mouth. He reaches down and begins stroking himself. Using his hand, he turns my foot and licks the entire footpad, finishing by taking each toe, one at a time, in his mouth to suckle. Kent's fingers press on the arch of my foot, and his tongue dances between each toe. Tiny slurping noises echo with his moans in the shower as he licks and laps. I never imagined such attentiveness to my feet would make my heart pound so hard, but here we are.

He gingerly rests my foot on his bent knee and pulls me closer, kissing the head of my dick. My head falls back at the relief of finally having my cock touched, even just by his lips.

'You ready?' he asks.

Ready for what? I have no idea. My chest tingles, and I remind myself to breathe.

'Yes. I'm ready.'

'Good boy.'

Kent takes the head at first, his lips surrounding it, and he draws my hips closer, slowly taking more of the shaft in his throat. The hair in his beard tickles the sensitive skin as I enter him, but I drop my shoulders, take another deep breath, and ease into the sensation.

Moving his mouth off me, he looks up at me and says, 'Now, fuck my mouth like a good boy.'

Nodding, I hold on to the sides of his head and do as I'm told. Being bossed around makes my insides boil. Kent makes gurgling, gagging noises as I plunge into his mouth. Each thrust sends waves of desire crashing over me with the cascading water.

'Are you okay?' I ask.

He moans and gives a quick thumbs up, cramming my cock in and out of his mouth. He's sucking, slurping, and sapping all of me. When he glances up, Kent's pupils have gone wide.

He stops stroking himself, both hands moving from my waist to my shaft, stroking when it's not in his mouth. He's attending to every inch.

'I love your sweet cock,' he says, pulling back and taking it all in. 'Slippery. Sloppy. Wet.'

He devours me, getting his lips almost to the base. The fingers from one hand creep under, cupping and massaging my balls. He removes my cock and begins sliding his lips up and down, stopping at the base, licking and flicking his tongue as he holds my balls in place. Observing his throbbing dick and recognizing his fondness for my feet, I position one foot between his legs as he kneels. My first two toes, which were in his warm mouth minutes ago, glide along his shaft with a teasing touch.

'Fuck, Vincent,' he says, pausing. He falls back to a seated position. Legs spread, Kent leans against the tile wall.

'Are you okay?' I ask.

'Fuck yes,' he says, grabbing my ankle to keep my toes in place.

'Do you like that?' I ask.

'Oh yeah, I love it. You just knocked me down.'

'Why don't you stay there?'

Kent's forehead creases and that adorable grin appears. 'All right,' he says.

With him safely on the shower floor, I move closer, leaning down on his shoulders for support, and do my best to rub the length of his cock with my toes. As I concentrate on satisfying Kent with my foot, I let out a gasp when he leans forward and devours my dick. He seems determined to suck me dry, and I'm perfectly content to let him have his way with me.

His fingers crawl under my cock, massaging my balls, and when he slides back further, he pauses and again asks, 'Is this okay?'

Right now, with the hot water pouring around us, I'm thrown into overdrive, and a finger is totally on the table.

'Yes. Please. Go for it.'

And then, a single finger delicately traces the perimeter of my opening, and the sensitive flesh quivers under his gentle touch. My foot finds the cool tile, bracing for him to enter me.

'I want to feel you,' Kent says. 'All of you.'

With one hand on my cock and the other gently holding my ass as he toys with my hole, he continues sucking. The combined sensation of his fingers and mouth have my eyes rolling back. It takes all my resolve to hold on to his head, my feet firmly on the ground, my thighs shaking from the pleasure.

'Am I being a good boy?' I ask, craving his approval.

When my cock slides out of his mouth, Kent says,

'Vincent, yes. Yes. You are such a good boy. You're fucking my face like a champ.'

His words pick at threads of a knot inside me, and I slowly unravel. A tingling floods my entire body, and my orgasm slowly starts to crawl up.

'Kent, I'm close.'

He seems to take this as confirmation what he's doing is working, and he's absolutely correct. Another finger joins the first, slightly teasing my hole with just a smidge of pressure. Occasionally, he uses them to spread me, one finger sliding in a tiny bit. He's careful not to enter past his fingertip, but the tension he's using is perfect. Combined with his head bobbing up and down, my balls and cock begin to contract in anticipation.

'I'm going to come,' I say, but he doesn't stop, and I'm unsure what to do. I start to pull away. I'm a gentleman, and I want to be good for him. Please him. But Kent draws me closer, determined to drain me.

'Kent, I'm . . . oh fuck.'

My cock explodes, filling Kent's mouth as he continues sucking, guzzling every drop I shoot toward the back of his throat. My hands grab his head, hanging on for dear life as he jolts me around like a rickety roller coaster. Gulping noises echo against the shower walls, and each spasm empties not only my balls but a sliver of my resolve.

When I finish, my dick still in his mouth, his fingers still teasing my hole, all the tension in my body, not just from the day, but maybe from forever, seems to spiral down the drain with the water.

'Holy shit,' I say.

Finally, moving off my cock with a trail of cum dripping

onto his beard, Kent says, 'Leg cramp!' He reaches a hand toward mine and says, 'Help me up. Please.'

I hold on to the shower handle and pull, and when Kent's standing, he wraps his arms around me. His damp chest hair brushes against my torso, and my thoughts scatter. What is this man doing to me?

'Hey,' he whispers into my ear with warm breath.

'You've got a little . . .' I point to his chin.

Touching his face, Kent wipes my seed with his thumb and pops it in his mouth, making a show of licking it clean.

'You're scrumptious.'

'That was . . . unexpected,' I say, tugging at his damp beard.

'Were you into it?'

'Um, you couldn't tell?' I ask, kissing his shoulder. My lips linger, longing for closeness.

'No, I could tell. Just wanted confirmation.' He pulls me closer, the pressure soothing my soul, and his cock, still firm, pokes my own dick, now only semi-hard.

'Let's get you off,' I say.

'Um, I'm okay. That was amazing. It's not necessary,' he says. 'I'm kind of out of breath.'

Kent's heavy breathing and small laughter mingle with the sensation of his unyielding erection prodding against me.

'I have an idea,' I say. 'Let's get you clean first.' I take two pumps of soap and begin lathering his chest. Warmth radiates from my cheeks, adding to the steam between us. 'I think you'll enjoy this.'

18

Kent

Vincent wraps a white towel around his waist, the fabric snug against his skin. He hands me another from the shelf. 'Come,' he whispers, his voice soft and soothing, guiding me gently to the main room. The dining table, covered in LEGO Paris, has more streets and buildings than the last time I was here. He slides the small coffee table away from the deep chocolate leather sofa and lays the extra towel on the hardwood floor, doubling and smoothing it like a picnic blanket.

I have no idea what he's up to, but having his feet in my mouth, licking and lapping his toes, I never in a million years thought that would happen. How, at fifty-two, am I only now discovering a fascination with feet? It never crossed my mind with Corrine. She probably would have let me explore if I'd suggested it. But I never did. A few times at the beach, I've noticed men, mostly their legs, thick thighs, strong calves, and, yes, their feet. Sturdy toes, with a dusting of hair and defined tendons, have caught my gaze occasionally, but I never thought much about it.

My cock, still thick and firm, has never been this hard without a pill. Even with Vincent's napkins, wipes, and LEGO-filled condo, this man does something to me I've never quite experienced. He's my medicine.

He sits on the sofa, the leather creaking softly under his body. Unwrapping his towel, he exposes his beautiful package, now soft but still exquisite, spreads his legs, and nods to the towel.

'Sit. Rest your back here.' He pats between his legs. I lower myself to the ground with a few grunts, throw my towel aside, and lean back between him, still unsure what he has in mind.

'Relax,' he says, his hands rubbing my shoulders.

I hear him squirt something onto his hands, and the smell of coconut takes over. He's lathering something, the sounds and aroma intoxicating. And then it happens. My breath hitches, and the air vacates my lungs as Vincent Manda's legs wrap around my torso and his delicious feet seize my hard cock. Carefully, he begins stroking, his slick soles gliding up and down the sensitive skin of my shaft, sending shivers through my body. When his big toe brushes over the tip, I let out a moan, and he reaches down and cups my chest. Holy fuck.

His hands, lost in my chest hair, massage my pecs, and he teases my nipples. His feet never stop jerking me, and yowsers. The sensation of having his feet and hands on my body makes my insides quiver in anticipation. My body wants to relent, give over, and allow my orgasm to happen, but this is too good. Too amazing. Too much. Grasped by Vincent's extremities . . . I yearn to stay in this moment forever.

'Do you like this?' he asks, leaning forward enough so his breath tickles the hair on the back of my neck.

'I love it. You're such a fucking good boy,' I tell him, the pleasure bubbling over. My hands glide up and down his smooth calves as they guide his feet.

With my last words, Vincent's dick, now semi-hard, surges against my shoulder.

'That didn't take long,' I say, surprised at his recovery time.

'It's you, Kent.'

Angling my head back, I'm able to give the tip a small kiss and take the head in my mouth. He continues using his fingers on my chest, getting lost in my salty fur while his feet glide around my cock.

'I love your chest. So hairy. So thick. So fucking sexy,' he says.

'Mmmh. My best boy.'

With closed eyes, the nerves in my body take over, tingling and vibrating. With a woozy head, I'm fairly certain all the blood in my body has traveled south. I cannot remember the last time I was this hard. Maybe high school? College? That one time, Corrine and I had sex on a hotel balcony in Barcelona. But something about Vincent and the complete attention he's giving me sends me over.

'Do you think you can come like this?' he whispers.

Not wanting to remove his delectable dick from my mouth, I simply give a quick nod.

Vincent's toes hover over the sensitive tip and my body trembles. My brain knows his disdain for the ensuing eruption, but I'm unable to signal my mouth to warn him. And he's got to sense it. My chest heaves, my balls seize, and I suck him harder as my cock shoots thick ribbons all over Vincent's toes and feet. The warm liquid coats us both, but he doesn't flinch.

He doesn't relent, even after I've come and my body shudders at his touch. My hips tremble with each slick stroke as he slathers cum up and down my shaft.

'Okay, okay,' I say, leaning my head back against his thigh.

He leans over, hands on my ears, and kisses my sweaty forehead. When he pulls away, his eyes open, I see his beautiful face, and my body fills with warmth. My breathing becomes deeper and more relaxed. I'm completely present, immersed in the bliss coursing through my veins.

'Did you enjoy that?'

Did I enjoy it? Is water wet?

'Um, yeah.' My entire body still hums with pleasure. 'What the hell was that?'

'It's called a foot job.' His chin now rests on the top of my head.

'A foot job? That makes sense,' I say, still not quite ready to move. 'But how the fuck did you know about it?'

'From the internet.'

'Excuse me?' I ask, my eyes agape.

'Kent, you can learn about almost anything on the internet.'

'Apparently.'

He hands me a washcloth, and I start with a few swipes at his feet before carefully rubbing in between each toe, ensuring he's perfectly clean. Once his toes shine, I take care of myself. Vincent watches as I clean us both, a soft smile on his heavenly lips. A shift is happening between us. Slowly, this man is letting me in, and I know his trust isn't something to take lightly.

Sitting at Vincent's kitchen island, our takeout in front of us, my stomach reminds me it's late, and after the physical exertion he put me through, I'm ravenous. We both wear plain white T-shirts and gray sweats, all Vincent's, a bonus for being relatively the same size. He's about an inch shorter, and I'm several inches wider around the middle, but thankfully, the stretchy material is forgiving. Matching dinner outfits wasn't part of my first-date re-do plan, but neither was the wine, the water, or the foot job. Oy.

'Are we over pretending we're just friends?' I ask, motioning to our matching outfits.

'Kent Lester,' Vincent says, a fork in one hand and a napkin in the other, 'only you were pretending.'

'Are you teasing me?'

He leans over, wipes the corners of my mouth with his napkin, and then kisses me. His lips brush mine; it's longer than a peck, but he pulls away before it escalates . . . only to return for another. He folds his napkin, wipes his mouth, and continues eating, the unique fusion of Mexican and Korean spices creating a cozy aroma.

'Do you think we'll make the go-live date?' I change the subject as thoughts of Dr Cutler swirl with her questions and continual obsession over the board. One bonus of being Jewish . . . anxiety runs like the electric company. It may have occasional outages, but generally, you can count on it being there. 'The clock is ticking.'

'For sure,' he says. Watching Vincent's meticulous use

of chopsticks, his luscious lips welcoming them, a small smile meanders across my face. He's really quite precious.

'Geoff never drops the ball.' His chopsticks pause, and his chin drops to his chest. 'That's my role.'

I reach over and put my finger under his chin, hoping he's okay with the contact during a meal. He doesn't recoil, and I gently lift his face until his eyes find mine. I take a deep breath and smile.

'Stop beating yourself up all the time.'

'Easier said than done. My whole life, I've been the problem.'

'I find that hard to believe,' I say, leaning over and kissing his forehead. 'You seem very ... unproblematic to me.'

Vincent steps to the sink and faces out the large window. Bathed in the moonlight, he talks into the darkness, his words hanging in the air.

'We were on schedule at the last school in New Hampshire. Geoff had the system tuned and ready for launch. I was working on outlining the needs assessments with teachers, and he called a meeting to look at the summarized data to make some critical decisions.'

I turn to face him, but Vincent continues talking to the window. He rubs the back of his neck, occasionally moving up to take a glide over his head, momentarily blocking the reflection from the moon.

'Even though the data suggested having teachers use their laptops would be more cost-efficient, the anecdotal interviews told me tablets would be more efficient and offset the difference.'

'What happened?' I ask, wanting to go to him. Wrap

him in my arms from behind, hold him close, smell his neck, and comfort him through this story. But I sit. Waiting. Listening.

'I did a quick workout the morning of the meeting, and afterward, in the shower, I got stuck.'

I purse my lips. Stuck. Like with the data in my office. Washing his hands in Gillian's bathroom.

'I started with my head, like I always do, and things were fine. When I got to my arms, I couldn't stop scrubbing.' – Vincent holds out his arms, flexing until the veins in his forearms pop – 'In hindsight, I realize the stress of the implementation, the meeting, knowing I had to convince Geoff and the team to do something more costly, it all triggered me.'

'Oh, Vincent.'

'I was late. Really late. By the time I got there, the meeting was over. They decided without me. The school saved money using existing laptops, but the launch failed. The software usage didn't meet benchmarks. Just as I predicted. Geoff made it clear that if I had been there, maybe they would have made a different decision.'

'But you weren't there.' I work my throat through a sandy swallow. 'They decided without you.'

'But I'm the specialist. I should've been present. And I wasn't. That's all Geoff cares about. My fault. Not his. He was adamant about that.'

Unsure what to say, I stand to join him at the sink, and my hand smacks my resting chopsticks, sending them flying across the room, catapulting a few bits of my Seoul Bowl with them. Even facing away, Vincent knows. He winces at the sound of tiny flying wood.

'I'll get it.' I scramble for the extra napkins.

I'm on the floor, searching, cleaning, trying to erase the mess before Vincent reacts. If I can clean it up quickly, it won't upset him further. With a handful of napkins, I rush forward. Suddenly sensing Vincent's presence, I snap my head and accidentally crash into his chin.

'Fuck!' he shouts.

'Oh my gosh, I'm so sorry,' I blather, pivoting my attention toward him.

Vincent closes his eyes and winces. He takes a deep inhale through his nose and pushes the breath through pursed lips.

'Are you okay?' I ask, grabbing at his face.

'I'm fine.' He rubs his chin and says, 'Kent Lester, has anyone ever mentioned you have Tasmanian Devil energy?'

A broad smile overtakes my face, and I laugh. 'Not that specific reference, but I mean, yeah, I can see that.' A flush creeps across my cheeks. 'I'm sorry.'

'Why? He's kind of cute. In a chaotic way.'

We finish cleaning, and seeing it's almost midnight, I pull my phone out.

'I'm going to call a car,' I say.

'Why don't you stay?' Vincent's eyes grow large.

'I don't want to impose. And I'd have to get up early tomorrow,' I say.

'But it's Saturday.'

'It's my day to take Lia. Plus, Sweetums couldn't care less about the weekend. He'll be looking for me. For his food.'

'Stay and go home early,' he says, and I'm not sure I can

say no to those batting eyelashes. The thought of another night cuddled up next to Vincent. Holding him. Being held. My heart yearns to be close to him.

'Okay, I'll sneak out in the morning. I won't disturb you.'

In bed with Vincent, with our shirts off, facing each other, our breathing the only sound in the room, my heart trots before taking off at a full gallop.

'Would it be okay if I . . .'

'C'mere,' Vincent says, grabbing my hand, rolling over, and wrapping me around his smooth body.

'Good night, Mr Lester.'

'Good night, Mr Manda.' I inhale the orange and honey aroma on his skin, pull him close, and let the warmth of our bodies quiet my mind. With Vincent so near, so sweet, so beautiful, how am I supposed to not fall for this man?

19

Vincent

'This is Sweetums.'

Kent holds a creature that appears to be an overfed cat on growth hormones. Featuring an orange coat, long wild fur, pointy ears, and paws like baseball mitts, he's the biggest feline I've seen in my life. Not that I've been searching. Does Kent know it's illegal to keep wild animals as pets?

'Holy mother of god,' I say, gulping down a breath, 'what the hell is that?'

'Sweetums. My cat.' Kent attempts to cradle the giant beast like an infant, and to my surprise, it lets him. He bends down and kisses the top of its head, covered in wispy whiskers that must be half a foot long.

'He's a Maine coon.' Kent rubs under the monster's chin, which seems to cast a spell on it. The cat's eyes close, and it begins purring. The sound expands until it fills Kent's rather cluttered apartment.

When Kent began getting dressed just after five this morning, it was clear to me that I needed to drive him home. Sleeping in isn't something my brain understands, and on weekends, I'm typically up by six, anyway. I planned to drop him off, get a workout and shower, do an abbreviated scrubbing of surfaces, and spend my afternoon working on LEGO Paris. But after our night together, when Kent invited me up to meet his 'baby,' declining felt rude.

'They're larger than most domesticated cats,' Kent says, once again holding the cat up under its arms for my inspection. 'Adult males usually weigh around eighteen pounds, but Sweetums is closer to twenty-five. He's got a little extra love on him. Like his daddy.'

The cat climbs over his shoulder, and its hind legs poke at Kent's soft stomach. He really has the perfect dad bod. Fluffy, furry, and perfect for cuddling.

'Anyway, let me feed him,' Kent says. 'He's starving, right, Sweetums?'

The cat makes a noise, something between a meow and a guttural growl.

My eyes survey his space while Kent takes care of the ravenous feline, and – much like Kent – the word disorderly comes to mind. There's so much . . . stuff, and it's everywhere. The built-in bookshelves are tightly packed with an assortment of books, small decorative items, and cherished family photos. Over by the large bay windows, there's a cat tree, easily over six feet tall, overflowing with more cat toys than a small animal shelter requires. Sweetums is clearly one spoiled feline.

I search for a place to sit. The sofa is completely covered. Blankets. Pillows. Magazines. A tattered sweatshirt. A random selection of remotes, coasters, and books surrounds a hopefully empty pizza box on the coffee table. There's not a vacant spot to be found.

'There we go,' Kent says, drying his hands on a paper towel. 'He's all set for at least five minutes. That's how long he takes to inhale a can of cat food. Sit,' he says, and then notices the state of his sofa, seemingly for the first time. 'Oh gosh, look at this mess.'

He begins folding blankets, plumping pillows, and stacking magazines on the coffee table.

'It's fine, Kent. I really shouldn't stay.' My skin itches in such disorder, and the unhygienic cat, only a few feet away, doesn't help.

'Why not? There. Sit.' He points to a cushion he's managed to clear.

The sofa, a deep navy fabric, has a few patches on the arms, probably from monster feline scratches. Doing my best to take up as little space as possible, I nod and sit. With my hands resting in my lap, I try to avoid unnecessary fidgeting.

Kent joins me, pushing more clutter aside, pulling his feet up, and grabbing a blanket to cover his lap. 'Where's my good boy?'

I'm tempted to crawl over and let him pet me, but alas, he's summoning the cat.

Sprinting over, Sweetums bounds into Kent's lap and immediately flops over, presenting his stomach.

'This is our little ritual. He eats and then gets massive belly rubs.' As promised, Kent massages the fur, kneading until, once again, the cat's purr roars like an engine.

'How did he get so, so . . .'

'Enormous?' Kent cradles Sweetums's face in his hands and then returns to running his palms up and down his stomach. 'Maine coons are the largest domesticated cats. And Sweetums, well, he's super-sized.'

For a brief moment, the cat looks at me, and before I can scream, run, or set the place on fire, he flips over and crawls toward me.

'Kent, I don't really like . . .'

His paws land on my thigh. Plump and hairy, the pressure of his body creates an indentation in my joggers. As he purrs, the sensation travels through my pants. My entire body vibrates and hums under him. When I work out, I can easily manage twenty-five-pound dumbbells, but out of nowhere, the same weight becomes an overwhelming burden. Sweetums peers at me, his eyes a deep amber, and his nose twitches.

'What is he doing?' I ask.

'Checking out his competition.'

'I'm not competing with a cat.'

'No, but he doesn't know that.'

Kent leans over and begins petting the back half of the cat.

Sweetums's rear rises at his owner's touch, and he immediately headbutts my bicep.

'He likes you. Well, your arm. You do have great arms,' he says.

'Flattery isn't going to distract me from the filthy creature currently walking all over me.' Usually, I'd take deep breaths to center myself, but there's no way I'm consuming massive gulps of air in such close proximity to this animal.

'Sweetums is very clean. He gets a bath every day. Sometimes twice a day. And I brush him weekly,' he says, burying his face into the cat's back. Kent's face. Kent's lips. That I've kissed.

'You bathe him?'

'No, he bathes himself, right, Sweetums?' Kent lifts the cat off me and returns him to his lap. 'I think Vincent has had his fill for now, buddy.'

My body relaxes, but only the tiniest bit because while he may not be on me, he's still only a foot away. I haven't located Kent's bathroom yet, and the need for a quick scrub down overtakes me.

'Can I . . .' My head darts around, searching.

'Of course. There's a guest bath right off the kitchen,' he says, pointing. 'You don't want a shower, do you? Because if you did, that's fine. I'm happy to get you a towel. A toothbrush. Whatever you need.'

A momentary calm washes over me as my heart slows down. He appears completely unfazed by the situation. By me. By my need to flee and scrub myself.

'No, I'm good, just want to wash up after the . . .'

'His name is Sweetums. He won't hurt you. I promise.'

My chin takes a nosedive and I hurry to the bathroom. My brain knows people have animals. My dad and his damn goats. People love their pets. Sleep with them. Dress them up like lumberjacks for Halloween. My mother sent me a photo of one of the goats wearing a crown and tutu. I think it was supposed to be a princess. Or queen. My dad was kissing it on the snout. The filth. The grime. The contact with an unclean beast.

Kent wouldn't make me do anything I'm not comfortable with. Deep breaths. After triple scrubbing my face, hands, and arms, I return. Sweetums has fallen asleep next to Kent. With his head nestled on Kent's lap, his stomach slowly rises and falls with each breath he takes.

'He's down for the count once he's eaten and gotten a little love.'

'Well, I should go,' I say, eyeing the door.

'Oh, sure. If you need to go, of course. I really appreciate the ride home. Didn't think out the whole water, wine fiasco, and then spending the night at your place when I asked you to pick me up. But if you wanted to stay, I mean, I can make you some toast. Plain. We could just chat until I need to pick up Lia. I can put Sweetums in the bedroom if you want.'

Do I need to go right now? No. The unfamiliar place. The clutter. The germs from having a living animal inhabiting your home. But Kent's face. His sweet smile. That beard. The way he held me all night long like the bed was the ocean and I was his life ring.

'I can stay for a little. Sure.'

Sitting as far as possible from Sweetums (and Kent by proxy), I do my best to remain still and focus on Kent's face and not the hibernating cat next to him.

'There you go, see, he's harmless. Maine coons are known for their friendly temperament,' he says. Sweetums stretches out his long body, his paws flexing and retracting. 'And for their silliness.'

'I'm not really an animal person.'

'Really? I'd never have guessed that about you.' Kent's mouth falls open and twists into his full smile, a hint of a dimple under the beard, and a sliver of his front teeth shines across his face. 'You didn't have pets growing up?'

'Gosh, no. My parents always said I could have one if I wanted, but I never did. They kept asking and waiting, and it never happened. I think that's why my dad is infatuated with his goats now. My fear of germs began early, and well, animals are generally dirty.'

'I get it,' he says. 'I always wanted a cat, but Gillian is allergic. She can only be around him in small spurts. When she went to college, Corrine and I split, and then she gifted me Sweetums, and well, he's really just a big baby.'

'It's really sweet she bought you a cat.'

'I mean, she was trying to distract me from the pain of hearing she was remarrying, but it's all good. She's happy. I'm happy. And I got Sweetums.'

He pets his cat, and this time, Sweetums doesn't move – his heavy breathing a sign he's finally asleep.

'And you,' he says, pushing his glasses up. 'You like working for Hopscotch?'

'It's a job. And I'm good at it. Mostly. The intersection of technology and people. Making the data and techie stuff mesh with the human side. I've always known how to integrate systems and make things work. Before Hopscotch, I worked for a statistical software company that catered to corporate clients and when I met Marvin, he told me about this new educational software company. It was an opportunity to get in on the ground floor.'

'Can I be honest with you?' he asks.

'Of course.'

'You don't seem to love it.'

My pulse quickens, and I cross my arms as I shift on the couch.

'I mean, who loves their job?'

'I do,' Kent says without a hint of irony.

'I need a job. What else would I do?'

'Plenty of things. You love building. Working with your hands. Keeping things organized. There's lots of things you could do.'

'Taking this position was new enough. I can't imagine a whole new direction.' My chest tightens, thinking about the uncertainty and newness even taking the job with Hopscotch elicited.

'Sometimes you have to imagine something in order to will it into existence.' Kent reaches over Sweetums and rests his hand on my thigh. 'Is my job perfect? Of course not. Is there more stress than the paycheck warrants? Yup. But education is entirely underfunded. I'm not there for the money. Would I like to earn what I'm worth? Of course. But I'm there for every adult who shows up to make it the best experience for our kids. And the students. I'm there to help each one of them be as successful as possible. I genuinely love what I do.'

'It's obvious,' I say. 'The way you interact with your staff. Brodie. That kid clearly adores you. Even if he loves Theo a little more.'

'I mean, Theo's a big grumpy bear. It's hard not to fall in love with him.'

I laugh, remembering the scowl he gave Brodie. 'Yeah, I can see that.'

'And that's why this is so important to me. Hopscotch. We need to show Dr Cutler and the board that our scores aren't an accurate representation of our school's performance.'

'Do you really think they aren't aware?'

'I suspect Dr Cutler knows. She visits. We meet. But the board, they're only looking at data.'

Kent inhales deeply. With a puff of his chest, he blows air through his nose, and Sweetums's back flitters. He's so clearly invested in his school. The people. It's more than a job to him.

'Well, I'm going to do everything I can to help,' I say, reaching over and placing my hand on his thigh – the one without a massive cat's head on it.

After I dropped the ball at River, there's no room for error at Lear. Or with Kent. Whatever happens between us can't distract us or create problems at work. We both need this too much.

Standing, I brush my pants swiftly. 'Well, I should get going.'

'I have to pick Lia up in . . .' Kent says, checking his watch, 'thirty minutes.' He tilts his head, his bushy brows jogging up his forehead. 'Why don't you join us?'

'Me? I wouldn't want to intrude on her Poppy time.'

'Oh gosh, she'd love it. And I think you'd love where we're going today,' he says, a small glint in his brown eyes.

'But I haven't showered. I need to change, and . . .'

'Go home. We'll pick you up in forty-five minutes.'

Kent eases Sweetums onto the blanket and stands. Taking my hand in his, he kisses my knuckles. His whiskers prickle my skin, sending a warm shiver up my arm. This isn't what I had in mind for my day, but Kent has a way of making it hard to refuse.

'Are you sure?'

Kent leans in, his lips brush my neck, and he whispers in my ear, 'Absolutely.'

20

Kent

'Poppy!' Lia shouts from her father's arms. Louis opens the door with my granddaughter in one arm and a giant meat baster in the other.

When I cock my head and stare at the utensil, he lifts it and says, 'Roast beef. No way mine will be dry.'

I extend my arms, and Lia transfers from her father to me, clutching my neck and burying her face in my beard. She moves her tiny mouth toward my ear, whispering, 'Where are we going, Poppy?' Her breath smacks of fruity cereal and toothpaste.

'Yes, where are you going, Poppy?' Gillian asks, her turn to parrot Lia. She stands behind Louis, her hands moving near his waist as she ties his apron. As she pulls the dark blue fabric taut, the words come into focus – *May I suggest the sausage?* I contain my groan and step inside.

'It's a surprise.'

Gillian's eyes widen, and she replies, 'Oh really?'

'Let's grab your coat, Lia,' I say, snatching her gear piled by the door.

'Have fun with Poppy!' Louis calls from the kitchen.

'Almost ready,' I say, pulling a pink hat over Lia's head. 'Listen, we're going to pick up Vincent and . . .' Lia eyes me as her mother zips her jacket, and knowing the way she loves to chat, I refrain from telling Gillian where we're headed. 'We'll be back by dinner. I'll call you when we get there.'

'Vincent.' Gillian hands me a backpack of supplies I might need for a day with my four-year-old granddaughter. 'Give him my best.' She arranges her lips into a knowing smile.

'We will,' I reply, slinging the bag over my shoulder and taking Lia's hand.

'Where are we going?' Lia asks as she buckles herself into the car seat that lives in my backseat for her.

'You're such a big girl,' I say, attempting to distract her while I wait for her to finish.

'I am a big girl.' *Click*. The final strap locks into place, and I give everything a quick tug to check it's secure. 'But where are we *going*, Poppy?'

'Someplace special. I can't tell you until we arrive because I want it to be a surprise.'

'For Vincent?'

'Yes.'

'But I won't tell him.'

I love Lia to the moon and back, but she cannot keep a secret to save her life. It's one thing I adore about her. I always know what my birthday presents are, because to keep them a secret, Gillian would have to buy and wrap them without Lia . . . and she doesn't have time for that.

'Well, I want it to be a surprise for you, too,' I offer.

'Can I have a hint?'

'Sure, sweetheart. The place we're going is close to Boston. So, it's going to be a bit of a drive.'

'Can we sing?'

'Of course we can sing.' I hope Vincent doesn't mind Kidz Bop.

> Kent: We're downstairs.

> Vincent: Be right there.

> Kent: I missed your face.

> Vincent: You saw me less than an hour ago.

> Kent: Exactly.

'Hi,' Vincent says, hopping into the front seat. He turns and waves to Lia and I spy her checking him out in the rearview mirror.

'Hi, Poppy's boyfriend.'

Vincent gives me a stare.

'Vincent is my friend, sweetie.'

'Mommy says he's your boyfriend.'

'Well,' Vincent says, 'we're both boys. And we're friends.'

Lia tilts her head, pondering the idea, nods, and says, 'Okay. Let's go to my surprise.'

I back out of the small parking lot for Vincent's building, and we head for the highway. Knowing my granddaughter will eventually take a nap if we sing first, I turn the music on, and a loud guitar sweeps through the cabin before a chorus of children sing loudly. Lia immediately begins crooning along to 'Sk8tr Boi.' I'm only familiar with the song because *Kidz Bop 4* lives in my car for this very purpose. The tune's ridiculous spelling pops up on the audio display, taunting the educator in me.

I glance over at Vincent. His face stretches and bunches like he's tasted the sourest lemon ever grown. I'm not sure if it's the music, the singing, the lack of Fleetwood Mac, or all of the above.

I lean over and whisper-shout over Lia's singing, 'Twenty minutes, she'll be asleep.'

He nods and asks, 'Where are we going, anyway?'

Hearing the possibility of a co-conspirator, Lia pauses her singing and shouts over the music. 'I've been asking Poppy since he picked me up. He won't tell.'

'Not even a hint?' Vincent asks.

'Near Boston,' Lia calls from the back.

'A Red Sox game?' Vincent asks.

I form a cheeky smile and shake my head.

'The 'quarium?' Lia asks.

'Nope.'

'But I love the fishes. And that giant turtle. And the penguins. Poppy, the penguins are so cute. Can we please go see them?'

'We went last summer. And we'll go again this year,' I assure her.

Vincent scratches his sexy head. 'The Freedom Trail?'

'Yes, we're taking my four-year-old granddaughter on a two-and-a-half-mile historical walking tour.'

'I'm almost five!' she bellows. 'In May. And then I start kindergarten.'

'Yes, sweetie. And you'll have a big cake.'

'I want a pink cake with pink frosting and pink sprinkles!'

'Lia, can I ask you a question?' Vincent swivels his head to face her.

'Sure!'

'Is your favorite color pink?'

I peep in the rearview and Lia's eyes go wide, her tiny mouth dropping open.

'Yes! How did you know?'

Vincent opens his mouth, and I spy his beautiful smile when I give a quick glance. A deep guffaw rumbles from his core, spills out, and overtakes the singing children. He may not love cats or children or messes, but even he can't deny the complete charm of Lia.

'She's very cute,' he says through laughter.

I nod quickly in agreement and push back against the headrest, enjoying the intersection of Vincent and my granddaughter.

After four more mangled pop songs, Vincent asks, 'Is she asleep?'

I glance in the rearview mirror, and as predicted, Lia is out in her seat. Her sweet face rests on the padded strap across her chest. Strawberry-blonde hair, a perfect match with her mother's, veils most of her face.

'Yes,' I whisper. 'If she were awake, we'd know. Trust me.'

'How?'

'She'd be singing. Or talking. Or asking a million questions.'

'You're really lucky,' Vincent says, glancing back at her.

'I have no complaints,' I say, patting his knee. Being here with both of them, Lia snoozing and Vincent next to me, warms my soul.

A group of guitars fills the car, plucking and strumming the familiar opening to 'Landslide.' And then the voices come in, a choir of children, harmonizing and singing about being afraid of changes and getting older.

'This is Fleetwood Mac, you know.'

Vincent cocks his head, and his beautiful lashes frame his eyes, which roll like a log down a steep hill.

'The song. Not the kids,' I say.

'Obviously,' Vincent says. I lean over and gently squeeze his thigh. My thumb rubs up and down his khakis, longing for a hint of what's beneath.

'Where are we going anyway?' he asks. 'She's asleep. You can tell me.'

'The surprise isn't for her, silly. It's for you.'

'Oh.' Vincent's voice squeaks in the most adorable way, and I tickle his knee, delighting in catching him off guard.

'This is our exit,' I say.

We pull off and drive down the ramp, heading for what I hope is a day that blows Vincent's mind in all the best ways.

'We're here,' I say. Pulling around the corner, I slow the car to find parking and the giant giraffe and store sign finally reveal my surprise.

I gently bring the car to a stop and steal a quick glimpse of Vincent's face. His mouth opens slightly, and he blinks a few times, his eyelashes pulling my attention.

'What? How?'

'Surprise!' I shout.

'Surprise!' Lia repeats from the back. She still has no clue where we are or what the surprise is, but she's never one to miss out on an opportunity to yell enthusiastically.

'Are you excited?' I ask.

Vincent leans over, takes my hand, squeezes it hard, and with a raw emotion in his voice I've not previously heard, says, 'Yes. Thank you. Thank you.'

A relaxed smile crosses his beautiful lips, and Vincent covers it with his hand. As I examine his hazel eyes, they widen in astonishment, tears glistening in the corners. I wish there was a way to tuck this moment in my pocket and savor it forever.

21

Vincent

'Poppy! Look at the giraffe.' Lia skips between us, clasping Kent's hand as we walk on the sidewalk. What if she wants to hold mine at some point? I pat the small bottle of hand sanitizer in my front pocket.

My heart races and I hope the drawn look of astonishment on my face doesn't betray how fucking amazing this surprise is to me. Had he planned this with Lia all along, or was this something for me? My hand finds Kent's shoulder. A quick squeeze is all I'm able to get in with Lia between us, but I hope it conveys how over the moon I am about this.

'His name is Gio,' I say. The giant, twenty-foot giraffe, made completely of LEGO DUPLO bricks, took an entire day to assemble. According to the article I read when the center opened, they constructed it using over 22,000 bricks. I close my eyes for a moment and think of being part of creating something so monumental.

'Gio?' Lia asks.

'Yeah, he was named after a little boy who –' I pause,

wondering if she needs to hear the story about the boy who died of congestive heart failure. '– really loved LEGO.'

'Vincent loves LEGO more than . . . well, almost anything, I think,' Kent says. 'I thought this would be fun for both of you.'

As we get closer to Gio, the sign behind him comes into view: LEGO Discovery Center. I have been itching to come here since they reopened last year after a twelve-million-dollar renovation. That would buy a lot of LEGO. Thinking about what awaits us inside, my pulse quickens, and my insides vibrate like my electric razor skimming over my scalp.

'I've wanted to come here . . . well, since forever,' I say.

'Why haven't you?' Kent tilts his head.

'Technically, it's for kids. And you need a child to get in. I thought about asking Marvin. He could bring Illona and let me tag along, but it's a long drive and, well . . . Illona doesn't really love LEGO.'

Lia reaches up, pulls at my fingers, and says, 'Well, I do. I mean enough.' She smiles, attempting to show me every tooth in her tiny mouth. 'I mean, we're here!'

We buy our tickets and I wait outside the men's room, while Kent takes Lia to the bathroom. Inside the elevator, vibrant LEGO decor surrounds us as we ascend to the top floor. Lia grabs my hand and says, 'I washed after. Real good. Poppy helped me.'

I smile at her and then Kent, and he shrugs. Right now, I am about to spend the day around LEGO. With a bottle of sanitizer, bathrooms everywhere, and Kent with me, I've got this. I exhale deeply, and Kent asks, 'You okay?'

'More than okay. I can't believe you did this.'

'I've been thinking about bringing Lia here.' Kent shrugs. 'As soon as you agreed to join us, I knew this had to be today's adventure.'

The urge to pull him close consumes me. When the elevator doors open, Lia bolts out, running toward the Build Your Mini Figure attraction, and I clasp Kent's hand for a moment.

'Thank you.'

'You already thanked me.'

'I know. I may never stop.'

We catch up to Lia and help her pick parts for her mini figure.

Kent and I both make our own as well. Giant bins are filled to the brim with hundreds of different variations of components. As she searches, Lia runs her hands through the head bin, creating a cascade of LEGO heads.

'This one is me,' she says. She holds a small head with pink and blue glasses and a huge grin. 'When I'm wearing my sunglasses.'

'I see it,' Kent says.

Continuing to dig and search, Lia finally hands another to Kent. 'Here, Poppy.'

She hands a piece to Kent. It has glasses, a gray beard, a kind face, and a sweet smile. She couldn't have picked a more perfect match.

'Oh my, do I look like this?' Kent holds the head up.

'Exactly,' I say, with a wink.

'Let's find one for Vincent,' Kent says.

'Okay! I'm a good head picker,' she says. Kent and I

share a smile, and maybe if I'm surrounded by LEGO, children aren't so terrible.

'Here!' she shouts, holding it up for our inspection. The head has a snarky smirk and furrowed eyebrows. It's almost like it can't decide if it's worried or carefree.

'Perfect,' Kent says, winking at me. 'Now, let's find hair.'

'That will be easy for you, Vincent,' Lia says. 'You don't need any.'

She giggles, pausing her trek to the massive bin of hair pieces to bend over with laughter and relish her own joke.

'I think she likes you,' Kent says as we follow a few feet behind her.

I hold my mini-fig head between my thumb and index finger and show him. Mini Vincent smirks with crooked brows.

'Really?'

'She's teasing you. That's her love language.'

We stand behind Lia as she turns over what appears to be thousands of pieces of plastic hair, taking the entire place in. 'I think LEGO is my love language.'

'Noted.' Kent bumps his shoulder on mine.

With our mini-figures intact, we explore the rest of the center. When we board the Kingdom Quest ride, climbing into a LEGO-themed cart on a track, we're handed small plastic pink and purple guns. The voiceover instructs us to shoot to save the princess, but when we enter the harsh darkness of the main area, Lia climbs into my lap and cuddles into me.

'Are you scared, sweetheart?' Kent asks.

'Oh, I thought you were Poppy,' she says, her sweet breath on my chin.

'I've got you,' I say, wrapping my arms around her small body and holding her close. Her tiny frame in my arms must be the most precious and delicate thing I've ever held.

The room comes to life with treasure chests that open and various other moving targets for us to fake shoot. A screen shows clips of the story. Something about a kidnapped princess, and even with the manufactured drama, the change in lighting seems to settle Lia. She turns around but stays firmly on me, her weight providing pressure on my torso that's oddly soothing. We shoot at skeletons, spiders, and various animatronic creatures, Lia never leaving the protection of my lap.

After saving the princess, we disembark and head to the vast open building area. Inside the room, there's a towering LEGO tree that stretches all the way to the ceiling, adorned with hidden nooks and crannies showcasing incredible creations.

'Vincent, look!' Lia tugs at my hand. 'A unicorn.'

I kneel to see what the fuss is about, and a princess, queen, or someone who looks vaguely royal and important sits atop a white unicorn in the hole Lia's spying.

When I spot a massive building table covered in LEGO mountains, excitement builds inside me. Eager to create, my fingers twitch. 'Let's go build.'

Holding all three of our mini-figures, Lia tells a story. When I kneel to watch closer, Kent rests his hands on my shoulders, gently kneading as we listen.

'Let's go to the LEGO center for Vincent,' Lia says, doing her best to imitate Kent's deep voice. 'Vincent loves LEGO, and I love Vincent because he's my boyfriend.

Even though I said he was my friend. But Mommy said boyfriend.'

Kent's fingers massage my shoulders, and I can't help but smile at Lia's ability to perceive what's growing between her grandfather and me. Does Kent love me? He certainly loves parts of me. Sharing meals even though I always order the same thing. Cuddling and kissing. What I did to his cock with my feet last night. His finger exploring my ass. Having me suck him off. But me? All of me? I'm not sure if anyone's capable of loving me entirely.

'And I love you,' Lia says, changing her tone to a slightly less deep tone, her attempt at . . . me. 'And LEGO, and now I might think I love Lia. She's a nice little girl.'

A laugh escapes my lips because this sweet child, who adores her grandfather beyond measure, simply wants me to love her.

'She is,' Kent says, moving toward his granddaughter and kissing the top of her head.

After Lia's dramatic play with our minis, we head to the café for a quick bite. Kent brings Lia to the bathroom again because four-year-olds apparently need to pee more than I realized. I buy slices of cheese pizza for each of us and find a booth. They have dispensers with napkins and I grab the largest stack I've had in a long time. Something tells me eating with Lia will be its own adventure.

When they return and settle in, I head to wash up myself. The bathrooms are LEGO-inspired, with LEGO handles on the urinals and sink, and I wonder how challenging it must be to keep all the crevices clean. As I scrub and wash, I catch my reflection in the giant mirror.

For a split second, I see myself as a stranger. My shiny

bald head. My hazel eyes and long eyelashes Kent seems so fond of. For forty, I'm fit enough, and I'm ... handsome. Maybe this is what Kent sees? But my appearance isn't the problem. It's me. Inside. My brain. My compulsions. The warm water continues to embrace my hands, only to be abruptly cut off by the sudden stop of the automatic faucet. One more hit to rinse again, and I dry my hands and head back to join Kent and Lia.

We feast on the salty pizza and Lia, surprisingly, doesn't make a massive mess. There's pizza sauce and cheese over most of her mouth, but she wipes every few bites and when we finish, Kent grabs a wet wipe from his bag and she does a fairly good job cleaning herself before he gives her a final once-over. As I observe their interaction, a warmth washes over me, touched by his sweetness and patience. He's a genuinely good man.

We spend another hour on various LEGO-themed activities. I help Lia make a rocket, and then a machine scans and projects it on an enormous screen while we use it to play a game of shooting asteroids. There's a LEGO replica of Boston that's easily ten times as big as my Paris, but hey, they have the space and a team of professional builders. After a quick visit to the gift shop, where Lia buys a LEGO set from a recent princess movie, we head to Kent's car.

'Will you help me put it together?' Lia asks, clutching the box to her chest in her car seat.

'Maybe Mommy or Daddy want to help,' Kent says, driving us back toward the highway.

'No way. They'd get flustrated.'

'Do you mean frustrated?' I ask.

'Or flustered?' Kent asks. 'It means nervous.'

Lia shrugs and repeats, 'Flustrated. I want Vincent to help me. He's patient.'

Patient. Nobody's ever called me that, but I suppose I can be. I certainly was today.

I glance back toward her and smile. 'You're easy to be patient with.'

Kent starts up the music, and Lia sings along, but it only takes three songs before she passes out. Resting my head back, I glance out the window, watching the giant cables of the Zakim Bridge. My eyes grow heavy as they fly by, creating a pattern of light.

'Are you tired?' Kent rubs his palm over my thigh. 'Close your eyes.'

I respond by placing my hand on top of his, ensuring it stays put. He went out of his way to make this day special for me.

'Thank you.'

'You have to stop thanking me,' he says.

I shake my head. 'No, I don't think I do.'

Wrapping my fingers around Kent's hand, I hold it until, exhausted by the tremendous joyful experience, I doze off after the most amazing Kent, Lia, and LEGO-filled day.

22

Kent

'A foot job? Are you trying to tickle my labia?'

The March mini warm spell prompts Ruth to tie the jacket of her tracksuit around her waist, and her toned, fit arms sway back and forth with each step, showcasing her strength.

'I wasn't sure what was happening at first,' I confess. 'His feet. On my shmekel.'

'Your what?' Ruth asks, and I chuckle, knowing I used a Yiddish word she doesn't know yet.

'Shmekel. Penis.'

She nods, committing it to memory. 'But you liked it. His feet on your . . . shmekel.'

I give her a crisp nod, place my hand on her back, and say, 'I was verklempt.'

'Feet can be hot. Take it from me. Being creative in the bedroom will only win you points.'

'Points? Is someone keeping score?'

'Of course they are. But from where I stand, you're scoring big. All the touchdowns and home runs. I like how this is playing out for you, Mr Lester.'

Ruth's bright smile and wise eyes comfort me. There's safety in our conversations, never judgment. I need her cheerleading and support as I explore some of this unfamiliar territory with Vincent. The companionship of other queer people is something I didn't know I missed, but having Ruth's counsel and confidence makes my heart smile.

'I brought him on a LEGO date with Lia. We're keeping things casual. The Hopscotch rollout needs to go off without a hitch. For both of us.'

'Oh, screw that,' Ruth says with a pinched expression on her face. 'Listen, I've told you this before, but I understand sometimes men need to hear things more than once. Lear is perfectly fine – more than fine. Test scores aren't everything.'

'I know, but the board cares about –'

'Fuck the board,' she spits. Gosh, I love riled-up Ruth. 'Someone needs to explain to them what really matters.'

'Are you volunteering?'

'Don't tease me with a good time, Kent.'

One more lap, and we head back to start the day. I'm an early bird, and my walks with Ruth get me to school by six-thirty. A few minutes freshening up in the bathroom, and I'm ready before most of the staff arrives. Heading to my office, I bump into Theo, rolling his mop toward the cafeteria for breakfast duty. 'Mr Berenson, how are you on this fine day?'

A shrug and a huff.

Theo isn't a man of many words, but he hasn't given me the silent treatment in years. His furrowed brow and pursed lips prod me to investigate.

'Theo. Come with me.'

'Breakfast.' He holds up the handle of his mop.

'Breakfast can wait five minutes.'

We walk to my office, and when Theo enters, leaving the mop and bucket outside, I close the door.

'Sit. Tell me what's going on.'

He saunters to the table, plops himself down, and mumbles, 'Nothing.'

Sometimes, the patience I need with children comes into play with staff. If Theo thinks this behavior will stop my prodding, he doesn't know me very well.

'Theo Berenson, if something is bothering you or something happened, you can tell me. You pouting around school like someone stole your favorite toy isn't going to help anyone. Most of all you.'

He rolls his eyes and sighs. All the air leaves his body, and his shoulders slump.

'It's not job related. Well, he works here.'

'Mr Soleskin? Sheldon. You can talk to me about anything. If you're comfortable.'

Staring out the window, Theo rests his palm against the frame. 'My parents want to fly us down for Passover, and he's "not sure" it's a good idea.'

'Because . . .'

'He didn't say, but . . .' Theo turns toward me. His big brown eyes glimmer, and I quickly understand this is emotional for him.

'My parents do a lot for me. And well, now Sheldon. This is how they are. We're together, so he's part of the family. It's not a big deal. I mean, I'm used to it, but he's . . . not.' The pieces begin snapping together.

'I know Sheldon doesn't have a relationship with his parents,' I say. 'It's going to take some time for him to adjust to the doting. Jewish parents are next level.'

'They can be a lot.'

'They're a lot for us. And we're Jewish.' I touch Theo's shoulder. 'Give him some time. Talk about it. I promise communication will only help.'

Theo pastes a smile on and nods.

'Thanks, Mr Lester.'

I smile, knowing Theo's use of my honorific and last name in this private conversation is his way of expressing gratitude.

He leaves for the cafeteria, and my nose twitches from the aroma of bacon and eggs traveling down the hallway. Today's hot breakfast item is Delores's famous English muffin sandwich. Made of identical ingredients as McDonald's, it magically tastes a million times better. And Delores knows it. Her cooking motivates the children to make healthy food choices. Relatively speaking.

As I move my bag to the seat Theo vacated, he and Sheldon return to my mind. Their relationship is progressing nicely. Theo seems much happier, but dating a ray of sunshine probably has that effect on you. Most of the staff know, and Sheldon's students couldn't be more supportive. But even when everything appears shiny and pleasant on the outside, there are often tiny tremors below the surface.

'Mr Lester.'

Vincent walks in, wielding a massive smile on his beautiful face. He's wearing a slight variation of his button-down and khakis uniform – a short-sleeved polo. Thank you, warmer-than-usual late-March weather. There are three buttons at the collar, and he left them undone. Way to live dangerously. My gaze lingers on the area, wondering if, from the right angle, I might get a glimpse at his firm chest and perky nipples.

'Mr Manda, how are you?'

He sets his bag down, darts to close the door, and gives me a soft kiss on the lips. No teeth brushing. No gum. No mints.

'That good, eh?'

'I missed you.'

'You did?'

Vincent nods and pulls me into an embrace. Not for another kiss, simply to hug. As he squeezes my torso, I breathe in his comforting aroma of orange and honey. Holding him here, in the relative privacy of my office, my body so connected to his, I wish I could stop the world and let us remain locked this way forever. There's an urgency in the way he clutches me and I relish being needed. He pulls away, lingering near my face. 'Maybe you could come to my place again . . . soon.'

'Maybe.' I kiss his neck, and the chime of the arrival bell reminds me we have work to do.

Vincent sits at the table and begins his setting-up ritual. Laptop. Water bottle. Wipes. And then he begins cleaning. The table, keyboard, screen, chair, everything gets a generous rubbing with disinfectant.

I open the office door and take a moment to watch him. A large, savoring breath enters my nostrils, and a silly grin overtakes my face. I'm falling for this man. When Corrine and I split, I was pretty sure that was it for me. Forty-five isn't the ideal age to reenter the dating pool, so . . . I didn't. Each year, I thought, maybe now, but then, meh. Nope. Too busy. Too much effort. Too many distractions. Corrine convinced me to try SWISH, and I agreed mainly to get her off my back. But there was a curiosity deep down, and well, Vincent scratched it like a nagging summer mosquito bite on your ankle.

'Mr Lester.' Helen stands near my door, holding a stack of papers.

'Helen, good morning. How are you?'

'The Bruins won last night so I'm fantastic.' She's wearing her black, yellow, and white team sweatshirt. 'These need your signatures,' she says, handing the papers over. 'Everything's highlighted.'

'Awesome. About the Bruins, and I'll get these signed right away.'

'Shreya was looking for you,' Helen says. 'When your door was closed.' Helen's smirk hints she has a clue what's brewing.

'Oh, well, if you see her, please send her, or I can call her.' I move back into my office and trip on the carpet. Catching myself on the door, I stammer, 'Heh, all good.'

When the Hopscotch logo flashes on Vincent's screen, an animated pebble skipping down numbered boxes, I'm reminded why he's here. To work. To help me show Dr Cutler and the board that Lear's test scores aren't an accurate representation of the impact that happens here.

'Kent, we have a problem.'

Shreya's face pokes in, her brow wrinkled. This isn't a social visit.

'Ms Shaan, I was about to call you. Come in.' I pull a chair out at the table for her. 'What's wrong?'

'I was up until three this morning fixing code. This damn game isn't going to build itself and the compute quotient and remainder had a bug in it . . .' I nod, trying to catch slivers of understanding.

'Oh, I'm sorry. Is that what you wanted to chat about?'

'No, sorry. Still trying to wake up.' Shreya takes a long slug of her coffee. 'We're having a performance latency issue.' She plops down, clutching her mug like her life depends on it.

My eyes widen, and I softly shake my head.

'Shreya. I'm going to need the Gen X translation, please.'

Shreya's chest expands, her dress's dark purple and blue abstract flowers swaying.

'There's a delay. We're still loading the test data from yesterday. It's not following instructions yet. Technically, the data is there, but taking its sweet time to populate. Screen load times are topping out at fifteen minutes.'

'What do we do?'

'Wait. Watch. Pray. Geoff is monitoring the transfer, and it looks good so far.'

'Oh, well, why did you say we have a problem?'

'Because the data should populate quickly, and so far it's not.' Shreya tips her mug upside down, attempting to get the last drops.

'It happens,' Vincent says. 'I'm sure it will be fine. Let's just give it a few hours. We're not testing until tomorrow. We have the day.'

'Okay. Give it a few hours,' I say. 'Good plan.' The

lightness overtaking my brain begins to settle. I'm so in over my head, it's ridiculous. It's like the time I subbed in kindergarten on Halloween. Twenty-two five-year-olds in costumes with candy – what could go wrong? Oy.

'Sit tight,' Shreya says, returning to the conference room.

'Well, I guess we have a few hours to kill,' Vincent says, turning back to his screen.

'Principals do not have free time.' I glance at my watch. 'It's first-grade recess. I'm going to cover one of the teachers. Wanna join me?'

Vincent smiles, nods, and grabs a stack of napkins and wipes from his bag.

'Come.' I give his shoulder a squeeze and the contact sends a thrill of delight zinging through my core.

23

Vincent

'Nolan, Norah, Noah, lovely morning.' Kent waves to three blond children.

'Are they triplets?' I ask, the sun struggling to warm my naked head.

'Nope,' Sheldon says, 'not remotely related. Although they look and act like siblings. And like a good parent, I call them all by the wrong name at least seven times daily.'

With its vast area, Lear's playground is a paradise for children, complete with slides, swings, climbing structures, and various outdoor activities. Woodchips carpet the ground under the equipment, and there are open grassy and paved areas for games. According to Kent, currently, only first grade is outside, but there seems to be an endless flow of children running, screaming, and creating complete chaos.

'How do you keep them all . . .' I begin.

'Safe? Clean? Fed? Quiet?' Sheldon tilts his head.

'Yeah,' I say with a laugh.

'Mainly, with lots of routines and procedures.' Without

taking his eyes off me, Sheldon kicks a rogue ball back to a group of children playing in the grassy area. 'You can't expect them to know how to do everything we need them to do at school. At least not the way I want them to. So I show them. And then have them practice. And then practice some more. Most really want to please their teacher, so I have that going for me.'

'Makes sense.' I shield my eyes from the sun.

'Vincent knows a thing or two about the value of routines,' Kent says. Our eyes meet, and my stomach takes a tiny topple.

'Hey, I take comfort in familiarity.'

'And kids do, too. Predictability is the key to everything in the classroom,' Sheldon says, nodding his head toward the children. 'Martha! I'm coming! Well, duty calls.' Sheldon waves and jogs off toward a little girl who appears stuck at the top of a tall structure.

'He seems like a wonderful teacher.'

'Oh, Sheldon is the cream of the crop.' Kent's brow arches. 'Having him transfer here was a blessing. I know his former principal hated losing him, but we're reaping the benefits.'

'What he said about routines and procedures, I never thought about it that way.'

'Oh yeah, it's key for running a smooth classroom. Kids like to know how and when to do things.'

'Interesting.' I rub my chin.

All of my rituals. The napkins. Wipes. Cleaning. Washing. Scrubbing. It provides safety. The work I do with Hopscotch, collecting requirements, inputting data, and running reports, there's a routine or procedure for almost everything I do. Maybe I don't find joy in it, but there's an assurance of security. Sure, unpredictable roadblocks can cause a hitch in the process. I suppose teaching is similar. Children are erratic creatures. And filthy.

'Mr Lester!' a voice calls. Two boys march toward us. Brodie, the boy I had lunch with, has his arm snugly wrapped around a slightly taller blond boy with ivory skin.

'Brodie, what's up?' Kent's voice is calm and collected.

'Kaden fell playing wolf pack,' Brodie says with his squeaky voice.

'Sit.' Kent points toward one of the many benches that line the perimeter.

They do as he instructs, and Kent kneels.

'Can I look?' Kent asks.

The hurt boy nods his head. Tears sting his eyes, and he winces as Kent carefully rolls up the leg of his pants, exposing the damage. My head becomes light and woozy the moment the scrape, easily six inches long and a half inch wide, comes into view. There's blood, but also dirt. Mud. Grime. It's all mixed, creating an awful deep maroon swath on his leg.

'Just a scrape, Kaden. The nurse can get this cleaned up for you.' Kent folds the boy's pants so they stay off the area.

'Brodie, can you take Kaden to Ms Kelly's office?'

Brodie nods with wide eyes. His arm hasn't left Kaden's shoulder, offering unwavering support.

'Mr Manda, would you mind taking the boys?' Kent's voice softens. 'I'd rather them not walk alone.'

'Oh, um, sure. Of course.'

The boys stand and hobble toward me. Brodie extends

his free hand. It's covered in dirt, wood chips, and something wet. Foul. He stares at me with pleading eyes. Waiting.

With a quick breath, I take his hand, and we walk to the office silently. Brodie squeezes my fingers. There's a squishing of fluids and dirt, but I don't let go. When I look down, his arm still around his hurt friend, he smiles at me. I remind myself I can scrub soon. Plus, Brodie loves LEGO. Returning his grin and grip, the three of us head to the nurse's office.

'You survived?' Kent's fingers fly across the keyboard on his laptop.

'I stayed while the nurse cleaned Kaden's wound, and then walked the boys back to class,' I say. 'My hands needed washing.' I hold my clean hands up. 'But, but, I'm fine.'

'Of course you're fine. Why wouldn't you be?'

Kent stands and sticks his head out of the office. 'Helen, Mr Manda and I have some work to do. Buzz if you need me.'

'No, you don't understand,' I say, Kent shutting the door behind me. My heart races, and a massive grin erupts across my face. 'There was dirt. Mud. Blood. Germs, so many germs. Like billions, I'm sure. And I took Brodie's hand. Held it.' I put my hand out, staring at the previously soiled skin. 'Stayed with them. Remained calm.'

I grab Kent's shoulders, holding him in place.

'I was fine. How? How was I fine?'

Kent chuckles, and his entire torso shakes.

'Sometimes, when you need to step up, when someone needs you enough, your fears and anxieties fade into the background.' With a smile stretching from ear to ear, I catch a subtle glimpse of the dimple tucked beneath his beard.

'They don't disappear completely, but they retreat. Long enough so you can handle the crisis. It's adrenaline.'

'Adrenaline? Can I buy it somewhere?'

More laughter erupts from Kent's mouth, drawing my gaze, and without thinking, I pull him close and capture his lips. His breath blows into my mouth with each guffaw. Coffee. Sugar. Cream. I can taste it all. A sweeping sensation overtakes my chest, and sunbursts appear in the temporary darkness when I close my eyes and deepen the kiss.

Pulling back, Kent says, 'Nobody's figured out how to bottle adrenaline yet. But it can reveal things to you. Like how capable and amazing you are.'

Kent kisses me gently, gathers me in his arms, and squeezes me. 'Kent,' I say into his ear.

'Yeah.'

'The mood. It's right.'

There's no hiding my hard, firm cock pressing against his thigh.

'Vincent, it's eleven o'clock. We're at school. In my office. We have work to do.'

'I know, but I wanted you to know.' I squeeze him close, grinding softly.

'How about tonight?' he asks. 'I'll bring takeout.'

I'm tempted to drag him by the collar to the supply

closet for a quickie, but I know he's right. Even if my dick disagrees.

'Sounds like a plan.'

'May I have chocolate milk?' Illona's tiny hand clasped in Marvin's triggers a vivid recollection of Brodie's hand in mine just a few hours ago.

The experience at school left me buzzing with energy, and I'm fired up to share.

'Of course. I might skip my espresso tonic and get one myself,' he says.

'Adults don't drink chocolate milk,' she protests.

'Miss Stone, haven't you realized yet? I am no typical adult.'

'Very true.' Illona nods and the two puffs on either side of her head shake.

Without being told, Illona sits, pulls out a tablet and headphones from her backpack, and plugs herself in. Do all children behave this way?

'How's the wedding planning?' I know the topic has overtaken Marvin's life.

'We've almost landed on a venue. The Ocean Inn. It's a little further out of town than we wanted, but we'll get a shuttle to bring people from the airport. And the thought of getting married on the beach, at a beautiful inn, where everyone can stay . . . perfection.'

'Sounds ideal,' I say, sipping my coffee. 'What's the holdup?'

'We just have to coordinate with their availability. What works for us, that type of thing. And Olan's family. They're all flying in, and we need to make sure the dates work for them.' Marvin rubs the back of his neck and takes a deep breath. 'Then the real work starts. Menus. Seating. And my favorite, cake tasting!'

'Of course, you like that best,' I say, knowing Marvin's fondness for sweets.

'I want a strawberry donut tower, but Olan says we really should have a cake. So, we might get both.'

'You can never have too much dessert,' I say.

'Exactly. Quit distracting me with wedding planning questions.' He waves his hands, shooing the topic away. 'What happened at school?' Marvin hands Illona her drink. Without taking her eyes off the screen, she opens the straw and milk and begins drinking.

'I was on the playground, and this boy got hurt.'

Marvin's lips make an oval. 'Is he okay?'

'Oh yeah, only a scrape. But there was blood. And dirt.'

'Typical.'

'And mud. And it was gross and germy, and I took this other boy's filthy hand and walked them to the nurse and stayed with them the entire time.'

'How many napkins and wipes?'

'None!' My cheeks rise, and my face absorbs the sunlight, bright and warm.

Marvin's eyebrows shoot off like fireworks, retreating behind his curly mop.

'I know. Kent said it's adrenaline. But after, I was so . . .' I pause, glancing at Illona, pull my lips in, and shake my head.

'Use pig latin.'

'Excuse me?'

'Pig latin. My mother always used it on the phone when she didn't want me to understand. Take the first sound off the word and add it to the end with an "ay" after. So I'm Arvin-May, and you're Incent-Vay.'

'Marvin Block, from the first moment we met, you've confused me. You still do.'

'Just try it . . .' he says. 'The adrenaline. You were so . . .'

I look around, wondering if anyone at the nearby tables understands pig latin, and quietly, through clenched teeth, say, 'Orny-Hay. For Ent-Kay.'

Marvin nods, a smirk on his lips.

'You wanted his ock-cay, right?'

My ears burn, and warmth creeps over my head.

'Up-yay. In my . . . oat-thray.'

Marvin's smile erupts into laughter, and I join him. Illona, sipping her milk, never breaks contact with her tablet. I've come so far in the last year since we've become friends. Talking. Sharing. Opening up. The smiles and laughter we share make my heart so damn happy.

'You like him. A lot. I can tell,' Marvin says.

'How can you tell?'

'You have a look on your face.' He nods slowly. 'I can feel it in my bones. You're bashert.'

'I do. I like him. A lot. That's what worries me.'

'Stop worrying.'

'Says the self-proclaimed King of Worrying.'

'It's my crown.' Marvin mimics placing a crown atop his curls. 'You can't have it.'

I smile at my ability to volley so playfully with Marvin. But how did Kent and I get to this place? 'Sure, it started with . . .'

'His ock-cay in your outh-may.' Marvin winks.

'Yes, but there's more. He's sweet. Patient. But also,

clumsy. A mess. And kind. Sweet. And yes, hot. I thought we'd just be friends. Then the benefits kept showing up.'

'Ah, the benefits. We love a tasty ow-job-blay.' Marvin looks off, surely reminiscing about his own escapades with Olan.

'Yeah, but then, these damn feelings snuck their way in.'

'That's what love does to you. Allows you to see someone, even their flaws, and want them anyway.'

'Me seeing him, wanting him. That's not what worries me.'

'Vincent, stop that right now. Remember, we're owning our love lives. Taking action. As Mariah sings, "Make It Happen."'

'But what if he realizes I'm . . .' The words get stuck in my throat, and my fingers fold the napkin's edge. Over. Fold. Over.

Fold.

'Bald?'

'He knows I'm bald. I can't really hide that.' I pull my beanie off, point to my head, and pop it back on. 'No, my OCD.'

'Vincent, he knows you have OCD. You can't hide that either. I knew after five minutes.'

I purse my lips.

'But maybe when he sees how bad it can get . . .'

'You're catastrophizing. Stop. Take a breath. I'll take one with you.'

He puts his hand out, and I take it. His fingers wrap around mine, and he nods. Together, we take a prolonged inhale. I wait for him, and slowly, we exhale together. Marvin lets go of my hand and smiles.

'There. Now, when will you see him next?' he asks. 'I mean outside of school.'

'Tonight. He's bringing Purple Giraffe over.' I grab the small bottle of sanitizer from my bag and squirt a generous amount on my palm.

'But you're not hungry for Korean-Mexican fusion.'

'Nope.'

'You want that ick-day.'

I nod and smile, and again, we burst into giggles. This time, our laughter is disruptive enough to draw Illona's attention. She rolls her eyes and says, 'Grown-ups. Oy.' I look at Marvin. He looks at me, and once again, we crack up.

24

Kent

'Hey.'

Vincent greets me at the door wearing a white V-neck, cream joggers, and bare feet. The man knows I'm a sucker for him in a V-neck. The area below his Adam's apple invites my gaze, and I do my best not to stare.

I hold the takeout up. 'Got your regular. And extra napkins.'

Vincent smiles, takes the bag from me, and heads to his kitchen. 'Thank you. And I have plenty of napkins.'

From behind, his thin shirt hugs his back, and I can make out his shoulder blades. I slip my shoes off at the door and follow him into the kitchen, my eyes wandering down to his plump ass. With each step, it seems to taunt me. First, his feet. Now his ass. Maybe everything about Vincent Manda excites me.

'Are you hungry?' Vincent sets the bag on his island. 'Or did you want to take advantage of . . . my mood from earlier?'

He's in my arms, nestling into my neck. The skin of his

head rubs against my beard, and I can't help myself – I give the top a little peck. I want to kiss and lick his entire head, but Vincent probably wouldn't like that. I'm here one minute and he's got me going. 'That was,' I say, glancing at my watch, 'almost seven hours ago. Your mood, it's still . . .'

With his head still cradled on me, he nods. He turns toward my face and plants a kiss on my mouth. Soft. Lips closed. There's a deep urgency.

'Bathroom,' he says, and I follow him, tossing my coat on a stool as I walk. It misses with a loud thud on his hardwood floor, but neither one of us pauses.

We stand at the vanity, brushing our teeth, and when I look in the mirror, Vincent's gaze never leaves mine. This 'mood is right' thing is fucking hot. He's a horny bugger when it happens, and well, who am I to complain? Having an inkling the night might lead to this, I popped one of my magic blue pills in the car. Even though I haven't needed them with him yet, I'm not taking any chances tonight.

Vincent rinses, spits, and says, 'We're just showering.' My face falls and my stomach clenches. Have I misread him?

'Oh. Okay.'

'I'll be a good boy for you after.'

His words send a surge of blood and energy to my groin. My lips part, and I exhale through my nose as my cock thickens in my pants.

Under the hot water, side by side, we wash. Water droplets cling to Vincent's eyelashes, sparkling under the shower light. I could stare at him wet like this all night. When he reaches for his back, I take a pump of soap, the citrusy sweetness filling the stall, and lather him up. My hands glide bubbles over his strong back muscles. Besides scrubbing him clean, I get a few good grabs at his sides. Being so close, his energy radiating through my hands, sparks fire in my core. As the pill begins to perform its magic, a surge of excitement barrels through me.

When my hands reach the base of his back, his ass only inches away, I pause. Ruth said to 'ask for what you want,' and heeding her advice, I swallow and say, 'May I?'

Vincent's hand reaches back and lands on mine. Carefully, he glides my soapy palm down until it's cupping his ass cheek. With the same care I took on his back, I lather and wash him, taking my time to enjoy every ounce of muscle and spot of skin.

And then, for all that's good and mighty in this world, Vincent Manda reaches back with both hands and spreads himself wide, exposing his magnificent hole.

'Can you get it all? Please?'

My cock, now fully firm and throbbing, may not survive this. And my heart, fuck, my fifty-two-year-old kicker races, and this would not be the moment to have palpitations. Closing my eyes, I steal a few breaths to calm myself. Easy, Kent.

Another pump, and using my index and middle fingers, I carefully apply the soap to Vincent's opening. Patting the tender skin, my fingers tingle with electric jolts of pleasure. Using both hands, I lather and rub, being careful not to enter him. Not here. Not now.

Not yet.

'Oh,' he moans, 'So gentle.'

I lean my forehead on the nape of his neck. 'Let's get my good boy nice and clean.'

Glancing toward the large mirror over the vanity, I get a better view of Vincent's arched back. His perfect ass tilted upward, allowing me to massage and get him clean enough to feast on.

'So sweet,' I say into his back. 'Spotless.'

My fingers gently spread him wider, and my middle finger lingers. 'Okay?'

'Fuck, yes.'

With permission granted, I carefully enter, only a bit, the bubbles and water providing enough slickness for my fingertip. Our reflection sends sparks to my core. I've never seen myself doing such things to someone this way. The view of our bodies in the mirror, Vincent slowly pushing back into my finger, my left arm wrapped around his waist, might be the sexiest thing I've ever seen. He slopes his head back, and it lands on my forehead. I can't resist moving my lips to his neck, tasting his scrumptious wet skin.

My cock rubs on his thigh, and I'm lightheaded from the contact. Or maybe all the blood has left my head for my groin.

'Kent?'

'Mmmh.'

'Bedroom. Now. Please.'

There's a pleading in his voice. He turns around, his erection rubbing against mine, the water rinsing the lubrication of the soap and bubbles down the drain. I take his chin in my hand and hold him steady while I kiss him. The spearmint from both our mouths creates a cool crispness that makes my lips tingle.

'Look.' I nod toward the mirror.

Vincent's gaze catches mine in our reflection. 'You like watching?'

'You? Yes.' I guide Vincent in front of me, palming his cock, as I observe over his shoulder.

'Are you ready for me to be your good boy?'

Words escape me, and I moan into his neck, turning him toward me. Vincent's tongue traces my lips before he returns to kissing, and his hands hold our hips firmly together. I'm so ready to ravage this scrumptious man.

We towel off, our hard cocks caught on flying fabric and stimulated by the contact of soft cotton. I keep drying myself until Vincent places his hands over mine and says, 'Enough.'

He takes my towel and tosses it into the hamper with his. It lands on the edge, not falling all the way in. He shrugs and pulls me by the hand to his pristinely made bed. Vincent lies on his back and puts his hands behind his head. Not a hair on his body, and his nipples and the head of his cock the same rosy pink, I'm tempted to lick every inch. He's on full display, and my eyes can't decide where to land. 'Come,' he says, patting the spot next to him.

I lie on my side, pressing against him, and he kisses me. There's enough pressure to make my cock twitch against his thigh, and an adorable laugh spills from his plump lips.

'What do you want to do?' he asks.

Ask for what you want. Ruth's words swirl in my head. I'm a grown man. More than grown. There's no harm in asking.

'Would you like to sit on my face?'

Vincent kisses me again, harder this time, his lips pressed on mine, and when he pulls away, he takes tiny nibbles at my lower lip.

'I'd love that.'

Gently, he pushes me on my back and climbs over me on all fours. Facing the foot of the bed, he lowers himself back, pauses, and says, 'Ready?'

His ass, about a foot away from my face, the familiar orange and honey swirls, and all I can think to reply is, 'Fuck yes.'

Bracing himself on the bed, he maneuvers into position. My hands grab his waist, guiding him back. With my head propped up on two pillows, I rest my neck and start by giving each ass cheek a little kiss.

'Your ass is so fucking sweet.' I pepper his soft skin with kisses. 'I'm going to devour it.'

Vincent's breath hitches, and he shivers, but he stays where my mouth can reach him. Repeating the motion from the shower, I use my hands to spread his cheeks. But this time, my tongue takes over, licking the pink skin around Vincent's hole. He's calm. Still. His hard cock hangs down, brushing the hair on my chest occasionally, letting me know how turned on this makes him.

'Vincent?'

'Uh, huh?' He sounds intoxicated.

'If I do anything you don't like, you tell me.' Once again, I give his cheek a small kiss. 'Understand?'

'Okay.'

And with that, I spread him wider than before, take a breath, and dive in. My lips kiss the entire perimeter. Dotting wetness on every spot. Finally, landing on his gorgeous hole, the whiskers of my beard brush the sensitive skin, and his body pulls slightly, but he doesn't protest. My tongue enters him, and again he shudders.

'Fuck, Kent. Fuck.'

He likes it. Loves it, maybe. I do my best to stick my tongue as deep as it will go, slurping, licking, flicking, and lapping up all I can of Vincent Manda's hot gripping hole. My cock, throbbing from the pleasure of eating him out, calls for attention, and I let go of one cheek to reach down and jerk myself off.

'Let me,' he says, pulling my hand off.

I move it back to join my other hand in keeping him spread open, and his mouth, his fucking delectable mouth, kisses the tip of my cock. The sensitive head, so grateful for the touch but wanting more. My hips rise as I go back to devouring Vincent's ass.

Slowly, Vincent takes more of my dick in his mouth until he's as far as he can go without choking. There's a gagging noise, and he pulls off. I quickly stop and ask, 'You okay?'

He turns his beautiful beet-red face around and replies, 'I'm awesome. I love choking on your massive cock.'

Okay, then. I caress his cheek, damp with spit, taking his beautiful face in.

'You suck it like such a good boy.'

I've fallen right into this dirty talk with him. Each word dispatches more blood to my dick. I resume coloring the inside of his hole with my tongue, and Vincent goes back to blowing me. Small grunts and choking noises escape his lips, but he's definitely enjoying himself, so I don't pause again.

Pushing himself up, he shifts to jerking himself off. With his body raised, gravity takes over, and his ass completely covers my face. My mouth attaches to his hole like a siphon, with my tongue working overtime to keep him pleasured.

'Deeper,' he moans, and I ram my tongue in further. 'There you go. I love being good for you.'

Exploring his warm sweetness makes my heart race, and I'd be content to stay this way forever. He gently rocks back and forth, helping me fuck his hole even deeper. My beard becomes a sloppy mess, but Vincent seems to enjoy it. His fingers crawl through my chest hair, lost in the moment. If I looked up heaven in the dictionary, I'd expect to see a photo of Vincent Manda riding my face like a professional surfer on a massive wave.

'Kent, you're going to make me come like this.' His words spur me on, but replying isn't possible in my current state. I slide my hands to his hips and pull down, attempting to get my tongue even deeper. His opening contracts slightly around my tongue, but I persist. Vincent grinds my face, jerking himself off, my own hard cock pointing right at him, patient and waiting.

'Oh fuck, fuck. Kent, I'm coming . . .'

My tongue, lodged deep inside him, senses it first. The pulsing. Vincent's ass clenches with each spasm, and his warm cum showers my cock and thighs. He's whimpering, the release undoing him from the inside out. My face warms, the heat of him unloading, letting go, literally raising my temperature. I don't stop because I can tell he's not finished, and I'm determined to squeeze every ounce of pleasure out of him. The last few spurts coat my hairy belly, and Vincent slumps over, lying motionless on his side.

If I died right now, at least I'd have a giant, ass-eating grin on my face.

'Holy fuck, Kent. Holy fuck.'

My lips pull into a satisfied smile, knowing I've rendered him boneless.

Vincent raises his head to take in the damage. 'You're a mess.'

'You drenched me like a good boy,' I say. 'I fucking love it.'

Lying still seems like the right plan of action, at least for the moment.

'Can I kiss you?' he asks.

'Um, of course, but I'm kind of covered . . .' I point to my mouth. 'In you.'

Vincent leans over and kisses my forehead. It's so damn tender and sweet. His lips move to my nose, and then he kisses each of my eyes. Baby steps.

Reaching down, I grab my cock, hungry for attention, and begin stroking.

'Wait.'

'Vincent, I'm good. It won't take me long.'

'I know, but I bought something . . . for you.'

He props himself up, reaches over to his nightstand, opens the drawer, and pulls out a small toy. It's about two inches long, wider in the middle, and looks like something you might use in the kitchen. A juicer, maybe? And it's hot pink.

I tip my head and run my fingers through my hair.

'It's a butt plug,' he says, biting his lower lip.

'A what plug?'

He laughs and shimmies over next to me. His face hovers close to mine, and my reflex is to turn away. He's all over my lips. My beard. My entire face. Corrine never cared to kiss after oral, and I never argued with her about it. Vincent leans over and delicately kisses my lips.

'A butt plug. I bought it for you. I thought you might like to try it.'

Would I like to try it? I have no idea. When Vincent told me he was a side, I just thought that wasn't something we'd do. 'Thank you?'

Vincent smiles, sliding the toy across my chest.

'I just figured my ass was off the table,' I continue.

'Well . . .' Vincent holds the plug closer so I can inspect it. 'This is on the table.'

'I haven't . . . prepared,' I say, unsure what that might entail for the toy.

'It's small. We haven't eaten.' Vincent places his hand on a clean area of my stomach. 'Do you feel okay?'

'Yeah. I think so.'

'Good,' he says with a wink.

And because everything with Vincent is like a new adventure, I shrug and say, 'Why not?'

Vincent grabs a small bottle of lube from the drawer and sits up. He squirts a good amount onto his fingers and says, 'Open, please.'

I smirk and do as I'm told, moving my legs apart enough to give him access.

When the chilly liquid lands on my hole, I shiver and say, 'Um, hello, cold!'

'Sorry, I should've warmed it up. It's so . . . sticky.'

Vincent's face contorts in discomfort, indicating his dissatisfaction with the texture, yet he doesn't stop. Even the simple pressure of applying the lube creates a new sensation.

'There you go,' he coos. There's more lube. More fingers. 'Yes. You've got a hairy hole.' Vincent licks his lips and my cock throbs with each swipe. If this is any indication of what's coming, I'm not sure I'll last long. He adds a few more squirts and then moves the plug into place.

'Ready, Mr Lester?'

I nod and close my eyes. The tip goes in rather quickly, but where the toy becomes wider, there seems to be a disconnect. It's not very big, but I've also never had anything in my ass before.

'Take a deep breath. Try to relax,' he says. 'Let's take two together.'

My eyes locked on his, I follow his lead, inhaling and exhaling slowly, and on the second exhale, Vincent slowly pushes the toy inside. At a certain point, my muscles relax enough to accept it, wrapping around the plug and sending frissons of pleasure through my body. My cock, still hard, becomes even more rigid. Somehow, at fifty-two, Vincent unlocks something inside me I didn't know existed. But there it is. A new delight. Waving at me from inside. The pressure of the plug creates such an intense buzz that it's possible I'll come at Vincent's first touch.

'Good?' he asks.

I sigh, my stomach deflating, and nod. 'I, I, um, yes, good. Fantastic.'

Vincent's lips twist up, and he moves down to my dick. Swiping his own cum from my belly and chest, he takes it in his hand and slowly begins stroking. The tension from the toy and his hands, slick and slippery, is almost too much to handle. This might top him riding my face. He moves a foot toward my hand, and I grab it and massage his toes. My eyes roll back in sheer delight at the intensity of bliss. Thinking about eating his ass, my tongue buried inside him, while all this happens, starts my orgasm. It's happening quicker than usual, and I blurt out, 'Vincent, I'm close. I'm gonna come. Very soon.'

My cock fills his hands. He uses long strokes, the back of his head in full view. My heart bursts with desire, watching him from this angle. I can't hold back any longer, and when the first drops of cum break free, Vincent takes my dick into his mouth, sucking and slurping, sending me right over the edge of glory.

'Oh fuck, Vincent. Fuck.'

More words than I thought possible, but I got them out. My dick gushes, the relief of each spurt threatening to rip me in half. Pressure from the toy causes more volume than I've shot in some time, and Vincent, his mouth wrapped around my rigid cock, drinks it all in.

'Look at you, taking my cum like a good boy.'

'Mmmh.'

My chest pounds as Vincent continues to suck, finally licking the head clean. When I finish, he takes my dick out of his mouth, turns around, holds his index finger up, and hops off the bed. I lie there, motionless from the most intense orgasm I've ever experienced. Mind-blowing. World changing. Life altering. Louis's brisket has nothing on this. What happens now?

I lie there, unable to move. The shower turns on,

followed by music. Guitar strumming. Bright and airy. Joined by a bass guitar, and finally, the drums kick in. Vincent has it turned up so loud that surely his neighbors can hear it. The voices, male and female, in unison, join in, and when the hand claps finally start, I can't help but smile. They're singing about love. 'I Don't Want to Know' – his reward for the euphoric experience we shared.

I probably should remove the toy from my ass before he returns. Maybe clean up. But I'm not sure where to put it. What to do with it? Where to go? Or if I'm able to move yet. Am I in a sex coma? I simply lie still, basking in the ecstasy and aftershocks of what just occurred.

Vincent returns wearing a T-shirt and flannel pajama bottoms. His sweet face stares, those eyelashes flutter, and I want to grab and cuddle with him for eternity. But that would require moving.

'Here,' he says, handing me a damp washcloth. 'You might want to hop in the shower.' I push myself up, take the washcloth, and head for the bathroom. Before I leave the bedroom, Vincent takes my hand, pulls me close, and says, 'Don't take too long.' He gives me a soft kiss on the cheek and whispers, 'I'm starving.'

25

Vincent

'So, does this mean we're dating?'

Kent's question catches me off guard as I unpack our takeout on the kitchen island. I open the napkin drawer and procure three . . . one for him and two for me.

'Excuse me?'

'The first date do-over. LEGO Discovery Center. The kissing in my office. The . . . shower and what just happened in your bed. Does it mean we're dating? Because Corrine is going to want to know. And Ruth is already asking if we're "friends with benefits," or something more and I'm not sure myself.'

'Well, we're friends.' A ribbon of anticipation twirls inside my stomach.

'Um, yeah, but friends don't typically sit on my face.' Kent cocks an eyebrow.

'Noted.'

He comes up behind me. His hands wrap around my stomach and travel to my chest, cupping my pecs. He pulls me close, his beard tickling my neck, and I smell the minty freshness. The man brushed his teeth. Before eating dinner. After eating me.

'Would you be okay if we said we're dating?' He kisses my neck softly.

'Why would you want to date me? I'm . . .' I stop talking and grab another napkin from the drawer. I place it between our two plates, just in case. All the time we're spending together, the bubbling emotions, Marvin saying we're bashert . . . does Kent want more? With me?

'Sexy. Amazing. Kind. Sweet. Did I mention sexy?' Kent's hands grab my chest, and he gently massages.

My heart pounds, and in the quiet space, I can almost hear it thumping. I reach for my glass of water and take a sip, the cool wetness pacifying my parched mouth.

'But, I'm the extra napkins guy. The joke you tell friends at a party.'

Kent kisses my neck four times and whispers, 'Vincent Manda, you are not a joke.'

'Kent, I've never had a boyfriend. I'm forty. I've kind of given up on romance.'

'That's not true,' he says, spinning me around on the stool, our faces inches apart. 'You go on all those first dates. You know what that tells me?'

He waits for me to reply. I'm silent, laying my head on his shoulder. Closer.

'It tells me you're hopeful. Optimistic. You keep trying. That's not someone who's given up. Sometimes it takes time for the right person to wander into your life.'

An itching tingles my ass, a reminder of Kent's beard. My stomach churns, the bulgogi taco salad taunting me.

My head rests on Kent's shoulder, facing away. I take a

breath, and the security of his closeness allows the truth to pour out.

'You'll be the end of me. Once you figure out just how damaged I am, you'll run for the hills.' Finally, I'm able to admit my genuine fear. 'And honestly . . . I'm not sure my heart could take it.'

Tears sting the corners of my eyes. Sharing my vulnerabilities with Kent is a mix of relief and a sense of being overwhelmed, like treading water in an endless ocean.

'Vincent Manda. Look at me. Please.'

I lift my head and catch his eyes. Unable to contain them, salty drops stream down my cheeks. And certainly, this will be the icing on top of the chaos cake that sends Kent running for the hills.

He reaches up, wipes a tear away with his thumb, and says, 'Oh, my sweet Vincent.'

I blink, waiting for him to continue.

'Don't you understand? I already see you. All of you.' He pokes my chest. 'And I'm here. I'm not going anywhere. Look at me. Tripping over my own feet. My hair will be all salt, no pepper soon. Who else would want me?'

'I love your hair,' I say, running my hands under his V-neck. The softness under his shirt creates a charge when my fingers graze it. 'It's soft and cozy and fuzzy. Just like you.'

'Well, my hair loves you.'

Kent smiles, and I gently kiss him. His hands wrap around my neck and then migrate to my head. He pulls me closer, deepening the kiss, and my heart melts a little. We stand in my kitchen, our food and LEGO Paris in the background, and connect. With our mouths. Our words.

Our hearts. Being honest and open with Kent might not end me. Maybe being truly vulnerable will save me.

'Are we ready for training?'

Hunched over his laptop in the conference room, Geoff's brow furrows as he completes the back end of the test data prep. This is where my expertise wanes, and I'm grateful for Geoff's technical brain. I've gathered the requirements and data from first grade. We'll use that for testing and training. Kent downloaded the data from the school's current legacy system, GradePlus. It's an antiquated, manually coded system, and each data point needs to be mapped and then meticulously transferred to the corresponding Hopscotch field. That's my job, and being anal is my forte. Well, where work is involved.

'Locked and loaded,' I say. 'I logged in this morning. Load times were acceptable. The test data looks good.'

Geoff glances up from his screen and cocks his head. 'And you're ready for the training? The principal knows what to do?'

The principal. Kent. He most surely knows what to do. With his hands. His tongue. His cock. Sweat pools on my brow, and I grab a napkin from my pocket to wipe it.

'He knows. Or he will. I'll make sure.'

Besides providing the data dump, Kent's job is to champion and cheerlead the process. People don't love change. Teachers are busy. Any way we slice it, this is a pain in the ass for them. I need Kent to sell it and bring teachers up to speed quickly.

Shreya arrives, holding a carrier with coffee and a white paper bag. She's wearing a yellow and purple plaid dress belted at the waist and her signature black combat boots. The short sleeves let her tattoos shine, and she's pulled her hair up into a messy bun.

'Coffee and cronuts,' she says, placing the tray on the conference table.

'What the hell is a cronut?' Geoff asks.

'What are you, a Neanderthal? It's a croissant–donut hybrid. Flaky. Sweet. Heavenly,' she says, opening the bag. 'I was up most of the night coding. Why I thought going live with Avandia and a project here at the same time was a good idea is beyond me.' She pulls a large pastry from the bag. It looks like a donut on steroids. 'If you don't want yours, I'll eat it. Or split it with Vincent.' She gives me a mischievous grin.

'Oh no, I'm good,' I say, patting my stomach. The sticky, crumbly treat would require a truckload of napkins.

'I'll eat it.' Geoff grabs the cronut, shoves it in his mouth, and resumes typing with his free hand while the other holds the treat.

'Okay, well, I'm going to make sure Kent is ready,' I say, heading to his office.

When I arrive, Kent and Ruth, the PE teacher, sit at his table, so I knock softly.

'Am I interrupting? I can come back.'

'No, come in,' Kent says, standing, 'and shut the door.'

'So, this is the famous Vincent.' Ruth stands and extends her hand. I shake it, and the woman could strangle a rhino into submission with that grip. Her biceps flexes and expands as we greet each other, and I make a mental note not to piss her off.

'Oh, there's nothing famous about me,' I say.

'This guy,' Ruth says, motioning her thumb toward Kent, 'would disagree. He hasn't shut up about you.'

'That's not true.' Kent's face tinges pink and, fuck, he's adorable when he's embarrassed.

'Um, excuse me,' she says, sitting. 'We've barely talked about my escapades for weeks.'

Kent nods to the empty chair, and I join them at the table.

'I used to be the one with all the action,' Ruth says. 'At least, more action than this one. But now? Who cares about an old lesbian when the principal is shtupping the hot software guy?' Ruth laughs, her bright teeth shine, and I glance at Kent to gauge his reaction and how to respond.

'Ruth Parrish, first, you are not old,' Kent says.

'I'm going to be fifty.'

'In three years. You're a forty-seven-year-old ex-Olympian with a body most thirty-year-olds would envy.' Kent dips his chin, and a shadow of a smile peeks from behind his beard.

'Quit objectifying my body, Mr Lester.' Ruth smirks, and Kent chuckles. 'Anyway,' she says, giving me the once-over, 'I can see why Mr Lester has been so smiley lately. You're gorgeous.'

My face flushes, followed by my ears, and finally, the top of my bald head warms like a radiator. I know I'm not unattractive, but with all the issues I deal with, my appearance never seems to be the focus.

'Th-th-thanks,' I stammer.

'You're embarrassing him.' Kent places his palm on the small of my back, rubbing little circles. I silently count each pass around. One, two, three, four, five . . .

'He's a keeper,' Ruth says. 'I can tell. I know queer people, and this one's special.'

'For sure. He's a mensch.' Kent nods, stopping the circles on my back at odd number seventeen.

'When are you meeting the wife?' Ruth says, and my eyes go wide.

'Ex-wife,' Kent corrects. 'And we haven't talked about it.'

'You have to meet Corrine. She's lovely.' Ruth takes a sip from her water bottle. 'She'll adore you.'

I look at Kent and give a small shrug. He pats my back twice.

The pressure soothes me, but I wish he would press even harder. 'Well, gentlemen, I'll leave you to . . . be gay.'

I smile, and a laugh escapes. 'I'm quite good at it,' I say. 'Years of practice.'

'Oh, Kent. I like him.'

Ruth heads for the door but turns back before leaving. 'Have a dinner, Kent. Invite Corrine. And me. I want to see her face when she meets this hot man.'

'Um,' Kent mumbles. 'Sure. Okay.'

Ruth leaves us, and Kent removes his hand from my back.

'You up for that? Meeting Corrine?'

'Sure. She won't hate me, right?'

'Vincent, I can't imagine anyone hating you. Ruth is right. Corrine will adore you. Mainly because I do,' he says with a wink.

I nod quickly.

'I'll arrange it.' Kent jots something on a sticky note.

'Now, let's talk about this training,' I say, opening my

laptop, firing up the presentation, and attempting to shift gears. Meeting Kent's ex-wife definitely means something. Sure, the stress might be triggering, but Kent will be there. If Kent and I are going to be more than friends, meeting the ex-wife he's still close with probably needs to happen. Deep breaths. I've totally got this.

26

Kent

'You roasted a chicken?'

Corrine's question doubles as an accusation. She knows the comforting effects of my roasted chicken well. Thyme, rosemary, with a pinch of crushed red pepper, soothes the soul with the added benefit of creating leftovers for chicken soup. My bubbe would be proud.

'It's my most impressive meal, and this is the first time I've cooked for –'

'Your boyfriend.'

'I was going to say Vincent.' I stir the mashed potatoes on the stove, they're thick and creamy. 'I'm not sure we're calling each other that.'

'Why not? You're dating, right?' Corrine asks.

'Yes.'

'And neither one of you is seeing anyone else?'

'No.'

'Kenny, my friend. You're boyfriends.'

'You sound like Gillian.'

'Where do you think she gets it from?' A satisfied smile spreads across her face.

She grabs the apron from the hook behind the pantry door, and when she fumbles with the ties behind her back, Sweetums, sensing playtime, jumps into action. He swats and paws at the apron's strings and Corrine's legs.

'Shoo!' she shouts. 'Get this creature away from the kitchen while we cook.'

'Let me,' Ruth says, hanging up her coat by the door and scooping Sweetums up. He instantly melts into her arms. 'Bedroom?'

I nod. 'But don't shut the door. He'll only protest. He'll snuggle up on the bed on his own. Maybe.'

'Got it,' Ruth says, cradling Sweetums during his temporary relocation.

Corrine presents her back to me, ties dangling, and I fasten them into a bow.

'So, dating then?' she asks.

'Yes. Dating. Definitely dating.'

'And shtupping,' Ruth says, returning empty-handed. 'There's definitely more than dating happening.'

My face blushes with embarrassment, but Ruth only persists.

'Listen, I know a thing or two about this. Amy and I started this way. Insta-lust. Like a new star exploding into existence. The heat could fry the Eastern Seaboard.' Ruth smirks and momentarily seems distracted.

'I liked Amy,' I say. 'She was hilarious. And cute.'

'She was a pain in my ass.'

'Sounds like she was a good match for you,' Corrine says.

'At first. But our star burned out. I prefer to explore . . . many stars and solar systems.' Ruth washes her hands, readying to assist. 'That's not going to happen here, though. Wait until you see Vincent. This guy is smoking. I wouldn't be able to keep my hands off him either.' With her hands dry, Ruth snaps the dish towel at my ass.

Corrine's pursed-lips smile hints this is unfamiliar territory for her. Our conversations about her and Charlie are firmly closed-door, and I was hoping to keep it that way about anyone I might date. But Ruth Parrish doesn't understand PG-13.

'This is some next-level shit, Corrine. We're talking –'

'Anyway,' I interrupt, throwing a bag of frozen peas from the freezer at Ruth, 'let's get these going and maybe not mortify my ex-wife and new whatever-we're-calling-him, thank you very much.'

Ruth opens her mouth to reply, and the buzzer saves me from her retort.

'That'll be him.' I peer at Ruth. 'Behave.'

She smirks mischievously. The sounds of pots, lids, and running water usher me into the hallway, and I head downstairs to let Vincent in.

When I open the door, Vincent's standing, shifting his weight from foot to foot, holding a bouquet in one hand and rubbing the back of his neck with the other. He's wearing his long wool coat, and his standard 'uniform,' but the top two buttons of his dress shirt are open. That spot, an appetizer of his neck and chest, beckons, but when he looks at me, there's something in his eyes I haven't seen before. He's blinking rapidly, and there's a tightness around his beautiful eyes.

'Hey,' I say. 'Are you okay?'

He doesn't speak but shakes his head quickly. 'I almost didn't come.'

'Come here.' I open my arms. All of his weight sinks into me, and he completely melts. When I gather him up, his torso shakes in my grasp. My teeth bite at my lower lip. Corrine and Ruth are upstairs. Waiting.

'Listen, there's nothing to worry about. Corrine is harmless. Truly. And Ruth, well, she'll behave. I promise.'

I pull him back. The color has drained from his face.

'Let's sit,' I say, and we settle on the front step. He leans on me, breath heavy. The weight of his body presses so firmly on me he'd knock me over if the door wasn't supporting me.

'This is why I don't get past the first date,' he says. 'This is what happens when I like someone.'

'What happens? Tell me.' My arm hasn't moved from Vincent's torso, and I squeeze tightly, attempting to soothe him.

'My OCD. People meet me and that's it. It's not what anyone's looking for.'

'Vincent, I'm not anyone.' I gently kiss his head. 'And Corrine and Ruth love me. They want to love you, too.'

A huge sigh escapes Vincent's lips. 'But am I loveable?'

My heart balloons. I pull him closer and say, 'Oh, my smoothie.'

'Excuse me?'

I chuckle. 'Smoothie. Vincent, you don't have a single hair on your body. And you're ridiculously sweet. Like a chocolate peanut butter smoothie. But way fewer calories.'

He smiles and lowers his head.

'Listen, I like you too,' I say, wrapping my other arm around him. 'A lot.'

'Yeah, but it's me liking you that's the problem. Because now,' he says, clasping his hands together, 'your ex-wife and your friend will see what a mess I am.'

'Vincent Manda. My smoothie. Look at me.'

He glances up, and the color has partially returned. His hazel eyes focus on me as I do my best not to get lost in the brown eyelashes sweeping over his brow.

'Look.' I nod down at my shirt. 'I'm covered in butter. And carrot peels. And' – I poke at something on my shirt – 'maybe black pepper. Or paprika. I don't know, but the point is I'm the definition of a mess. And those ladies upstairs?' My lips brush his temple. 'They still love me. Loving someone means cherishing every imperfection. Because those are what make you special.' I lift his chin, my thumb rubbing along his lower lip. 'They're going to love you too. Ruth already has a crush on you.' I give his forehead another peck. 'Vincent, you're quite loveable.'

He brushes his lips on mine. The kiss is short and soft, like two well-loved LEGO pieces melting into each other.

'Okay. Okay. Let's go,' he says. 'Before I change my mind.'

I take his hand, give it a squeeze, and we head up.

'Couldn't wait to get it on –' Ruth's wisecrack greets us as we enter, but she's interrupted by Corrine, who moves toward the door, wiping her hands on a dish towel.

'Vincent. I'm so happy to meet you.' Corrine tucks her hair behind her ear and offers her hand. Vincent glances at her hand, me, and then takes it.

'Same,' he says, handing her the flowers.

'For me? That was thoughtful.' Corrine smells the flowers and a sweet smile blossoms on her face. 'Daisies are my favorite,' she says, and slips the apron over her head.

'Nice move,' Ruth says, winking at Vincent.

'Kent has told me so many lovely things about you.' Vincent hangs his coat next to Ruth's.

'Don't believe any of it. This one' – she nods at me – 'is full of platitudes, but how am I supposed to play the role of evil ex-wife if all he does is fawn over me?'

'Corrine's an honorary lesbian,' Ruth says. 'Friends with your ex. Even after you've moved on . . .' Ruth nods. 'I wholeheartedly approve.'

'Is that really a thing?' Vincent asks.

'I'm still friends with all my exes,' Ruth says. 'It's how I have so many damn friends.'

'Come, sit.' Corrine nods toward the stools under my island. 'The peas are almost done. Kent made everything else.'

'He roasted a chicken for you,' Ruth says. 'A whole fucking chicken.'

'It's the only thing I know how to make,' I say with a shrug.

'Because I taught you.' Corrine uncovers the peas and steam escapes into the room.

'And you taught me well.'

Vincent tucks himself on a stool next to Ruth and grabs a wineglass from the collection on the counter.

'Sir,' Ruth says, lifting the bottle and giving Vincent a generous pour. She fills her glass and holds it up. 'Cheers. To queers!'

We take turns clinking glasses, and when my glass touches Vincent's, we make eye contact briefly. I do my best to give him a warm, reassuring look.

'And you, Corrine,' Ruth adds.

'Hey, I'm an honorary lesbian.' She winks at Ruth.

'We welcome everyone,' Ruth says, and a small laugh escapes from Vincent's mouth. Corrine joins him, followed by me, and finally Ruth.

The wine flows ... we finish two bottles, and Vincent continues to be utterly charming. When the serving fork slips out of my hand, and breast meat falls onto his plate, splattering chicken juice and a smattering of potatoes on his freshly pressed shirt, he doesn't flinch. He takes an extra napkin from Corrine, does his best to wipe himself off, smiles at me, and moves on. He's trying so hard. My heart kvells.

With Ruth's pineapple upside-down cake almost finished, Corrine yawns and gives me her patented I'm-ready-to-leave-now look.

'Well, it's almost this old lady's bedtime,' she says.

'Corrine, is this what happens when you near fifty?' Ruth asks.

'Pretty much,' she replies, 'although I've been an early bedtime girl since Kent began teaching.'

'Valid.' Ruth stands and folds her napkin. 'I'll walk you out. We can leave the men to do ... manly things.' She raises her eyebrows at me and smiles. I chuckle because her heart really is pure. Ruth just wants everyone to have as much sex as she does, and well, I'm starting to understand her viewpoint.

'Vincent. I can see why Kent likes you so much,' Corrine says at the door. 'You're wonderful.' She gives Vincent a sweet smile and then leans over and gives him a peck on the cheek. When she pulls back, his ears have flushed pink. The smile that creeps across my face confirms what I'm realizing. Vincent Manda's blush definitely gets my heart racing.

'Thank you,' Vincent replies. 'I'm so glad we got to spend a little time together.'

'We'll do it again,' Corrine replies. 'Maybe go out. I'll drag Charlie.'

'If you can get him to stop hitting other men with sticks,' Ruth says. 'Hockey. Officially the least gay sport in existence.'

'Any sport with a locker room is gay,' Vincent says, and when both Corrine and Ruth laugh, my smile beams.

Finally, alone, Vincent leans against the closed door and sighs.

'You were amazing.' I grab his waist and press my torso against his. 'I told you she'd love you.'

'How can you tell?'

'I know Corrine. If she didn't adore you to bits, she would've been polite, but calling you wonderful? No way.'

'I'm exhausted,' he says, resting his head on my shoulder and nestling into the crook of my neck. As his warm breath caresses my skin, I realize being close to Vincent Manda is quickly becoming one of my favorite places in the world.

'I have an idea,' I say. 'To help you wind down.'

'What?'

'Come.'

I take his hand and tickle his palm with my fingers as I lead him into my bathroom, hoping he'll enjoy my surprise.

27

Vincent

Kent's bathroom is surprisingly enormous. A long double vanity with under-mounted sinks takes up most of the far wall. There's a shower stall, covered entirely from floor to ceiling with glass tiles in different shades of blue. The large round soaking tub, big enough for at least three people, near the window, has an edge at least a foot around dotted with candles and small plants. I'd never have guessed Kent to have such an opulent bathroom.

In the corner, a hamper overflows with laundry cascading to the floor. Amid the overall tidiness, it's the one moment of disorder.

'How is your bathroom so . . .'

'Large?' Kent shuts the door, giving us some privacy from the cat. 'The previous owners combined the existing bathroom with a small nursery to create the spa getaway of their dreams.' He motions to the tub. 'They split. And I got custody of their luxurious bathroom.'

My stomach clenches as Kent starts the tub and grabs a bag of Epsom salts from the vanity's cabinet. Pools. Tubs.

The thought of soaking in my own filth makes me queasy. I need to be honest.

That's the only way this won't blow up in a fiery blaze.

'I don't really do pools. Swimming of any kind.' I wince and wait for his reply.

'It's a tub. Not a pool.' Kent scratches his chin, his fingers lost in his whiskers. How is confused Kent even sexier?

'I know, it's just . . .' I sit on a small wood bench against the wall. 'Being in water. In my own . . . grime, let alone someone else's . . .' I shake my head.

Kent offers a thin smile and gazes up at the ceiling. He walks over, puts his hands out, and I give him mine.

'What if we showered first?'

My fingers fidget in his hands, and the skin on my scalp prickles. How long would we have to scrub to be clean enough for a bath together? Kent lets go of my hands and opens a cabinet. A jumble of items comes tumbling out, and he attempts to capture and shove them back in.

'Well, this is what happens when you tidy up quickly,' he says, scrambling to pick up a box of cotton swabs, a nail clipper, and various small bottles. Turning around, he's holding a new toothbrush out to me.

'Let's start with our mouths and go from there.'

'Wha . . . how . . .' I stammer.

'This old guy has a few tricks up his sleeve.' Kent winks and grabs a tube of toothpaste. 'Especially for you.'

I unwrap my toothbrush. The bristles are soft, and I prefer medium, but it'll suffice. The gentleness of the brush isn't the end of the world. And Kent did this. For me.

Kent finishes with a spit and asks, 'What do you think?' He comes from behind, his minty breath on my neck. 'How's your mood?' He runs his palm over the dome of my head, and my cock surges in my pants. His thoughtfulness, patience, and empathy create a tiny firework display in my core.

I nod slowly, his beard prickling my neck. He kisses me right where his whiskers tickled and pulls away. 'There's my Vincent.'

My Vincent. His. I'm his.

He starts the shower, then the tub, as I undress. When I slide my briefs off, my cock snaps up, aroused by Kent's appetizer of attention. He chuckles when it slaps my stomach before pointing at the floor, and I'm rewarded with a soft kiss on my neck. Kent palms my erection, whispering, 'Be a good boy and get nice and clean.'

I turn my face, and our mouths connect. There's no hesitation. My tongue darts in to meet his, and he slides his thumb over the tip of my cock, already slick with precum.

'The shower isn't big enough for both of us. Why don't you go first, and I'll get the tub ready.'

With the hot water running, I get in and do my best to scrub every molecule of my body with the bottle of soap Kent hands me. A bar of green soap rests on the shower's shelf, but I have no intention of touching it, thank you very much. I open the liquid soap, and a cool, crisp aroma fills the shower. Peeking at the bottle, the tiny print reads 'Cucumber and Mint.' While it's no orange and honey, it does the trick. As the soap reaches my ass, a tingling sensation spreads, reminding me of the lingering irritation from Kent's whiskers, and a smile crosses my face as I recall his beard buried in my backside.

As I exit the shower, Kent kisses my cheek, takes my hand, and walks me to the tub.

'So damn clean,' he says with a mischievous grin. 'I scrubbed the tub. There's a little salt, some lavender, that's it.'

I shake my head. Still damp from the shower, I can't hide the tears in my eyes.

'What's wrong?' He takes my face in his hands, his fingers rough. 'We don't have to.'

I take a deep breath, blow it out, and say, 'No, it's not that. It's you.' Kent's soft smile pulls my focus. 'You make me feel like I'm the only man in the entire world.'

'Vincent Manda. To me, you are.' He kisses the top of my hand and says, 'Now, watch your step.'

I climb into the tub, only about three-quarters full, and the moment my feet hit the bottom, my shoulders drop as the lavender scent washes over me. Kent doesn't let go of my hand until I'm seated.

'I'm going to jump in the shower and scrub every inch. You relax.' He walks to the stall, but before jumping in, stops and says, 'I almost forgot.'

He jogs over to the vanity, his dick flopping with each stride, and pushes a button on a small black box.

'For my smoothie.'

Scooting down, I rest my head on the back of the tub, and strumming guitars fill the room. The sound is small, only slightly louder than the shower, but when the flute joins, and Christine's voice arrives, 'Oh Daddy' covers me like a weighted blanket. Fuck yes.

With my eyes closed, the sound of water and Fleetwood Mac takes me away, and when I open my eyes, Kent stands naked before me.

'I think I dozed off,' I murmur.

'Good.'

He steps into the tub, and peppers my head with kisses, migrating down to my nose until I let out a small whimper when his lips brush mine. He lies at the opposite end of the tub and clasps on to my legs. With closed eyes, he lays his head back, completely relaxed, as he massages my calves.

Kent's fingers press and push, and when I pull my legs up a few inches, they slide down to my ankles and feet.

'Oh, fuck, yes,' he moans. His thumbs press into my arches, and I spy his cock stiffening under the still water.

With both hands, he gently massages and caresses my right foot, focusing on each individual toe. I ease my left foot to the base of his dick and glide the ball of my foot up and down his shaft. Kent releases a tiny sigh, followed by more moaning. I slide the foot in his hand up to his chest. My toes tangle in his thick chest hair, and he grabs my ankle, pulling my foot up and kissing my big toe before taking it in his mouth and softly sucking.

'Kent?'

'Mmmh,' he mutters, with my toe still lodged between his full lips.

'My mood,' I say. 'It's, um. Peak.'

His eyes pop open, and without removing my toe from his mouth, he mumbles, 'Fuck yeah.'

Laughter pours out of me. The sound of him

attempting speech with my toe in his mouth tickles me more than his tongue lapping at my foot.

Removing it, he says, 'Come. Sit.'

Kent places a small, white towel on the ledge, smoothing it out with a few soft pats. I push myself out of the tub and do as I'm told, relishing relinquishing control.

He lowers himself between my legs, glances up at me, and smiles, his goofy grin driving me wild.

'My handsome boy.'

Now, I've just turned forty, for god's sake, but also, when Kent calls me his boy, every ounce of blood rushes to my groin to celebrate.

'Yes,' I whisper. 'Sir.'

Calling him this, something I've never done but flies out of my mouth like a T-shirt in one of those silly cannons at sports events, just clicks. Surrendering myself to Kent, letting him praise me, have his way with me, and be submissive to him is the ultimate act of power, and my body vibrates with arousal.

My shoulders shudder as he licks the tip of my cock. He pushes himself up and places his hands on my chest. Cupping and massaging, his fingers find my nipples, stirring up more heat in my center.

'Lean back,' he says, and when I do, I'm startled by the warmth of the wall. 'Heated tiles.' He gives me a sultry half-smile and then takes the top half of my dick in his mouth. He begins to guzzle and slurp, his beard – damp from the shower – quickly becoming soaked with spit and precum as he makes a thorough mess of sucking me off. I fucking love it. My core gurgles with pleasure, and I think about what I can do for him.

With his attention elsewhere, I hoist my right leg out of the water and place my foot on the ledge. Inches away from my cock, which is currently down his throat, my toes are now within reach.

'Fuck, you're my best boy,' he says, saliva dripping from the whiskers on his chin. 'Letting me suck every inch of you.'

He licks my first few toes, covering as much surface as he can, before returning to my cock which is waiting patiently. He creates a pleasant rhythm, alternating between my foot and dick. Feasting on me, he grunts and groans, occasionally glancing up at me with his bright, beautiful brown eyes.

'Kent?' I say when he's moving in between my foot and shaft.

He looks up at me with an adorable toe-filled grin. 'Yeah?'

'My mood. I want your cock in my mouth now. Please, sir.'

He laughs and gently sets my foot back in the tub.

'Since you asked so nicely.' He stands, water cascading off him, and moves in between my legs, leaning his mouth to mine. Tracing my lips with his tongue, he cradles my face and whispers, 'Will you suck me like a good boy?'

I nod, and he kisses me, his beard damp and soft on my face as my tongue whirls in his mouth. My hands migrate to his shoulders, and gently, I maneuver him to the spot where I sat. Grateful the tub isn't full, I brace myself on the edge and lower myself to my knees.

Kent's dick is just as hard as last time. He must have taken one of those pills. Thank you, modern medicine for vaccines and rock-hard cocks. Before I take him in my mouth, his fingers find my chin and bring my gaze to his.

'You're amazing, you know that.'

With a gleeful flushed face, I nod, basking in Kent's praise.

My lips stretch around his long, plump dick, and the minty flavor of his soap coats my tongue. Cautiously, I move my head down, attempting to take as much of him as possible, but I only make it about eighty percent of the way before my gag reflex kicks in. Pulling back, Kent places his palms around my ears. He's trying to help me move off him.

'You okay?' he asks, again lifting my face. I can't hide my watery eyes, and he uses his thumbs to wipe the tears away.

I lower my head and nod, catching my breath and whispering, 'Yeah.'

'Go slow. It's not a race, and you don't have to share. I'm all yours.'

I slap Kent's cock against my cheek, the skin-to-skin contact dispatching a rush of arousal to my groin. Heeding his advice, I return to sucking, not taking as much in. I use my right hand to help cover the real estate of his massive cock while holding myself up with my left. Giving myself occasional breaks, I rub the head over my lips, kissing and licking the sensitive tip, and spanking my face with his dick. Kent leans back on the toasty tile, and quiet noises of pleasure escape his mouth, joining the music, filling my soul with affection.

My hand moves under his balls, massaging, remembering how he loved the butt plug, wishing I'd brought it over. With a bit of pressure on the spot he loves, Kent leans forward, his palms on my upper back. Taking his hint, I swing my right foot forward, allowing him access to his target. His fingers travel down until he reaches his desired location.

'Your ass. It's literally perfect. No notes.'

I smile the best I can with his cock lodged in my mouth and his furry stomach pressing on my forehead, the soft hairs tickling my eyelids. His hands land on my ass cheeks and pull them apart.

'Vincent Manda, do you have a license to be this hot?'

My small laugh gets lost in Kent's midsection as his cock throbs in my mouth. What he's doing, and perhaps about to do, is pushing the throttle for him.

A finger circles my hole, rubbing, patting, and applying pressure before another joins it, creating a symphony of pleasure I've never experienced. Using lube from a tiny tube on the tub's ledge, his fingers glide and slip around my ring, sending a shudder through me. Sucking his cock while he does this might be the end of me.

He leans over again, spreading me as wide as he can, and says, 'Are you ready to take me from both ends like a good boy?'

I mumble, 'Yes,' the best I'm able, and he slides the tip of his finger into my hole. I clench around him, and removing his dick from my mouth, press the side of my face into his thigh.

'Vincent? You tell me, and I stop,' he says.

'No, just give me a minute,' I say, counting breaths, sending relaxing energy to my body. My face, pressed against Kent's fuzzy thigh, makes me think of him as a big, cuddly bear. Right now, the bear's cock is pressing against the other side of my face.

He removes his finger. His hands cup my ass, and massage gently, occasionally stretching and rubbing the skin around my hole. I continue taking deep breaths, allowing the warmth from being between his leg and dick to settle me. I take him back in my mouth.

I'm more relaxed. More ready.

'Okay?' he asks.

'Uh-huh.' Now it's my turn to attempt speech with a dick down my throat.

'Spread those legs for me,' he commands, and I widen my stance. 'Good boy.'

He resumes pulling my ass cheeks, his fingers playing around it, until again, only the tip enters. This time, there's no discomfort, only pleasure. The pressure of his finger triggers nerves and sensations completely new to me. Cautiously, I arch my back, an invitation for more.

'Deeper?' he asks.

Pulling off quickly, I say, 'Yes, sir. Please.' Spit drips from my mouth. 'Deeper.'

'How far? Show me.'

Carefully, Kent's finger burrows. I pull off him and take deep breaths until it's all the way in, and when I resume sucking, he pats my ass with his free hand. 'That's my good boy.'

My insides smolder, and I buck against his hand, finally pausing, saliva dribbling on my chin, to say, 'Try another. Please.'

There's more lube, and then Kent adds a second finger. The walls of my ass press against them, creating the most glorious friction. Suddenly, a slap on my ass creates a loud *whack* that echoes against the walls and startles us both.

'Sorry, I got carried away.'

'Damn,' I say. The sweet sting tingling. 'Do it again. Please.'

Authorized to continue, Kent now adds slaps to his repertoire of ass play, and the beautiful bite stirs a jolt of pleasure in my body.

Lost in the moment, I tremble when his other hand reaches under and grabs my cock. Delighting in him taking up so much space inside me, the added sensation of him jerking me off sends shockwaves down my spine.

I pull off for a second and smile up at him. A stream of spit and precum stretches from my lips to the head of his cock, and his wide grin makes my chest radiate with comfort.

'There you go,' he says. 'You look so beautiful taking my cock and fingers, Vincent.'

As his fingers swirl inside me, unfamiliar sensations ignite. My whole being surrenders to the overwhelming pleasure of Kent Lester. It happens quickly. My orgasm begins, and unsure what to do, I continue sucking and fucking his fingers, speeding up, moaning, trying to let him know I'm close.

'That's it. That's it.' Kent's voice, slow and steady, guides me like a skilled captain bringing his ship into port. 'I've got you, smoothie. Come for me like a good boy. Let it all go.'

The freedom. Having Kent inside me. Stroking my cock, my seed boiling over as he talks, praises, and unravels me from the inside. I exhale and welcome the release.

Shooting into Kent's submerged hand, my entire body vibrates as my orgasm rips through me. His fingers slip and slide, attempting to catch it all.

'Good boy. There you go. There you go. I've got you.' He's got me. All of me. His voice flows over me, and moans and quick breaths escape my lips, stretched around Kent's fat cock as he pumps the last drops from me.

'Vincent, I'm close. Can I come on you? On your back? Your ass? I'll wash you off. I promise.'

I pull off him and say, 'Please. Shoot all over me.' He stands, sending the bath water sloshing.

He continues jerking himself while maneuvering behind me. I rest my face on the tub's edge, the tiles warming the towel and soothing my cheek.

'Will you take my cum like a good boy?'

'Yes, sir. I want it. All of it.'

I do want it. Him. All over me. And then it lands on my skin in fast spurts. Warmer than the water, sticky, and glorious. With my permission, Kent solidifies his possession, covering my lower back and ass. His rigid cock presses against me as he spreads his cum in my every nook and cranny.

'There you go,' he says, and I hear an enormous sigh. He lowers himself into the water, mumbling, 'Vincent, you . . . I . . . fuck.'

He lies back, catching his breath, and I crawl onto his torso, snuggling into him. 'So fuzzy.' With Kent, I'm unhinged. Discovered. Relished. The talking. The checking in. Going at my pace. Equally concerned about my pleasure as his. It's like being truly seen for the first time, and my body practically floats from the euphoria.

Showered and naked in Kent's bed, I'm welcomed by fresh, crisp sheets and my sweet, fluffy, furry bear. I lay my head on his chest, wrap my arm around his soft stomach, and breathe him in.

'That was . . . hot,' he says, nibbling my head.

'Really?'

'Are you kidding?'

I chuckle, and my breath blows the thick fur on his chest.

'Even the . . . sir?'

'Vincent. You can call me whatever you want.'

Kent's nibbles morph into mouthing, and his slowed heartbeat and breathing signal me to relent to sleep. We lay quietly, my eyes heavy. And then it happens.

My heart trips in my chest as a surprise pounce pummels my feet.

'Kent . . . Kent!' I whisper-yell.

'It's Sweetums. He always sleeps with me,' he murmurs.

'I can't sleep with an animal.'

'Vincent, here's the issue . . .' Kent's voice sounds slightly more awake. 'If I shoo him out of the room, he'll cry and paw at the door all night. If we let him stay, I promise he won't move from the foot of the bed. He's a good boy.'

My belly stirs with Kent's 'good boy,' and I take a breath, attempting to return to the euphoric afterglow I was experiencing moments ago.

'Okay.'

I snuggle into Kent, doing my best to ignore the creature on the bed. Lying on his chest, I'm able to drift off, the sounds of Kent Lester's low breathing lulling me to sleep.

Cracking one eye, the sunrise bleeds through Kent's blinds, but something blocks my view. It's the cat. Sweetums. He's sitting six inches from my face. Staring at me with giant yellow eyes.

28

Kent

'Have you given leather any more thought?'

Ruth's words cause a temporary lapse in my balance, my body jerks, and I stumble on the track. She grabs my arm as I catch myself.

'Easy, easy,' she soothes. 'It's just a suggestion. Don't plotz.'

'Do you remember every Yiddish word and phrase I say?'

'Are you shepping naches?' she asks and then giggles, head back, her face brighter than the sun.

'Yes, Ruth, I am impressed and proud of you.' Truly, her ability and desire to integrate a plethora of Yiddish into her lexicon amazes me.

'Anyway, you'd look great in leather. A harness.'

'A what?' I ask, reestablishing my balance on the bouncy track. The cold is back, and frigid March air fills my lungs, but the bright, direct sun attempts to warm my keppie.

'A harness. It stretches across your chest and wraps around your neck.' She motions with her hands. 'So fucking hot. It gives your partner something to grab on to.' Ruth latches her arm in mine, perhaps to keep me upright. 'They make fabric ones, but a leather harness on that furry dad bod – you'd make Vincent's eyes explode.'

'Excuse me, how do you know the ins and outs of leather harnesses?'

Ruth's eyes roll up so far, I'm convinced she's exploring the recesses of her own brain.

'I have two. Black and purple. Sarah adored them. Whips and leashes too. A little light bondage play can really crank up the pilot light.'

'Whips? Leashes?' My mind races to put the pieces together. 'Is there anything you don't know about?'

'My friend. Lesbians know about . . . well, everything. It's a fact.'

'Okay, fair. Fair,' I say, patting her back. There really isn't much she doesn't know. She even changed my oil once. 'But what? How?'

Another eye roll, and Ruth pats my arm. 'Kent, Kent, Auntie Ruth will take care of you.'

'But where would I even –'

'The internet. Kent Lester, you can literally buy anything on the internet. Where do you think I bought my Gina Gershon pillowcase?' She taps my arm affectionately. 'I'll come to your office at lunch. We can shop together. I need a new strap-on harness.'

'A what?'

She erupts into laughter, pats my back, and hooks her arm in mine. Once again, I find myself asking what I'm getting myself into.

*

'Poppy!' Lia leaps into my embrace and wraps her arms around my neck.

Vincent waits a step behind me, rubbing his thumb and index finger together. Lia wears her warmest flannel pajamas. Pink with tiny rainbows and unicorns.

'You brought your boyfriend,' Lia whisper-yells into my ear.

'I did.' I don't want to correct her and I'm not sure what I'd call Vincent at this point, anyway. 'We had so much fun with him at the LEGO center, remember?'

'Is he going to be my new Poppy?' she asks louder, her words now devoid of any trace of privacy.

'Lia, let's not embarrass Vincent,' I say, hoping he didn't hear, but almost certain he did.

Vincent moves forward, his eyebrows drawing closer. 'I'm fine. And Lia, you never know.' He shrugs, attempting to assuage her.

'If you get married, can I be the flower girl?' Lia does a twirl. 'I could throw tiny LEGO pieces instead of flower petals.'

Gillian, hearing the commotion, joins us in the entryway. 'It's freezing! You're letting the cold in. Sweetie, let Poppy be for a minute.'

I put Lia down, and the moment her feet hit the ground, she grabs Vincent's hand and pulls him inside. The door shuts behind us, and Gillian's meatloaf, my mother's recipe, hits my nose, sending a smile over my face. When my mother passed away three years ago, Corrine and I spent hours combing and collating her recipes into a book. Knowing Gillian uses the index cards with my mother's horrible handwriting makes my heart swell.

'Vincent, nice to see you again,' Gillian says. 'Lia, go help your father set the table.' She shoos her off toward the dining room. 'Dad,' she says, nodding toward the coat closet. 'We're eating in five minutes.' Gillian leaves us in the foyer, and I shake off the cold from outside and let the coziness of being at my daughter's with Vincent envelop me.

Alone for a moment, Vincent hands me his coat, and before I place it in the closet, I give him a quick kiss. Soft. On the lips. Mouths closed. Warmth transfers from his lips to mine and my body relaxes at the contact. We came straight from school, and I could only pop a mint in my mouth on the drive over. These small, sweet kisses don't seem to bother him. Vincent's hands move around my waist. He pulls me close and places his nose on mine.

'Bathroom?' I ask.

He dips in, his lips connect with mine, and I smile into his kiss.

'Flower girl!' Lia shouts from behind Vincent. 'And I get to pick my dress!'

Caught in our small moment, we burst into laughter as we joyfully join the family.

Around the table, with freshly scrubbed hands, Vincent sits next to me, with Lia on his other side. She's staring at him, although I'm not sure he notices. Even after our LEGO outing, Vincent is new and interesting, and she's curious and determined to ensure he adores her.

'Mommy said boys can marry boys,' Lia says with half a piece of meatloaf hanging off her fork. She's taken a bite, and a full mouth mumbles her words.

'Sweetie, Poppy and Vincent know.' Gillian cuts Lia's meatloaf into bite-sized pieces.

'And girls can marry girls,' Lia adds.

'Yes,' Louis says. 'Anyone can marry whoever they love.'

'There's no need to talk about weddings,' Gillian says. 'Poppy and Vincent are just . . .' She stops and gives me her confused look. The same one she gave me when she came home from school at seven and asked me how the baby got into her teacher's belly. 'Just, just . . .'

'Very good friends,' I say.

'No. Boyfriends,' Lia says. 'Mommy said you were boyfriends. Right, Mommy?'

Gillian shrugs, and I say, 'Well, we're, we're . . .' The words stumble out of my mouth like loose change.

'Boyfriends,' Vincent says. His hand covers mine, and he gives me a soft smile. My heart trips in my chest, and I attempt to swallow. I'm fifty-two and have never had a boyfriend. Vincent rubs the back of my hand against his cheek, and my heart does a tiny cartwheel.

'I want a pink flower-girl dress,' Lia shouts. 'With roses!' Vincent laughs and this prompts her to blurt, 'Or LEGOs!'

After dinner, Vincent helps Lia with her LEGO Princess Castle. They sit at the small play table in her room, Vincent's knees in his chest, as he patiently explains the ins and outs of the directions. Lia watches him as if her life depends on it. Batting her eyelashes, smiling, and grabbing on to Vincent's arm, she's quickly casting her spell on him. As they work, I return to help Gillian and Louis clean up.

Louis buses items from the table as I rinse, and Gillian packs leftovers and loads the dishwasher.

'You like him.' Gillian spoons mashed potatoes into a plastic container.

'Of course he likes him,' Louis says. 'You don't call someone your boyfriend if you don't like them.'

'What do you know about boyfriends?' Gillian snaps the lid onto the container. 'You thought I actually wanted help with algebra homework in college. A yutz.' She hands me the bowl to rinse.

'Math is confusing.' Louis sidles up to her, poking at her ribs.

'Says the accountant.' Gillian bats him away.

'Yes. I like him,' I say. 'He's sweet.'

'And dating and working together,' Gillian says with enormous eyes.

'So far, so good,' I say.

'Be careful,' Louis says, handing me a stack of dirty plates. 'You don't want to screw things up. With work. With him.'

'Ah, my Louis, giving his father-in-law dating advice,' Gillian says.

'Not dating advice. Life advice,' Louis says. 'Just make sure you keep your head clear.'

'I don't want you getting hurt.' Gillian places the last plate into the dishwasher and comes behind me, resting her head on my shoulder.

'It's good.' I reach up and cup her face. 'We're not rushing into anything. We're just enjoying each other's company. And the project is on track. We go live soon. Then, the board meeting. It's been mostly smooth sailing. Vincent and his partner know what they're doing.'

'Good.' Gillian moves in front of me. 'Just take care of this.' She pokes my chest and taps my heart.

'If I need to kick anyone's ass, you tell me,' Louis says, handing me the last of the glasses.

'You're not kicking anyone's anything,' Gillian says, pinching her husband's bottom, starting a cascade of laughter in the kitchen.

A smile scatters across my face. Being here, even in the chaos, my soul settles. The picture of our family, painted with warm watercolor brushstrokes, comes into focus. And I glimpse a spot for Vincent on the canvas.

29

Vincent

'Your family is . . .'

'A lot,' Kent says. 'I know. They worry too much. It's kind of our thing.' He scratches his beard, and his soft sweatshirt lifts enough for me to steal a peek at his even softer tummy. 'They just want me to be happy.'

'Are you?' My stomach flips in anticipation.

'Happy?' he asks. 'Generally speaking, I think I'm a happy guy.'

'No, I mean . . . do I make you happy?' With us both freshly showered, I'm digging in my bag for Kent's surprise.

'Very,' he whispers, leaning down and kissing the back of my neck. Orange and honey envelop my senses, and I smile. Kent's thoughtful gesture of stocking my preferred brand and scent doesn't go unnoticed.

'I bought something for you.' I continue to poke in the duffel bag I bring when I stay over. Sweetums lies next to the bag, wishing, hoping, praying for me to leave it unzipped. No way. He'd sleep the entire night inside it. On my clothes.

Biting my lip, I pull my surprise out. After Kent's reaction to the butt plug, I decided he might like something a little more . . . interactive. Thank you, internet.

'What do you think?' I ask.

Holding the gadget out, Kent moves back, taking it in. Larger than it seemed online, the baby blue plastic casing cools my palms. Popping the cap off, I show him the opening. His eyes broaden, and his mouth opens a little.

'What, what is that?'

'It's a Fleshlight.'

'A flashlight?' Kent cocks his head back and forth, trying to understand what wild sex gadget I've brought into his home. 'I've never seen one like that before. Where does the light come out?'

'No. *Flesh*. Fleshlight. You, you, well . . . fuck it.'

Kent's mouth opens and he nods before moving closer to inspect it. He slowly circles the small hole on the end with the tip of his index finger, pushing and prodding at the material. His finger glides inside and he immediately pulls it out.

'It's so, so, realistic.'

I laugh and hand it over for him to inspect.

'It's supposed to be. It's made of something called ReelFeel SuperSkin. Apparently, it feels exactly like fucking someone.'

'Apparently? You've never used it?'

I shrug. 'Not really my cup of tea. But I thought we could use it,' I say. 'Together. I figured you might like the next best thing.' I nuzzle my temple into his neck.

'Vincent,' he says, moving back and taking my chin in his free hand, 'you are the best thing. I want you.'

'You don't care?'

'About fucking you?' Kent asks, placing the gadget on the bed. He removes his sweatshirt, takes my face in his strong hands, and holds my gaze.

'Vincent, don't you get it? You're all I want.'

My legs turn to jelly, and I close my eyes. The fingers on my right hand find my temple. Shaky and tentative, I inhale deeply. And again.

'You want me?' I peek with one eye, and Kent's sexy smile stares back at me.

'Of course, you silly goose. You're fucking amazing.' He takes my hand, and kisses each knuckle. 'I want to be with you. Whatever that means. Everything we've done so far has blown my mind. It's not only enough . . . it's perfection. You're perfection.'

'Oh.'

'C'mere,' he says, pulling me closer and holding me tight. 'Vincent Manda, you are all I want. You. Just as you are. And I will tell you that every single day if you need to hear it.'

With Kent's woolly body plastered against mine, each hair on his stocky chest brushes against my skin. He wants me. Even with my napkins. Wipes. Routines. He wants me. Me.

'I bought something, too,' he murmurs. 'Can I show you?' I nod with a smile, still woozy from his words. What's he up to?

Kent opens the top drawer of his dresser and pulls out something long, strappy, and black. The material shimmers and small metal rings sparkle as they catch the light from the bedside table.

'It's a leather harness. I have no idea how to put it on, but I . . . I thought you might like it. To grab on to.'

The smile plastered across my face gives me away. I've seen them online, in movies, and always thought how hot they were, but not something anyone would wear in real life. And here he is, ready to strap it on for me. Every inch of my body hums at the thought of him wearing it.

'Can you help me?' he asks, holding it up with his head tilted, turning it around, and examining every angle.

I inspect the harness, and the earthy smell of leather fills the air as I find the label and orient it toward the back.

'Here' – I hold open the two sides – 'slip your arms through.'

I guide Kent through putting it on, taking the time to adjust the straps on his back so they provide a secure fit without being overly tight.

'Comfy?' I guide him in front of the floor-length mirror against the wall.

'Yeah, I think.' Kent turns around, inspecting his reflection.

'Fuck. It's hot.' The leather bands cross and frame his chest, pressing the hair down slightly and creating the perfect place for me to grasp on to.

Just below his breastbone, the metal ring beckons, and I finger it, tugging him close. 'You are so fucking sexy.' My mouth lands on his, holding him near, lost in his beard, mouth, scent, all of him. When his tongue brushes against my teeth, poking, and he takes a small nibble at my top lip, I'm unsure how long I can wait.

'Now, why don't you get me nice and hard by sucking my cock like a good boy. Can you do that for me?' He's lowered his voice and my dick thumps against his. I'm so turned on that the atoms in my body seem to rearrange. Am I going to be the newest member of the X-Men? No, maybe their secret subgroup, the Sex-Men?

'Come.' I pat the comforter. 'Sit.'

Kent sits on the edge of the bed, leaning back on his propped-up arms. I've positioned him directly across from the mirror. He's getting a show.

'I want to suck you like this.' I lower myself to my knees on a folded towel. My eyes transfix on him. 'Do you know how fucking beautiful your cock is?'

He shrugs and smiles.

'Hasn't anyone ever worshipped your gorgeous cock?'

'Um, I don't think so. Corrine liked it. Maybe? But worshipped? Definitely not.'

'Well, let me be the first.'

From this angle, he looks so much bigger than me. I reach and place my palms on the harness, pulling at the warm, smooth leather, until he relents and rewards me with a kiss. As he breaks away, my hands find their way to the warmth and softness of his stomach. My fingers get lost in his furry forest, pressing gently, tugging, wanting to experience every bit of Kent Lester.

'Do you not like my belly?'

'No. I fucking love it.' The gentle touch of his tummy sends a buzzing sensation through my fingertips, as if each hair has a story to tell. 'All of it. You.'

My hands melt into his delicious carpet. The softness of his middle. He's so fucking sexy, and my mood meter is off the charts. Suddenly my amp goes to eleven. I slide my fingers down and comb through his pubic hair. It's thick, still mostly dark, although a few inviting silver strands peek through.

'Kent.' I cradle his cock in my hands like the most fabulous treat. 'May I?'

'Of course.' His thumb traces my chin. 'My handsome boy.'

My hands around the base, I gently kiss the tip. A sweet scent remains from his recent shower as I nuzzle into him. Slowly, I wrap my lips around the head and take him in as far as possible.

'Fuck. Your mouth feels like heaven.' Kent's breath reaches the top of my head.

Relaxing my jaw as much as possible, I take more length in. My hands move to the base, and remembering his fondness for it, I massage under his balls. With pressure right near his hole, Kent shivers, and pleasing him this way sends a jolt of electricity to my groin.

'There you go,' he says. 'Good boy.' A hand glides over my head. 'Good boy.'

Kent pushes himself forward. His hands pass under my face and land on my chest. While I feast on him, pulsing in my mouth, he begins lightly pinching and playing with my nipples. My knees spread on the towel, giving him a better view of my ass in our reflection, and a rush of excitement jogs through me as he playfully teases my chest while I struggle to catch my breath. And now, my dick, at full attention, craves contact.

With uncanny intuition, Kent's right foot slides up, applying pressure to my cock against my stomach. The smooth gliding motion from my precum heightens the sensation, and I tilt my pelvis back, giving him a better angle to view my ass in the mirror.

'There you go,' he purrs. 'Your hole wants some love?'

Unable to respond with words, I wiggle my butt and Kent's stomach rumbles with a low chuckle. 'Fuck. Look at you.' He moves his hands to my lower back, pawing at my ass, desperate for contact. Kent stands, his cock pops out of my mouth, and he slaps my right ass cheek. 'Such a sweet ass on my good boy.'

There's another crack, and I stare at his beautiful cock, my mouth watering for it. I push myself up to kneeling and am able to swallow him again. Kent leans over, massaging and spreading my ass. His fingers play with my hole and there's another slap as he thrusts into my mouth. As he slopes over my back, his cock pushes deeper down my throat, and a few small choking noises escape my lips.

Kent pauses, moves back slightly, and asks, 'You okay?'

Pulling off for a moment, I reply, 'Good. Amazing. I love choking on your long, fat, gorgeous monster cock.'

Kent's voice is deep and steady. 'Good boy. My balls are full of cum for you. Are you willing to work for it?'

My skin vibrates with desire. 'Yes, sir.'

I resume sucking and shake my ass again, begging for more. Kent takes this as permission to resume fondling. He grabs my cheeks, massaging for a moment, and then lets go before another *thwack*! The sound and sweet sting send a shiver of delight up my spine.

'Look at your beautiful hole.' He's staring at our reflection. 'It's so fucking perfect.'

When his fingers explore the tender area surrounding my opening, I pause and say, 'Wait. Don't move.'

I fetch the small bottle of lube that came with the toy. 'Here.'

While I engulf his cock, spit and slobber dribble down my chin and fuck, right now, I don't care. I swirl my tongue over the tip, and Kent's thighs shudder.

'That. With your tongue. Do that again. Please,' he says.

I comply and the sound of Kent rubbing his hands together above me tells me he's warming the lube up. When slick fingers spread me wide and then carefully place a generous amount on my hole, I'm unable to contain myself.

'Your ass. Delectable.'

'Now. Sir, please.'

Being a side means I get to decide what I want. I want Kent Lester.

With a few soft slaps on my ass, my skin sizzles. Starting with one finger, Kent enters me slowly, cautiously. His concern for my comfort doesn't go unnoticed.

'You're, you're,' he says, 'so fucking horny for me.'

'Mmmh,' I mutter into him, my head bobbing on his cock, because yes, I am.

'You've got my cock so fucking hard,' he says. 'Your beautiful lips wrapped around me.'

Focused on the current task at hand, when Kent slips a second finger in, I'm too distracted to stop, but I pause, inhale deeply through my nose, the sweet smell of his sweat mixing with the soap, and remind myself to relax.

Breathe. Relax. Breathe. Relax.

Kent's fingers move past the ring of muscle, and my ass welcomes him as a wave of pleasure flows from my hole outward, overtaking every nerve in my body. He's completely still. Waiting.

Removing his cock from my mouth, I beg, 'Please. Finger me. Harder.'

Kent slides his two fingers in and out methodically and carefully. Without warning, he stands, retrieves his glasses from the bedside table, and moves behind me.

'I need to watch this. Closer. See my fingers in your horny hole.'

Resting my head on the bed, I push back, allowing Kent's fingers inside further. He pauses. 'Your ass is fucking perfect. Does this feel good?'

'Oh yeah. So good. Don't move. Let me do it.'

I begin rocking back and forth, fucking his fingers, letting him simply witness the action.

'There we go.' Kent's voice, low and steady, compliments my movement. 'You're fucking me like such a good boy, Vincent. Such a good boy.'

I can hear his right hand jerking himself, the slick sound of my spit around his cock. He's speeding up, and I do my best to match his rhythm. My body thrusts and the tips of his fingers delve deeper, sending an electric current through me.

'There, Kent. Right there.'

I grab the Fleshlight from the bed, lube it up, and position it between my legs with the opening facing Kent. The cold plastic pushes against my balls, sending a quick chill through me before my thighs warm it.

I hold the toy in place with one hand while the other braces against the bed. 'Fuck it.'

With his two fingers still lodged deep inside, there's pressure when Kent tentatively slips his cock inside the toy.

'Um, that's wild,' he says. 'It feels ... .'

'Like my hole?'

'Yes.'

With a few thrusts, Kent matches the rhythm of his fingers inside me with his cock inside the toy. The room fills with a crescendo of grunts and gasps, echoing the desire crashing over me.

'Vincent, hang on . . . I need to . . .' Kent's fingers withdraw, and he collapses on the bed. My heart races, and I quickly move next to him.

'Are you all right?' His heavy breathing alerts me, and I gently kiss his cheek above his beard.

'Yes, just cramping. My legs. I can't do that, stand while . . . doing that for too long.'

I run my thumb under the smooth, soft leather across his chest, checking it's not too tight. There's plenty of room, and his breathing seems to steady.

'Why don't we stop,' I suggest.

'Are you kidding?' He lifts his head and points to his cock, still rock hard, aimed directly at us.

'Don't move,' I instruct.

Retrieving the toy from the floor, I sit next to Kent, take hold of his cock, and guide it in. Using both hands, I slowly begin fucking him with it. Soft moans escape his mouth, and when his hand reaches for my waist, I shift my hips, allowing him better access to my hole. Recognizing my hint, the two fingers sending me over the edge a few minutes ago easily slip back inside.

'Holy fuck,' he purrs.

'Am I a good boy now?'

'So good. The best boy. You get a gold star. No, two!'

My gaze ping-pongs between my hands clutching the toy and the mirror, and seeing his cock plunge in and out of the toy from both angles makes my mouth water. A laugh spills out of my mouth, followed by a whimper, when Kent's fingers burrow deeper again. Shockwaves pulse through my body as the suction noises from the toy being fucked by Kent's fat cock fill the room.

'I'm close,' he says. 'What do I do?'

I pull the toy off him, and there's a sudden, loud snapping noise when his dick pops out. Taking him in my hands, I do my best to take over, jerking him fast as his fingers fuck me deeper.

'Vincent, I'm going to . . . Do you want it? On you?'

Being covered in Kent Lester? 'Yes, sir. Please. Come on me.'

Moving my head closer, I aim his cock near my cheek. Kent shakes, his hips thrust up, and warm liquid blasts my face, pooling and then slowly sliding down my cheek. With a quick glance at my reflection, I see my face adorned with Kent Lester's orgasm, and I'm unable to hide my smirk.

'I'm so close.' I push back onto his hand. 'Keep fucking me with your fingers. Please.'

'How deep?'

I'm not sure how much further he can possibly go, so I say, 'All in.'

'Of course,' he says, taking over as I focus on my cock. His fingers, deep inside, my body fused with his, the thought of us being so close, connected, and with only a few strokes, I'm ready.

Sensing I'm on the brink, Kent says, 'On me. Come on me.'

Without taking my hand off myself, I kneel next to him and ask, 'Where? Quick . . .'

'Right here,' he says, pointing to his open mouth.

Reaching up, Kent thrusts his fingers inside, caressing and massaging depths I never knew existed. My orgasm charges through me like a freight train, shooting long, thick ribbons of cum toward his face. As he opens his mouth, some of it lands on his tongue while the majority finds its way onto his bushy beard. My hole clenches around Kent's fingers with each spasm, releasing any tension my body clings to. 'That's my good boy. All over. Every drop.' Kent pulls me closer and licks at the head of my cock. 'Good boy.'

Using his free hand, he wipes the cum from his beard, popping two fingers into his mouth and sucking as much off as possible.

Finished and drained, I collapse next to him, snuggling up to his chest.

'Wow,' he says. We're both momentarily still. 'That was fucking hot.'

He cranes his neck, and his lips brush the top of my head, slowly sprinkling my entire dome with mini kisses.

'Look.' He nods toward the mirror opposite the bed. 'Look at how beautiful you are.'

Our naked bodies, my arms wrapped around Kent, reflect back and seeing us like this stirs something in my soul. Like two LEGO pieces snapped together, we fit perfectly.

Unable to move, I lie on Kent's bed, enjoying the view.

'Do you want a shower?' he asks, but my buzzing brain

can't quite string words together. I nestle into his chest, the soft hair soothing me.

'Hungry?'

'Meh,' I eke out.

Kent lies next to me, and I bury my face into his torso.

'C'mere.' He wraps his arm around me. 'Whenever you're ready, my sweet boy.' Kent plants a soft kiss on my head and squeezes me close. 'I got you.'

30

Kent

'What exactly would you need to pet him?'

Sweetums sits on the edge of the island, staring. Not at me, the man who feeds, brushes, and scoops his litter. Not at the simple breakfast of toast with various butters and jams. At Vincent. Determined to win this new human over, Sweetums won't relent until he succeeds.

Vincent, with his long eyelashes, pulling my focus at the most inopportune times. Vincent. Last night. Lying on my bed. Naked. Undone. Because of me. The leather harness. The toy. The lube. My cock. My fingers. Inside him. My face warms, and I tilt my head and smile at Vincent. School. My apartment. Everything seems brighter with him near.

'An army of nurses in hazmat suits scrubbing me down. A giant vat of disinfectant. A truckload of wipes. A mountain of napkins.'

'If I were to arrange this for you,' I say, spreading peanut butter on my toast, 'exactly which option would you prefer?'

'Ummm . . . I have to pick one?'

A sly smile creeps across Vincent's face, and the urge to throw him on the island and kiss every inch of his body overtakes me.

'All of them. Got it. I'll begin preparations.' I bite into my toast, the creamy peanut butter coating my throat.

Hearing our plan, Sweetums lies down, exposing his belly to Vincent and bobbling his head back and forth.

'You realize he has a crush on you,' I say.

'The cat?'

'Yes, the cat. Look at him.' Sweetums reaches a tentative paw in Vincent's direction. 'He's flirting with you.'

'Well, please ask him to stop.'

'He's right there.' I nod in Sweetums's direction. 'Ask him yourself.'

Vincent wipes his mouth with a napkin, unfolds it, and holds it up, creating a makeshift shield between them.

'Cat. You can stop it right now, please. You're barking up the wrong tree.'

He lowers the napkin, sits, and takes another nibble of toast.

'You're ridiculously charming, but no,' I say. 'He knows his name. You have to use it. And cats don't bark.'

'He heard me.'

It seems monumental for Vincent to eat while Sweetums lies just a couple of feet away. Maybe they'll never be best buds but coexisting this way would be more than acceptable. I pet Sweetums's back, lean down, and kiss his giant head right between his furry pointy ears. 'Who's my good boy?'

Chewing his dry toast, Vincent raises an eyebrow and smiles at me.

'Are we ready for next week?' I ask.

'The go-live?'

I nod. 'The switchover. The staff. The systems. All of it.'

'The test data worked like a charm,' Vincent says, wiping his plump lips. 'The staff is prepared. I'll have the online documentation ready to supplement the binders we gave them.'

'Teachers love binders,' I say. 'So many binders.'

'Geoff assured me the tech side is set. Your servers have been upgraded. Shreya helped with all of that. Really, all we need is the new extract file for the entire school and to flip the switch. Once all the school's old data populates Hopscotch, we're done.'

'It's that simple?' I ask. 'And before you answer, remember, checking email on my phone confuses me.'

'It should be. I mapped the data. We'll bring GradePlus down on Friday after you do the final export, prepare the data, and start the transfer. Then we wait.'

'Wait for what?' I ask. Sweetums, momentarily giving up on Vincent, jumps to the bench in the front window to sunbathe.

'For the transfer. It should finish by Sunday morning.'

'And we just sit at school waiting?'

'Gosh, no. We monitor from home. The system will send an alert if there's an error or any issues.'

'Errors? Issues?' My stomach does a quick flip. 'We don't have room for errors or issues.'

'That's why we get alerts. Geoff monitors for tech issues. Servers crashing. Timeouts. Bugs. And I'll get any messages about the data transfer.'

'Bugs? Like ants?'

'Oh, you handsome man,' Vincent says, gently tugging at my beard. 'No, technical bugs. Flaws. Imperfections. Mistakes.'

'So, all weekend, you just sit at home?'

'Yeah, I'll probably work on Paris. Why don't you come over?'

'Can I help?'

'With what?'

'Paris.'

'No, mon ami,' Vincent says in a horrible French accent. 'I prefer to work alone.'

My teeth nibble at my bottom lip as thoughts of this major process and the associated steps swirl in my head. Vincent seems confident everything will go smoothly, and I'm choosing to trust him. He knows what he's doing. He's done it before. My role is minimal. The data extract is a few clicks. It's out of my hands after that. I slather blueberry jam on my toast and take a bite. Jelly oozes onto my beard, and Vincent hands me two napkins.

'Mr Lester,' Ruth says as I join her out front to wait for the drop-offs. The loop in front of the school allows car drop-offs to unload and depart quickly. That's the idea, anyway. Often, backpacks are open, lunches are on the car floor, children are stuck in car seats, and dogs need goodbye kisses. Ruth and I do our best to move the process along to prevent a backup.

'Ms Parrish, how are you?'

The line of cars reaches the street, but we don't start the process until exactly seven-thirty. This way, teachers are in their rooms, awaiting students. Ruth and I stand at the ready. We don't walk on Thursdays because she plays volleyball on Wednesday nights, so this is our time to chat.

'Tired.'

'Late game?'

'Nah. The game ended around eight. It was the after-game festivities that kept me up.'

I glance at my watch and nod.

'You have exactly three minutes until children come flooding out of cars.'

'Four words. Locker room shower shenanigans.' She puts a finger up with each word.

'Oh? Sounds . . . interesting.'

'Melissa. The new woman.'

I put a hand up. 'Wait, let me guess. You didn't know if she was queer. But now you do.'

Ruth closes her eyes and nods, relishing her ability to attract almost anyone.

'And you seem a little extra chipper this morning,' she says. 'Does it have something to do with a word that rhymes with "feather?"'

I make a fist near my head before opening it with a loud explosion noise crackling from my mouth.

'Damn,' Ruth says, her face split by an enormous grin, and right on cue, car doors fly open.

Like two whack-a-moles, Ruth and I pop in and out of cars, prodding children out to keep the cars flowing. We work in tandem, moving past each other to reach the next vehicle, and my chest swells when the line dwindles.

In the flurry of little bodies rushing into the building, I don't notice Brodie charging at me like a baby rhino until he crashes into me. His arms wrap around my waist, squeezing me with the force of a boa constrictor.

'Mr Lester, good morning!' Brodie's mom shouts from the driver's seat. In his eagerness to dart over, he's left the car door open, and she's trapped until someone closes it.

'Good morning!' I call back. 'Brodie, let's shut the door so Mom can get to work.'

I glance down, and his face remains hidden in the curve of my stomach. When Brodie's parents brought him to kindergarten screening, they informed us they 'knew something was off' and 'needed help.' They listened and nodded as I explained how we'd care for their son. The school was now part of Team Brodie. Almost two years have passed, and he's finally getting that evaluation.

'I got it,' Ruth calls, jogging over from the car behind and slamming the door.

'Thank you, Ms Parrish!' his mom shouts and drives off.

I pull Brodie's hand from my back and gently hold it.

'Want me to walk you inside?' His eyes finally meet mine and he nods. 'Let's go find Mr Soleskin.'

We head into the building, Brodie's small hand gripping mine, and make our way to his classroom. The warmth from his tiny fingers in mine travels up my arm and swells in my chest. The entire school is rallying behind Brodie, and I know he's going to be okay.

'Nice shirt, boss,' Helen teases.

With spring looming, I finally broke down and bought some new clothes. Short-sleeved polos, khakis, and new underwear. The old ones were falling apart, and it was time. Corrine used to buy most of my clothes, which I actually liked – one less thing to worry about. Understandably, after the divorce, she assured me she'd no longer be my personal shopper. With some suggestions from Ruth, I found an online store with basic and attractive clothes. I'm wearing a cream shirt with a solid navy-blue stripe across the chest today. Apparently, it's now my lot in life to have things splashed across my torso.

'Hey, we can't all pull off a denim jumper,' I say, and Helen's eyes crinkle as she smiles.

'The Hopscotch crew is already in the conference room,' she says. 'I told them we'll need it for the IEP meeting at eleven.'

'No worries. I'll handle it,' I say. Not only does Helen take care of the entire school, but she's also always watching out for me. Pausing at her desk, I ask, 'How are you, Helen?'

She pulls her cocked head back and dips her chin.

'Fine? Why?'

'No reason. Just wanted to make sure you're doing well. And if you ever need anything, you let me know.'

'Sure thing,' she says. 'I could use a large black coffee. One that lasts all day. And for my husband to put his dishes in the dishwasher. He doesn't even have to turn it on. Just put them in the dishwasher.' Helen laughs and turns toward her computer. Before I make it to the conference room, she yells, 'And for the Bruins to win the Stanley Cup!'

'The server is up.' Shreya holds a cup of coffee, and I worry it might spill as she motions with her hands.

Vincent sits a few feet away, and his pinched face tells me he has the same fear.

'The performance testing went off without a hitch. Now you have to do your part,' Vincent says.

'My part,' Geoff says. 'That's all dependent on the servers being ready. And they're ready. We're good. Vincent, let's do another performance run with the first-grade data. Better safe than sorry. We have the time.'

Vincent nods and begins pecking away at his laptop.

'Need anything from me, team?' I ask, unsure what I can do.

'We're almost ready for the final data dump,' Shreya says.

'All right. That's easy.' I smile, knowing my part is within my capabilities. 'I'll do it now.'

'You'll need this.' Vincent hands me a thumb drive. Too large for email, the complete file from GradePlus needs to be copied to the small device.

'I'll have this to you in a little bit.' I stand at the door, holding the drive up. 'If you need anything, just holler.'

Vincent's eyes glance up from his screen and the dawning of his magnificent smile appears. My lips tingle, and I quickly lick them, hoping he hollers.

31

Vincent

'At your service. Corrine is checking on Sweetums. I'm all yours.'

'Thank you, Corrine,' I say as Kent leans in to kiss his favorite spot on my neck. His lips land on the sensitive skin right above my collarbone, and his scruff scratches in all the right ways, dispatching goosebumps over my entire body. Heading into a go-live weekend should have me riddled with anxiety, but Kent's here with takeout. Kissing my neck.

Kent does a little bow in my doorway while holding plastic takeout bags with the familiar Purple Giraffe logo, a duffel, and a large gift bag.

'My favorite.'

'Wait, the food or the guy?' he asks, heading for the kitchen island.

'Both.'

Sometimes, the expected can be a salve for the soul.

'What's this?' I ask, lifting the sparkly present and attempting to gauge its contents. The shiny blue bag dwarfs the plastic takeout ones, but its contents seem relatively light.

'A gift.'

'For me?'

'Yes, smoothie,' he says, kissing my nose, 'for you. For later.' He puts the bag on the floor next to the island. 'So, we're really just going to go about our weekend like something huge isn't happening?' Kent unpacks the containers of food from the bag.

'I mean, sort of.' I place plates on the island, making their familiar clang as ceramic hits granite. 'If there are any errors, we'll know.' I shake my phone. 'Geoff's monitoring his end, and any data errors route to me.'

'Are you hungry?' he asks, pulling a stack of napkins from the dedicated drawer. My heart melts because he remembers where they are. That I need them.

'Yes, but first,' I say, nuzzling into his chest, the warmth of his breath on my head, 'I'd love a Mr Lester appetizer.'

'Oh, would you?'

I nod, and my hand moves to his pants.

'Vincent, I'm actually a little uneasy. About the go-live.'

A tiny knot forms in my stomach, and I sigh. If Kent's nerves are cockblocking me, I need to do my best to soothe him.

'It's going to be fine. I promise.'

'I hope so.' Kent's fingers tug at his beard, pulling and twisting. 'But after. Once you're done. I have less than three months with Hopscotch to show the board . . .'

'If they don't already know how amazing you and every human in that building are, what are they doing serving on the board?'

'That's an excellent question.'

With a heavy sigh, Kent drops his shoulders. 'Distract me,' he says. My hand tugs at his waistband. 'With food and LEGOs.'

'LEGO.'

'Excuse me?' he asks.

'LEGO, no *s* necessary. Per an official statement from the company. There are LEGO bricks, pieces, parts, but never LEGOs with an *s*.'

'You're a nerd, you know that?'

'I do.' My head lands on his shoulder, the softness of his fleece comforting.

'Distract me with LEGO.'

'Deal. Let's eat first,' I say.

'Once we know it's all working, you can be my good boy.'

'Yes, sir.' I wrap my arms around Kent's waist, my hands caressing his sides, as our foreheads touch and something magical conjures between us. There's a closeness – a sweetness. More than simply physical, somehow, we're becoming an *us*. Breathing him in, my body fills with a sense of warmth and comfort. I never thought this would happen to me.

With full bellies, cleared dishes, and washed hands and faces, we head to the dining-room table.

'Now, for your present.' Kent fetches the gift bag and hands it to me with a flourish. 'To celebrate the go-live.'

'We shouldn't celebrate until Monday. When it's all over.'

'Okay, then I'll just keep this until Monday.' He grabs the white corded handle.

'No, no,' I protest, pulling the bag away. 'Now. Let's celebrate now.'

Kent laughs and grabs me instead of his gift. He scatters kisses over my neck, crawling up to my cheek and landing on my nose. He sighs softly and whispers, 'My handsome boy.'

Sitting in one of the gray cloth-covered chairs around the table, I remove the tissue paper and spy a large black box. The logo on the bottom instantly clues me in. LEGO. My lips part, but only a small gasp escapes.

'It's The Louvre. For Paris,' he says. 'You don't have it yet. At least I didn't see it. I can return it. I kept the receipt.'

For a moment, I'm unsure what to say. My parents and I agreed to stop exchanging presents years ago, and I honestly can't remember the last time I received a gift. And this is LEGO. From Kent. I hug the box to my chest and squeeze it tightly. 'I love it. Yeah, LEGO definitely is my love language.'

'And I adore that about you.' He kisses my neck from behind. 'Were you planning to include it?'

'For sure. I hadn't decided whether to build it from scratch or with the kit.'

'Oh, I'm sorry,' Kent says, pulling his hands behind his back. 'I didn't mean to . . .'

'No. You helped me decide.'

I stand and wrap my arms around him, and when he exhales, and his body melts into mine, a lightness overtakes me. This kind, caring man, eager to please, unearths my heart. And with his head resting on my shoulder, I softly say, 'You know. Things seem to be better lately.'

'Things?'

Holding Kent. Here. I'm amazed at how relaxed I am. I've grown so accustomed to being tight, compressed, restless. Kent somehow has become the ultimate distraction. It's like I'm floating on a cloud. Even when I'm not with him, the power of his affection lingers. The urge to tell him more, connect more, prods me.

'Me.'

We stand in my living room, overlooking LEGO Paris, clinging to each other. 'Because of you.' I lean my forehead on his. 'You don't try to fix me.'

Kent sees me. All of me. He understands me. For once in my life, I don't shatter into a million pieces.

Kent brushes his nose on mine. His sweet breath blankets my face and he whispers, 'Because you're not broken.'

My mouth falls on his. His beard, needing a trim, tickles my lips, but the urge to have him near overrides the sensation. And breathing him in this way, the nerves on my face relent and settle.

Kent feels like home.

'Now,' I say, 'Paris awaits.'

Moving to the clearest end of the table, I open Kent's gift, carefully pulling out the plastic bags and placing each one on the table. Finally, the thick book of directions appears, and I hand them to Kent.

'I'm thinking you're a directions guy,' I say.

'Oh really,' Kent says, thumbing through the fat pamphlet. 'Well, I'll have you know . . .' He juts his chin out and says, 'I am *totally* a directions guy. Especially when I have no idea what I'm doing. Which is most of the time.'

'I'll empty the first few bags.' I pinch and pull the first

one. 'They're numbered, and each number corresponds to the instructions.'

'You realize there's no text.' Kent holds the book up, showing me the first set of directions. 'Only pictures. How am I supposed to tell you what to do?'

'Ah, this is where your excellent verbal skills come into play.' I smile brightly at him and dump the bag's contents into a small white bowl. The bricks clink as they hit the ceramic glaze, and the familiar sound prompts a contented sigh. 'LEGO markets around the world. Look how many pages that book has already. Now imagine it in dozens of languages.'

Kent nods as he flips the pages.

'And children who aren't reading yet are some of the biggest consumers. So' – I point to an image – 'pictures tell the story.'

'Okay, well, let's see . . .' Kent tilts his head slightly. 'I guess you take a . . .'

'What's the element?' I ask. 'Which kind of piece? A brick? Plate?'

Kent rubs his face, and the booklet falls from his hands, hitting the table and falling to the floor.

'Oh, babe,' I say. 'You need a LEGO lesson.'

'Be gentle with me,' he says. 'My brain is sharp as a tack, but my fingers don't always cooperate.'

'Kent, your fingers are fucking amazing.' I take his hand in mine, massaging the tips.

'Now, this is a brick.' I place a piece in his palm. 'It's the basic building block of LEGO. They come in all different sizes and colors. This one is cream and is a two-by-four. There are two rows, and each has four studs.'

'Who are you calling a stud?' he asks, curling his fingers around the brick and my hand.

'No, the brick's studs.' I lean over, and he kisses my neck. 'These,' I say, pulling back and pointing to the bumps on the top of the brick, 'are called studs.'

Kent's brow furrows, and he nods.

'This is a plate.' I grab a black one from a bowl. 'It's identical to the brick, only it's flat, and the brick is thick.'

'Thick, got it.' He thumbs the brick.

Tilting my head, I say, 'I thought you weren't in the mood.'

'I wasn't, but your enthusiasm is getting me all worked up.' Kent dots my nose with a kiss.

'This is a tile,' I say, handing him one. 'No studs.'

'Well, that's no fun.'

'They're decorative finishing pieces.'

He chuckles, puts the pieces back in the bowl, and gathers me up in his arms.

'You are something else,' he says. 'You know that.'

My heartbeat ramps up, and the warmth from Kent's embrace envelops me. Sharing this with him is a big deal. He's interested. Curious. Patient.

'There are plates, baseplates, jumper plates, even cheese graters,' I say, 'but let's go slow.'

Pulling back, Kent's fingers find my chin and pull my focus. His pupils study my face, and a tender smile pokes through his beard.

'I love you, Vincent.'

Tears prickle my eyes. Even before the words left his mouth, I felt it. From him. For him. How do you define something you've never felt? You experience it, and then someone presents you with the vocabulary. Kent's helped me grasp the true meaning of the word, and maybe, just maybe, even with all my imperfections, he actually means it.

If I could peer inside my torso, I imagine my heart glows with a soft, pulsating light. Radiating a warmth, an energy. I'm rarely comfortable in my own skin. I'm unsure of almost everything. But with Kent, I'm grounded. Safe. Cherished. Open.

I lean into Kent. My lips brush his and I pull back and meet his gaze. 'I love you, too.'

32

Kent

'There's my kitty boy.'

Sweetums, perched on my kitchen island, stares intensely as I walk toward him. His body retracts like he's pondering bolting away, but I snag him first, pulling him close and kissing his head.

'Did you miss me? I missed you.'

And I did. After an hour of unpacking, sorting, and preparing to build the LEGO Louvre, Vincent, spurred by my incessant yawning, stopped us and took me to bed. After twenty minutes of phenomenal kissing and cuddling, I dozed off. Gosh, how I've missed sleeping with someone in my arms. After the twenty-year mark, Corrine and I drifted to opposite ends of the bed with only occasional cuddles. Vincent craves to be right next to me. Like his life depends on it. His skin on mine. Swapping between big and little spoons all night.

My eyes flew open just before dawn, and as I lay next to Vincent, I couldn't help but watch him sleep. His lips parted a tiny bit, eyes closed, and those gorgeous lashes on full display as I studied this sweet man. I hadn't planned to tell him I love him. It just happened. There was no stopping it. Like a bud on a tree in spring — a force of nature. I said it because I needed him to know. There was no expectation for him to say it back. But he did. So quickly. His words bloomed like a blossom on the bud. Hoped for, but never taken for granted.

My phone vibrates in my pocket. Trying to balance Sweetums while removing it proves trickier than I thought. With a sudden burst of energy, he wriggles and jumps onto the sofa, and I lose my balance and crash onto the unforgiving wood floor.

I accept the call, lift the phone to my ear, and sigh.

'Dad, you there?'

As usual, Gillian's voice sounds slightly chaotic, frantic, and frazzled. Corrine swears she gets it from me.

'Lia, cheese goes in your *mouth*, not on the wall!'

'Cheese painting?'

'I want to nurture her artistic side, but not everything takes the place of paint.'

'Go, tend to your little artist.' I push myself up off the floor and move to the sofa, grateful for the soft cushion under my tush. 'If you don't intervene, all you'll be left with is de brie.'

'De what?'

'De brie. Brie? Get it?'

Gillian groans, but I know she cherishes my dad jokes.

'Go, call me back.'

'No, I do not want to call you back. I want to talk now, and if Lia can't paint nicely, then "NO CHEESE,"' she yells, and I momentarily pull the phone away from my face.

'How are you?' she asks, forcing sweetness.

'Good, just running home to check on Sweetums, grab a few more things, and then back to Vincent's.'

'How's it going?'

'With Vincent or the new software?'

'Both.'

'The software goes live this weekend. Or transferring. Or something like that.' Once again hungry for attention, Sweetums returns to my lap and I scratch his favorite spot, under his chin.

'And that's it? It's that simple?' she asks.

'I think so. I provided a new file from the old system. Now the young people take over. Vincent is on call. He has to push a few buttons on his laptop and check for things like errors and latency and mapping and bugs. Things I know nothing about. And frankly, I'd like to keep it that way.'

'That's it?'

'Well, then everyone uses it and hopefully it helps illustrate the impact staff are having on students. We'll have the last few months to turn the ship around.'

'Dad, you already know what an amazing school Lear is. Everyone knows.'

'I know. You know. Most of the community knows. The school board, I'm not so sure.'

'And you're spending more time with him?' I hear rustling and then crinkling.

'Sour cream and onion?' I know my daughter's taste in chips mimics my own.

'Guilty. Louis hasn't found this bag yet.' More crackling, and then the loud crunching begins.

'Thick ones? With ridges?'

'Yup.'

'Great, now I want chips,' I say, licking my lips.

'You should've come here,' she mumbles through a full mouth.

'It sounds like Lia is up to no gouda.'

Silence.

'Oh, come on,' I say. 'That was a good one.' I stop petting Sweetums momentarily, and he crashes his head onto my lap.

'Dad. No.' Gillian sighs. 'But really, you should've stopped by so we could kibbitz with chips.'

'I roasted another chicken and wanted to pack it up for dinner. Vincent likes it. And I needed to check on Sweetums.' Hearing his name, Sweetums crawls up and rests his face on my free shoulder. 'Corrine feeds him and leaves. This cat requires physical affection.'

'Do you love him?'

'Of course I love him. Sweetums is my baby.' Sweetums snuggles into my neck, purring like a motorboat.

'Not the cat. Vincent. Do you love him?' The chewing has slowed, and relative silence fills the air. Vincent. With his endless quirks, napkins, wipes, and showers. Vincent, who needs me to brush my teeth before a make-out session. And that sexy fucking bald head. And the way his eyes peer at me when my cock is in his mouth. Even at my age, I'm still learning new things about myself and a lot of that has to do with Vincent.

'I do.' Sweetums cuddles closer. 'I told him. Vincent. That I love him.'

'Wait, what? When? You didn't tell me.'

'I'm telling you now.'

'Spill it.'

'It just kind of happened naturally. Last night. I told him. He told me. It wasn't a big deal.'

'Oh, Dad.' She sighs deeply, and a few chewed chip pieces hit the phone.

'This feels right,' I say. Gillian, like all good Jewish children, has a propensity to worry about her parents. 'I promise.'

'No, that was a good sigh. It is a big deal. I'm so happy for you, that's all. It's been so long since . . .'

'I know,' I say, the weight of loneliness over the last few years finally subsiding.

'And what happens after this weekend?'

'Well, typically Monday.'

'No, with Vincent. Once the implementation is over.'

I'm slightly lightheaded, so I scoot myself down. With my head comfortably nestled on the couch and my feet resting on the coffee table, I inhale deeply.

'We won't see each other at school, but otherwise, I imagine nothing changes,' I say. Sweetums adjusts himself so he's lying on my chest, face burrowed into the crook of my neck – Vincent's favorite spot.

'I hope so,' she says.

And dear God in Heaven, hear my prayer. I hope so, too.

'What's that smell?'

Vincent perches at the kitchen island, on his laptop, pecking away at a screen I don't recognize. It's dark gray and filled with lighter gray text. No pictures. No sounds.

Only bland words scroll by as he scans with scrunched eyebrows, his fingers occasionally snapping keys.

'I roasted a chicken.' I hold the bag up, but he's too engrossed in his current task. Placing the bag on the far end of the counter, I come behind him, lean in, and gently kiss his neck. Orange and honey mix with the faint sweetness of a scent that's all him. A flavor that complements the others but is distinct. A deep inhale. Maple syrup. Fresh from the tap. Slightly earthy. It's so fucking fragrant. I wish I could bottle him up. 'The chicken is for you.'

'One second, babe.'

My stomach flips at this new term of endearment, and basking in the affection, I unpack the chicken and potatoes.

'I'll make you a plate.' Taking two from Vincent's cupboard, I carefully place four slices of breast meat and two spoons of mashed potatoes on each plate, ensuring nothing touches. As I bend down into the drawer for napkins, Vincent's arms wrap around my waist, and he pulls me close.

'Thank you.' Vincent's breath falls on my neck.

'You need to eat.'

'I do. We have a long night ahead of us,' he teases.

'Are things not going well?'

'Oh no, everything's fine. I have to check a few more times before bed, but I meant a long night in Paris.' He sits and places a napkin on his lap and another beside his plate. With each passing day, Vincent becomes more familiar – his touch, his presence, the way he looks into my eyes. This comfort we're falling into, the ultimate pleasure. I haven't felt needed by someone like this in years and my face beams as I hand Vincent his plate.

'I will do my best to assist,' I say, only slightly more confident in my ability to translate the coded pictures into coherent directions for Vincent. Of course, he could look at the book himself, but then what part would I play?

'Tonight, I think you might need to do more than read the directions,' he says.

'Wait.' I put my fork and knife down. 'You're going to let me . . . touch them?'

'If you're good.' A smile inches across his beautiful face, and a warmth sprouts in my chest. Being here. With him. Eating. Talking. Building. Vincent gazes at me with that half grin that sends my insides tumbling, and fuck. I want to drink his smile up – every last drop.

33

Vincent

'Gray? Which gray? There's like fifty shades of gray.'

Booklet in hand, Kent pulls at his beard as he cocks his head back and forth.

'Fifty shades of gray? Is that a hint?' I tease, but Kent's face remains focused on the booklet. Unaware of my joke, his fingers poke in his whiskers, searching for a clue.

'They printed the directions on black paper. The grays all look the same.' He points at a page, studying. 'Do you need a degree in engineering to do this?'

'Let me see,' I say, taking the booklet. He's right. The similar shades of gray mingle on the shiny black paper, making it almost impossible to distinguish them.

'Here's what we do. Sort all the pieces, count them, and then check the inventory numbers in the back.' I flip and point to the page near the back, listing every included element and its quantity. My finger glides on the glossy paper, and the smell of ink and plastic comforts me.

'Seriously?' Kent's chin lowers to his chest with a soft sigh.

'It won't take long. You start sorting by color,' I say, placing three empty small white bowls in front of him, 'and I'll count.'

Kent sorts, and I place a sticky note in front of each bowl, ready to document the pieces.

When the bowls are almost full, and Kent's pile grows smaller, I slowly count. Kent finishes and waits, watching me methodically pick and account for each one. After each bowl, I write the number on the corresponding sticky note.

'There. Now we know which is which. See?' I point to the back inventory page. 'Forty-one.' My shoulders prickle at the odd number. 'The darkest ones, so we'll know when you see them.'

Kent's face softens. He takes the directions from me and puts them on the table. With my hand in his, he delicately brings it to his face and presses a gentle kiss on each knuckle.

'My sweet, handsome boy. We're a good team, eh?'

'We are.' I lean forward and tilt my head, offering my neck as an invitation. Kent's soft lips, his beard adding a pleasant tickle that I've grown to cherish, brush my sensitive skin.

Almost two hours later, the set actually begins to resemble the photo on the box. With clear tiles for the glass pyramid out front and the large museum building behind, the Louvre, in all its glory, takes shape in the first arrondissement of LEGO Paris on my dining-room table.

'It's going to be perfect.' I take Kent's arm and cuddle into his chest. 'I love it.'

'How much longer?' His lips brush the skin on the top of my head.

'Probably twenty minutes. Just the plates on the roof.' I point to the open spaces waiting for their finishing touches.

'Is that how long it typically takes?'

'About. I'm faster than a novice,' I say, patting his belly. 'It really depends on the experience and expertise of the builder. I'd say together we were slightly better than average.'

'I'll take it.' He plants another kiss on my head. The pressure of his lips instantly causes my shoulders to drop. I certainly could've done this myself. It would have been easier. Quicker. But working with Kent, with his questions, curiosity, glances, and kisses, is a million times better.

My phone vibrates on the kitchen island, piercing our bubble of solace. Oh right. The implementation. The system. Not everything comes down to LEGO. As I reach for my phone, a notification brings me back to reality – an error.

'I need to log in and check something,' I say, heading for my laptop. 'Why don't you snap those last few tiles on? I'll check your work after.'

'Is everything okay?' Kent nibbles his bottom lip and I'm tempted to take over for him.

'Yes, fine. I just need to confirm something.' I open my computer. 'You put those last few pieces on.'

Kent's eyebrows spring up, and a smile appears. 'Okay. I'll be careful.'

The clicking of Kent handling and snapping tiles onto bricks in the background fills the room while I log in and wait for the status screen to load. When the system message flies across the screen, I scan the error to investigate.

SYSTEM ERROR: DATABASE > 500 GIGABYTES. TURN ON COMPRESSION? Y/N

'Did you fix it?' Kent asks me – more clicking noises echo.

'Not yet.' I lower my voice. 'It's asking me about compression. This didn't happen during our testing.'

'Compression? For what?'

'The system wants to confirm the database size.'

My mind clouds with pieces clicking, Kent's voice, and Geoff's face – less than 500 gigs. My head spins with uncertainty. Is it greater or less than 500 gigs that we need compression? Greater than. Geoff told me this – more than once. My head grapples with the information when a cacophony of bricks, plates, tiles, and joiner pieces engulfs the room, joined by Kent's scream. 'Fuck!'

As I turn to see what's happening, the entire baseplate, holding the Louvre and the surrounding buildings, crashes to the floor and shatters. Hundreds of pieces fly in every direction, plinking and clanking against wood and walls. Adrenaline shoots through my entire body. My heart slams into overdrive – less than 500 gigs. The room spins. I quickly hit NO and sprint over.

'I'm so sorry,' Kent says. He's on the floor, surrounded by elements. Hours of work ruined.

'What happened?' I grab a bowl to gather pieces. My breath quickens. Dark clouds gather in my head as a storm brews in the distance.

'I don't know. I got distracted. Talking with you. Thinking about the error.'

'It's fine. I handled it.'

'The pieces were so small. And my hand slipped, and then I tried to catch myself and made it worse, and then, and then . . .' He motions to the disaster, littering the floor. Tears dust his eyes, and my heart sinks.

'We'll fix this,' I say. 'Now.'

Sweat begins on my brow. My heart reverberates in my chest cavity. Every element. Found. Retrieved. Sorted. Rebuilt. I need to restore this – all of it. Finish. Now. My fingers twitch, and I get to work.

34

Kent

Why am I so clumsy? SO FUCKING CLUMSY. Sometimes, my brain and body run on different tracks at different speeds, constantly attempting to calibrate and sync up. Talking with Vincent. The tapping on his keyboard. An error. Hopscotch. The school's reputation. Dr Cutler. The school board. My job. I'm lightheaded. Weakness creeps over me. I'm about to unravel – I'm usually able to keep the stress caused by living my life and doing my job at bay. Now, it crashes down like the shiny, smooth tiles slipping from my grasp, conjuring a LEGO nightmare.

Paris. Shattered. At least half of the sprawling city flung into the air and destroyed. Sure, they made LEGO to withstand children's rough-and-tumble play, but not an out-of-shape fifty-two-year-old man slamming into them, sending them across the room like projectile missiles. And not with such intricate, small, delicate pieces so carefully planned and placed. By Vincent. Sweet Vincent. He finally sees what a complete disaster I am and will surely hightail it out of my life. Who needs this kind of chaos? I'm the epitome of a schlemiel.

Vincent's already moved into action. On the floor, surrounded by broken buildings, elements scattered everywhere. I grab a bowl and collect pieces.

'I've got it,' he says flatly, not making eye contact. My stomach churns with nausea.

'What can I do to help?'

'Nothing. I need to do it. Myself.'

My cheeks burn, and I take a chair from the table and slide it toward the corner of the room. I cringe and shake my head in my hands, knowing I've done this to him.

'Maybe I should go,' I say.

Vincent's head shakes briskly as he quickly sorts pieces into white bowls.

'Don't.' There's a furious symphony of pieces plinking. 'Please.'

So I watch. And apologize. Vincent's furrowed brow and set jaw offer some relief. As I watch him work, swiftly selecting, snapping, and securing pieces with precision, it dawns on me. He's not upset. He's determined. Fixated. Obsessed. He's fallen into an episode. Because of me.

I'm seated about five feet away from him. He's standing now, plugging away at the rebuild. Some of the larger sections attached to baseplates weren't totaled. There's at least a semblance of a foundation. And with no directions, seemingly from memory, he's snapping and clicking things into place.

'Vincent. I'm right here,' I say. 'I'm not leaving.'

There's no answer. He works. And works. He focuses on one structure at a time, quickly returning each to its original pre-Kent-disaster glory. Not hampered by my greenness and ignorance, he works rapidly. Fingers move. Pieces snap. His hands move so swiftly, at times, they become a blur. He's a man on a mission to build. Toiling into the night, Vincent is relentless. Quiet. Focused.

I ponder asking him to stop and go to bed. But there's no way.

He needs to do this. Finish.

'Smoothie, do you need a drink?'

He shakes his head, and I carefully place a glass of water on an open area of the table.

At some point, I walk over, softly kiss his neck, and settle into the sofa. Pulling myself into a ball, I lie, watching, hypnotized by the sound of Vincent's building. Unable to keep my eyes open any longer, I whisper, 'I love you,' and doze off.

I wake up groggy, unsure where I am for a moment or what time it is. The rising sun slowly pierces the darkness outside. At the other end of the couch, Vincent lies. He's in the fetal position, his head on a throw pillow, softly sleeping. Socked feet poke at my thighs, and I'm tempted to reach down and caress them. He's safe. Near. I'm not sure he needed me to stay, but him lying so close makes me glad I did. I move toward him and kiss the top of his beautiful head. If he senses my lips, he doesn't show it. He's out. Breathing deeply.

And then I see it. LEGO Paris stretches across Vincent's dining-room table. It's as if nothing ever happened. He rebuilt every single building and structure to completion – even the Louvre. Vincent finished what I destroyed.

Softly, he stirs, and I shimmy behind him, holding him the best I can in such close quarters. I wrap my arm around his chest. It slowly rises and falls, and he moves slightly when I nuzzle my face into his neck.

'Tickles,' he murmurs. My beard. Oops. 'You're still here.'

'I told you,' I say, kissing the back of his head, 'I wasn't leaving you.'

'Mmmh.' He pushes back into me.

'Vincent, I'll be right beside you, even when it's hard.'

He exhales, his warm breath blowing the hair on my arms.

'Do you believe me?'

He nods, and I pull him closer.

Surveying his work, I'm completely in awe of his skill and speed. 'You finished it.'

'Had to. Couldn't stop.'

I pull him closer, the heat of his body against me, yearning to be even closer and savor the sensation of his skin against mine.

'I'm so sorry.' My lips brush the warm, soft skin on his head.

'It was an accident,' he whispers.

'Because I'm a klutz.'

'My klutz.'

He clutches my hand to his chest and squeezes it. Tears nip the corners of my eyes, and I do my best to melt into him. Yes, I almost ruined his masterpiece. But he's not upset. He fixed it. I'm here.

We're okay.

'What time is it?' he asks. I have no idea. No clue.

'Early. Hold on.' I reach for my phone on the coffee table to check the time.

The screen lights up at my touch, and notifications assault me. They're layered on each other, jumbled, so many I can't make sense of the clutter. I touch one, and my phone flickers on. Eight missed calls. Fourteen messages. All from Shreya within the last hour. My stomach drops. What the fuck happened?

35

Vincent

'This isn't good.'

Geoff paces the conference room. There's no soft entry this Monday morning. No coffee and cronuts. Kent texted Shreya yesterday before five a.m., and the rest of the day unfolded in a blur. By mid-morning, after scrambling to figure out next steps, I sent Kent home. Sweetums needed to be fed, and I needed to focus. As the process wasn't finished and it was already Sunday, Geoff called for a post-mortem Monday morning – mortem as in death. Post as in after. After death. Clearly, taking my eye off the prize, I made a careless, stupid error. And once again, Geoff needs to fix my fuckup.

Greater than. Less than. Taught to most first graders, I should know these symbols. And I do. Usually. Mostly. Children need to know which one is which. I remember sitting in Mrs Willow's class. Her hair pulled into a neat bun. 'Imagine it's an alligator's mouth. The hungry alligator wants more, so that's greater.' But in my seven-year-old brain, when a gator turns around, he's still hungry. But that's less. The symbol doesn't change. The direction does. To this day, as a forty-year-old grown man, I'm still confused. I misread the error message. It was greater than 500 gigs. Not less than. I should have selected yes. Turn compression on. This is a disaster. My disaster.

'Greater than 500 gigs,' Geoff says. 'There's no compression. The data set is too large.'

'Okay, what does this mean for performance?' Shreya guzzles her coffee. 'How bad is it?'

Kent sits in a chair at the end of the long conference-room table. Quiet. His face pained and searching.

'The data loaded. The system works,' Geoff begins. Kent's eyes widen, a glimmer of hope sparkling.

'But . . .' Shreya says.

'But, the load times.' Geoff shakes his head. 'The system isn't really viable this way. Because the data wasn't compressed,' he says, glancing my way, 'load times will be exorbitant.'

'How long?' I ask, my stomach still unable to hold down much since yesterday.

'Login screens, two to three minutes; individual student pages, one to two; whole class entry, at least four. Maybe longer.'

'What does this all mean?' Kent asks, scratching at his temple.

'The data's all there.' Shreya taps her keyboard. 'Technically, we could go live.'

'But,' Geoff continues, 'it will take so long for screens to load that nobody can use it functionally.'

'Teachers won't sit and wait that long for screens to load,' Shreya says. 'Nobody would.'

'So what do we do?' Kent asks. 'How do we fix this?'

'Start over,' Shreya says.

Geoff nods his head.

'Start over?' Kent asks, rubbing his eyes. 'But the school board meeting is Thursday. I'm supposed to report out on next steps.'

'If we restart it now,' Geoff says, 'it should be done by . . .'

'Wednesday,' Shreya finishes. 'Afternoon. If we're lucky.'

'And this time, compress the database.' Geoff gives me a pointed stare.

'Okay, that's what we do then. What do you need from me?' Kent asks.

'Communicate with teachers,' Shreya says. 'Let them know there was an issue. Leave it at that. In the meantime, I'll run some data analysis tests on the live data behind the scenes. It's an opportunity to check it.' Shreya pokes at her laptop, opening windows and swiping them to corners of the screen. 'Hopefully, we'll be up and running with the optimized system by Wednesday evening. Thursday morning at the latest. We'll let them know. For now, continue using GradePlus.'

Kent stands and heads to his office. Shreya and Geoff huddle around their computers, talking, tapping, and taking action to restart the conversion go-live process. My body aches from the lack of sleep and the general malaise of defeat. This is it. There's no way I'm keeping my job after another misstep. I'm unsteady and dizzy as I stumble out of the conference room.

Kent's at Helen's desk. Her head is down, pen to

pad, taking notes as he speaks. I wander past them into Kent's office and collapse into a chair around his table. My heart, still beating faster than normal, seems to have migrated to my throat. The throbbing makes it difficult to swallow. I'm not sure if it's worth me even staying. Should I give Geoff my resignation and go home? Take a long, hot shower and lose myself in LEGO. Kent's got to be furious. Or at least disappointed. Embarrassed. I retrieve a napkin from my bag, clutch it in my fist, and wait for the tears behind my eyelids to emerge, but they don't.

The door clicks, and Kent stands above me. I shake my head and stare at his feet. Lowering himself to a kneel, Kent's face comes into view, and my eyes close.

'Vincent. Look at me.'

'Kent. I'm sorry. I know it's over.'

'The implementation?'

'No. Us.' The toast I choked down this morning creeps up, and I'm not sure I can hold it in. Naturally, I had to do something that would only further highlight what a disaster I am to Kent.

My eyes search his face for clues. There's no hint of a smile and the coolness he's exhibiting frightens me. My stomach swirls, and all I can think is that vomiting in front of Kent right now would be the feather in the shitstorm of a hat I'm wearing. Lightheadedness takes hold of me, and my cheeks grow cold as the blood drains from my face.

'Vincent Manda. You're not getting rid of me that easily. You made a mistake.' Kent wobbles before regaining his balance. 'And my clumsiness was at least part of the reason. This isn't the end of the world. We're only losing a few days. It will be fine.'

'But, but . . .' I stutter.

'But nothing. When I told you I love you, I meant it. No matter what. We'll get through this.' He takes my hand. 'Together.'

'Dr Cutler,' I say. 'The board meeting. We won't be ready. You won't be ready.'

My breathing becomes heavy. Tension builds in my chest as my heart begins to gallop.

'You need to breathe,' Kent urges.

'I can't . . .' I pant, clutching my torso. 'Can't get enough air.'

He rubs my palm with soothing circles. 'Breathe.' A hand moves to my chest. 'Let me be your air. Deep breaths.'

I close my eyes and inhale. Slowly. I push the air out of my lips. Kent whispers, 'There's my handsome boy.'

A loud knock startles us and Kent rises, but before he can say anything, the door opens.

'This is bad.' Shreya stands against the frame, staring at the laptop balanced on her arm.

'I know.' Kent pulls out a chair for her. 'It was a mistake. We lost a few days. We'll restart and go from there. I'll explain things to Dr Cutler and the board.'

'Not the database. The data . . .' Shreya sits and taps at her screen. 'Look.'

Kent and I lean over Shreya's shoulder, attempting to make sense of the tables and figures in front of us.

'These scores are too high.' She points to a document with comparison figures. 'This didn't happen during testing. How did these get inflated?' Shreya and I both turn toward Kent. The data extract came from him.

Kent's eyes go wide, and his shoulders make a beeline toward his ears. 'I have no idea.'

Shreya begins clicking, screens fly by in a blur.

'What happened?' I ask.

'Here.' She clicks a few keys, and then points. 'We're supposed to feed individual student data for each assessment. Hopscotch gives each one a weight and averages it. But this data export from GradePlus pulled averages.' There's more typing and pointing. 'And then populated those averages across each student's year to date. We're averaging averages.' Shreya shakes her head, sending her top knot into a tizzy. 'And it looks like we're cooking the books.'

'I-I-I don't know what happened. I extracted the data file like I always do,' Kent stammers. 'I wouldn't even know how to do what you're saying.'

Shreya clicks a few more keys and brings up the antiquated back-end settings screen for GradePlus. 'We had the setting correct in GradePlus, but when you changed the criteria to pull for the entire school, it reverted to pulling averages for the export.' Shreya clicks a tab near the top of her screen. 'Here. Right here. Look.'

'Why would it do that?' Kent asks.

'I don't know.' Shreya snaps her laptop closed. 'This software predates Nintendo 64. It could be a glitch, but we can't use this data. We need a new file. Stat.'

'Okay, hold on.' Kent's at his desk, opening his laptop.

'Let's do it together.' Shreya heads to Kent's side and I take her seat.

'There. You have to click that box.' She points at Kent's screen. 'The system reset it after you changed the criteria.' Shreya turns and the color drains from her face. 'Honestly, the database issue is small potatoes compared to this. We could have gone live with the slower load times, but this impacts the integrity of the entire system. We have to reload the data. Revalidate everything. Repeat user-acceptance testing. Get final sign off from teachers. This sets us back ... weeks.'

'Weeks?' Kent says with a heavy sigh as Shreya pecks away at his keyboard. 'We don't have weeks. We only have a few months left in the school year.'

With the thumb drive containing the new export in hand, Shreya heads back to the conference room to explain the error and restart the process.

'I wasn't sure the situation could get any worse, but somehow I found a way.' Kent slumps in his chair, his chin lowered to his chest.

'I messed up the database,' I say.

'And I provided inaccurate data. The process would have needed to be restarted regardless. I've derailed the project completely. By weeks.' Kent scrubs a hand through his beard, tugging. 'I'm meeting with Florence this afternoon. I'll explain it was my fault. I mismanaged things. Didn't provide accurate data.'

'But, we have a new file now.' My hands rest on Kent's shoulders, attempting to pacify him.

'Not now,' Kent spits. He jerks away and my fingers fall like rain. His voice trembles and my stomach ties in knots. 'How did I mess this up so royally?'

I stand back, my hands stinging from his rebuff. Kent's

brow beads with sweat and I eye the box of tissues on his desk.

'I'm sorry. I-I . . . I'll go.' My gaze falls on the door, but my feet don't move.

'I just need to think.' Kent's head falls into his hands. 'Please. I'll figure it out.'

I leave with tears stinging my eyes, and head straight for my car. My feet move under me, but I'm unaware of the ground. Something crunches underfoot, stopping me in my tracks. Glancing down, I see the culprit. Almost unrecognizable, a muddy two-by-four blue brick stares up at me. Even covered in mud and grime, it's the most perfect piece.

And then it hits me. All those first dates. All those men. It wasn't them having an issue with me. Not the napkins. Not the wiping. It was me. I was always searching for a quick escape hatch – a way to dodge potential pain. But Paris fell. The implementation failed. Kent's reaction. And I'm still here. Loving Kent Lester. And more importantly, finally loving myself. I need to find a way to fix this.

36

Kent

'Kent, please reconsider.'

Every wrinkle and line on the pale skin of Florence Cutler's face, a badge of honor from her almost forty years in education, emits empathy. This woman has a job I don't envy. The buck stops with her, and every complaint and major decision lies on her shoulders. Calling the snow days alone would turn the few remaining dark hairs I have gray. No, thank you. She's not buying what I'm selling, but I don't relent.

'I recognize this doesn't look good,' she says. 'But maybe if I explain it was an honest mistake caused by an ancient system we're trying to replace. Ms Shaan could walk me through it. Provide screenshots. This was a simple mistake. Anyone who knows you realizes you'd never do this on purpose.' Florence pinches her lips together. 'I can buy time with the board. We have a month until the next board meeting. It will cost the district . . . more, but they always have money tucked away. We're starting over. We'll have the accurate data in a few weeks. There's more time to train teachers. I can spin this.'

Sitting across from Florence Cutler, my job – no, my career – on the line, I should cling to her words. She's attempting to throw me a lifeline as I flail in open seas. I sigh at the weight of this failure on my shoulders. My breath catches in my chest, and when I open my mouth to speak, only a puff of air escapes.

'Let me do the talking at the board meeting,' Florence says. 'I'm used to taking heat from them.'

My head shakes softly. If Vincent and I had never met before this mess, would the outcome be different? Perhaps. But I love him. I want him more than anything right now. I want this to be over.

'I think this is it,' I say. 'For me. Here. I mean, after this school year.'

'Kent, no,' she says, putting her hand up.

'I'm going to offer my resignation to the board. I'll have my letter to you by Thursday morning.'

'I'm not accepting it.' Florence's jaw muscles firm into a rigid line.

I chuckle. Her stubbornness is part of why I've enjoyed working for her. The last few months with Vincent have shown me what a horrible job I've done with balancing work and life. Complete shit. Why do they call it work-life balance and not life-work balance? Why does 'work' always come first? My first date in literally seven years. Since Corrine. I owe her an apology for being such a career-focused schmuck. When did life become so complicated?

'Well, you'll have it. Thursday.'

I muster up my best smile for her and head back to my car.

Back to Lear. I want Hopscotch to be a success. If the team needs me, I'll be there for them. For Vincent. My heart thuds in my chest as I pull onto the road and return to school.

'What will you do now?' Gillian tucks her feet under her body, and Sweetums lies on her lap like a giant orange furry blanket.

'For work? To fill my time? To support myself?'

'Yes. All of it.'

'I'm not sure. I have some savings. Maybe bag groceries somewhere. Or stock shelves. I need health insurance until I'm fifty-five and can access the state program.'

'You can always come live with us.' Gillian rubs Sweetums's chin.

'I'm not living with you. Yet. But thank you.' I lean over and kiss her forehead – my sweet angel.

'Don't you think you should be there?'

'At the school board meeting?' I check my watch. 'No. It's already started. They'll be doing their opening business. It's over. Dr Cutler will explain what happened.'

'I'll go with you,' Gillian says. 'Louis is on bedtime duty.'

'I'd rather not.' I swallow rapidly at the thought of standing before the school board and admitting what happened. No way. Vacation starts tomorrow – a week off. The board will have plenty of time to find my replacement before next year, and I can deal with the fallout and begin the transition process afterward.

'And what about him?' Gillian asks.

'Vincent?'

She nods, Sweetums's purring providing a soothing soundtrack to our conversation.

'I'll see him tomorrow night. He's supposed to have a few more days at Lear to tie up loose ends before moving on to the next school. I'm not sure if they'll stay longer now. That's probably up to the board. But we're good.'

'Well, that's a relief,' she says. 'At least you didn't lose your job and your guy.'

I chuckle at her calling him 'my guy,' but she's right.

'I didn't lose my job.' I squeeze her shoulder. 'I resigned.'

'Noted.' Sweetums has gone belly up, and Gillian massages his stomach while he paws at her sleeve. 'You know I took an allergy pill for you,' she says as Sweetums stares up at her.

The ringing of my cell phone, which sits on the coffee table, startles us, mostly Sweetums, who darts off toward the comfort of his food bowl.

'Are you ready for Lia to start kindergarten next year?'

'Dad, your phone. Aren't you going to answer it?'

Shaking my head, I give a slight shrug to show my indifference. It's oddly satisfying, ignoring my phone. Gillian picks it up, gives it a quick glance, and then presents the screen to me.

'It's Vincent. Calling you. Answer it, or else I will.'

Recalling how he left my office, my heart aches to hear his voice. I slide the blinking arrow at the bottom of the display and put the phone to my ear.

'Hello?'

Gillian cocks her head and squints.

'Kent. You have to hear this,' Vincent whispers. 'Listen.'

The echoing sound of Dr Cutler's voice in the café-gymatorium. Her amplified voice bounces off folding chairs and the gym floor. Vincent's at the school board meeting. Alone. I close my eyes and focus on Florence's words.

'. . . after Mr Lester explained his error with the Hopscotch data, we discussed the idea of failure. I'd like to tell the board about this "failure" and why Kent Lester, Lear's principal, is to blame.'

I attempt to swallow, but the saliva gets stuck in my throat, and I cough instead.

'What, what's he saying?' Gillian asks.

I put my hand up and yank the phone away from my face, quickly jamming my thumb on the little icon to switch it over to speaker.

'I once gave a commencement speech for my alma mater . . . go Bears . . . where I urged the students to go out and fail. Fail big. Fail often. The successes we achieve. The big ones. The wins with trophies, prizes, and awards are all the fruit of our failures. Installing software like Hopscotch is a massive swing. And sometimes, when you swing, you knock it out of the park. This was not one of those times. This was more of a . . . what do you call it?'

'A whiff,' a voice from the crowd yells.

'Yes, a whiff. But it's from those . . . whiffs that we learn. And those whiffs, those trials and errors, and yes, complete failures, that's how we learn who we truly are. What we're made of. What we're good at.'

Sweetums returns from his temporary panic, Gillian picks him up, and scoots over. Snuggled up next to me like she did when she was smaller, I wrap my arm around her. Sweetums now drapes over both our laps, fully content to anchor us here with the phone in my hand.

'And Mr Lester, with this failure, revealed more of

who he is. What he's made of. What he's good at. Friends, would you please come up?'

I hear rustling, some commotion, and then a new voice fills the room.

'My name is Ruth Parrish. I'm the PE teacher at Lear, and I'm here to tell you what Hopscotch can't.' My stomach drops. Ruth has the capacity and desire to read the entire board to filth. 'I'm here to tell you how much the teachers and students adore Kent Lester.' Clapping begins slowly before erupting into applause. A tear falls from Gillian's right eye, and I use my thumb to catch it. My chest swells, hearing my friend's voice.

'Mr Lester is here before the crack of dawn and always one of the last to leave,' Ruth continues once the noise subsides. 'He puts his whole heart into making Lear a special place for everyone. It doesn't matter if you're the school custodian, the secretary, or one of the hundreds of children who come to school daily; Mr Lester takes the time to be present. To listen. To care.'

Moisture prickles the corners of my eyes. Giving praise has always been a strength of mine, but taking it? Not so much.

'And there's one more person who'd like to say something,' Ruth says.

There's noise: metal and feedback.

'My name is Brodie, and I love Mr Lester.'

And now the tears fall, and it's Gillian's turn to wipe my face.

'He lets me go with Theo the custodian when I earn points with Mr Soleskin. They're boyfriends.' Small laughter erupts from the audience. 'And he lets me eat lunch in his office when the lunchroom is too loud, which is almost every day. Kids are noisy. And he gives the best hugs. That's all. I'm done.'

More chuckles from the crowd, and again, someone adjusts the stand. Florence, back at the mic, says, 'Thank you, Ms Parrish. Brodie. You just heard how Mr Lester makes the people at Lear feel. That doesn't change where we are with the implementation. We've lost time and money. But there's a famous quote by Maya Angelou which I'd like to paraphrase for you. "The people we meet on our journey through life may forget what we say, and they may forget what we do. But they will always remember how we make them feel." Kent Lester makes people hopeful. Proud. Courageous. Loved.'

Gillian's arm wraps around my shoulders, and she leans her head on me.

'Therefore, we'll move forward with the Hopscotch implementation. We'll look at the new data. Figure out ways we might tweak instruction. And Kent will lead the charge because he knows, as do I, that what matters most is how the children at Lear feel. About school. About each other. About themselves. With Mr Lester at the helm, they're excited to learn. They feel safe to do so because he's created a rich, loving environment. Mr Lester will be at next month's board meeting to report on Hopscotch. Thank you.'

The room applauds, and Gillian wraps her other arm around my neck, hugging me. 'I love you, Dad.'

We embrace as the sound of clapping fills the café-gymatorium. Applause for Brodie. Ruth. Dr Cutler. And me.

'Kent? Are you still there? Did you hear all that?'

Vincent asks, his voice louder than before. 'You're not going anywhere. You're needed here.'

'Thank you,' I say, taking him off speakerphone. 'For going to the meeting. For calling.'

'You've given me so much. Taught me how to love. Be loved. I had to do something. Coming here felt daunting, but I chose growth over security.'

'Stay right there.' Urgency rushes over me. I'm already up, my keys jangling in my fingers. 'I'm on my way.'

There's no parking when I arrive at the school, so I pull into the drop-off loop. A definite no-no, but I'm not planning on staying long. Park, run in, grab my sweet guy, and head out. Just as I remove the keys from the ignition, there's a gentle tapping. I lower the passenger window to Vincent's handsome face, wearing a giant grin.

'Can I get a lift?'

It's warm for March. I roll down all the windows, press play on the stereo, turn the volume up as loud as possible, and hop out and rush over to him.

The magical twinkling synths of 'Everywhere' join the stars rising to dot the sky, and when Christine McVie's voice, layered with harmonies, joins the music, I gather Vincent up in my arms and kiss his neck. As my beard contacts his skin, he instinctively leans in for a kiss. Our mouths meet, and standing in front of Lear Elementary, with Fleetwood Mac blaring, kissing the man I love, my heart fills with so much joy my body almost levitates.

'Can I have this dance?'

'Kent . . .' Vincent juts his chin out. 'I don't dance.'

'Even with me?' My lips kiss his chin, and his beautiful

smile appears, cracking my soul wide open. The soft flutter of his eyelashes accompanies a gentle nod, and holding him this way, under the stars, I long to stay this close to Vincent Manda forever.

My hands migrate to his waist, and we sway gently to the music. As my head bops to the beat, I examine him. His face. His eyes. Those eyelashes. 'How did I get so lucky?'

'You deserve a little luck, Mr Lester.' I tip my forehead on his, close my eyes, and take him in. His smell. His warmth. His energy. All of him.

'You know, this isn't from *Rumours*,' Vincent says, his eyelashes brushing my cheek.

'I know. But I figured you might allow it. This once.'

'For you. This one time.'

He kisses me again – deeper this time. I'm grateful for the mint I popped on my way over, and the glittery ethereal sounds return. When the voices begin emulating a synthesizer, or maybe the synthesizer copies the voices, Vincent grabs my waist, pulls me close, and pauses the kiss. 'You're the perfect distraction, Mr Lester.'

'Happy to help.' My body vibrates with love for this glorious man as we sway and share a tender kiss under the moonlit sky.

Bonus Epilogue

Kent

Vincent's Move-In Day

'Is that the last one?'

Vincent stands with a small box, surrounded by others in the foyer of my condo. Ruth had offered her truck, but there wasn't much left to move after Vincent pared down his belongings. We made two trips with our cars and spent some time tidying up, but the cleaning crew will finish the rest this weekend.

I'm looking forward to ordering pizza and enjoying a long, hot shower.

'That's it,' Vincent says, placing the box on the island and turning on the sink to wash his hands. 'Part of me wants to stay up all night and unpack, so it's all done before Lia comes tomorrow.'

'Really?' I open the bathroom door, and Sweetums scurries out, immediately investigating the sea of boxes. 'She won't care. We can tell her it's a fort and let her climb on them. It could be fun.'

'No, for me.' He dries his hands with a paper towel. 'I don't like this.' He gestures to the boxes – no more than ten in total. 'It makes me feel . . . unsettled.'

I wrap my arms around him from behind, inhaling the sweetness of his neck. 'Smoothie, if you want to do that, I'll help. Whatever makes you most comfortable.'

Vincent sighs deeply, grasping onto my arms. 'I'll be okay. Lia will be here tomorrow, and then we have all day Sunday. You'll help, right?'

'Absolutely.' I kiss his cheek, the ripeness of his skin mingling with the warmth of the day and the scent of moving. 'Now, why don't you go take a shower, and I'll order dinner?'

'Can we get a salad too?'

'Yes, my love. Pizza and salad. Now, go.'

When I return with dinner from the delivery driver downstairs, I hear the shower running and 'Songbird' blasting from the bathroom. After leaving the takeout in the kitchen, I head in to investigate.

Standing in the bathroom doorway, I study Vincent. He's in the shower, standing outside the cascade of water, scrubbing. I can't tell if he's caught in a loop, but when he catches me watching him, he flashes a genuine smile, and I'm confident he's okay.

'Be out in a minute.' Vincent's hands glide down his lower back. He's turned, giving me a view of his beautiful butt. 'Why don't you hop in after me?'

'Is your mood . . .'

'Peak.' He cranes his neck and flashes his teeth. 'Something about moving. The shower. Being here. I'm all . . .'

'Worked up,' I say with a smile.

'Exactly.'

I tug my shirt over my neck and grab my toothbrush. Juggling the brush in one hand, I struggle to unbutton my pants with the other, finally managing to shimmy out of them.

Vincent laughs in the shower, watching me trip and almost fall. The urgency of his words prods me to hurry. When I'm naked with a clean mouth, sensing he's almost finished, I hop in. In the cramped shower, we're squeezed tightly together, barely able to move.

'Hey,' he says. Without taking my eyes off him, I can feel his cock poking against my thigh.

'Hey.'

Vincent leans over and kisses me softly. 'Don't take too long.'

I'm not sure I've ever washed so quickly, but I'm careful to clean well. If I want Vincent to enjoy this truly, I need to be spotless.

Toweling off, I enter our bedroom, and he's on the floor, kneeling near the foot of the bed.

'Why are you on the . . .'

'Sit.' Vincent pats the bed.

I do as I'm told, resting on the comforter, legs spread, my cock already springing to life at the thought of what he might be planning.

'Let me be your good boy,' he says, 'and you enjoy the view.'

He's positioned me directly across from the floor-length mirror. With his knees spread, his ass sways in the reflection, and I'm able to glimpse his beautiful hole.

'Fuck, smoothie, you're ready for me.'

'It was all the lugging.'

'Noted,' I say, followed by a quick gasp as he swallows me down. 'We should move you into my place more often.'

I lower my voice because I know the timbre drives Vincent wild. 'Now, take me like a good boy.'

Vincent pulls off and runs his tongue up and down my shaft, licking. 'I want to suck you dry. Is that okay?'

'Um, yeah. More than okay.'

He swallows me again, his tongue working the tip and doing that swirling he knows makes my thighs shudder. 'Good boy.' My hands grip the bed. 'Good boy. Just like that.'

He cups my balls, adding slight pressure right underneath.

'Vincent, if you keep doing that, I'm going to come quickly,' I warn.

He pulls off, saliva dripping from his lips. 'That's fine.' He wiggles his ass. 'As long as you're not too tired for this.'

'Never.' My eyes are glued to his plump rump shaking as he taunts me.

'I want to, can I, while I . . .' I stammer, the sudden need to taste him overwhelming me. Vincent doesn't move. He lets me have my way. Such a fucking good boy.

I'm up. Moving behind him, pushing him against the bed, spreading him wide, burying my beard between his cheeks.

'Fuck, Kent.' His body juts forward at the contact, but there's nowhere for him to escape, and he quickly pushes back. He tastes sweet. Fresh. Raw. All mine. Sometimes, I simply need to devour him from the inside while I come.

'Fuck, Kent. You're going to make me come if you keep at this.'

I want to tell him he's a good boy and I love him more than I ever thought possible. The need tickles my throat, but my mouth is preoccupied, so I flick my tongue and swirl it deeper, eliciting moans from Vincent's sweet lips. There we go. My Vincent. His ass twitches, and I reach under to take over stroking him. He's so close, and I have to work hard to jerk him while eating him out, but he's worth every ounce of effort.

'Right there.' Vincent pushes back.

'Right there. Right there. You're . . . Oh fuck, Kent.'

His hole contracts around my tongue as he shoots warm cum into my palm. I keep stroking him but do my best to catch as much as possible – no sense wasting it.

When Vincent's body stills, I pull my tongue out. 'Such a good boy for me.'

Vincent lays his head on the bed and sighs with the most decadent sound – pure pleasure. 'Give me just a minute,' he says in a tired, soft tone.

'Smoothie, don't move. Just let me . . .'

I take his cum, still warm, and slather it on my cock.

'This view. It's not going to take me long.' My free hand slaps his ass with a *thwack*, and I pull at the cheek, exposing his hole. My orgasm crawls up, provoked by the view and the slippery help of his cum.

'Can I . . .' I eke out, the gratification creeping up, slowly overtaking my body.

'Cover me in it.'

And that's it. Vincent's voice. Permission. I move forward, my cock right at the crack of his ass, and shoot long ropes. The first eruption lands close to his shoulder blades with the subsequent ones covering his lower back. The moment my dick touches his backside, I'm consumed by a wave of pleasure, heightened by the electric sensation of our skin meeting.

'Be a good boy and don't move,' I say as I stand. 'I'll get you a warm washcloth.'

Lying in bed, the smell of orange and honey mingles with the sharp sweetness of sex. Vincent's head rests on my torso, and with each exhale from his nose, the hair on my chest blows. If my entire body could smile, it would be ready for a school picture right now.

'Thank you,' I say.

'For what?'

'For being you.' My hand caresses Vincent's smooth head, and he lets out a half-laugh. I know it will take time for him to fully embrace his unique perfection, but I will never stop reminding him.

He nuzzles into me, making tiny noises as he gets comfortable.

'Now, get some sleep, my sweet,' I say. 'Lia will be here bright and early.'

He raises his head, kisses me softly on the lips, and whispers, 'I can't wait. I love you.'

'I love you, too.'

In the room's stillness, we lie motionless, anticipating sleep. Just as I'm about to doze off, I notice Sweetums curling up at my feet, completing our cozy family circle. With a feeling of utter contentment, I finally surrender to slumber.

*

'Poppy! Did you get books from the library?'

One of my favorite parts of being a principal is having access to the school library. On Fridays, when I know it's 'Poppy Saturday' with Lia, our thoughtful librarian Patti loads me up with her favorite picture books. In the summer, Patti lets me take whatever I like for however long I want.

Since we're taking it easy after yesterday's move, we decided to have a chill day here. I picked Lia up after breakfast and let Vincent take a shower before bringing my granddaughter into what is now our home. She seems unfazed by the boxes full of Vincent's belongings. Instead, her attention is on the bag of picture books on the coffee table.

'I have so many books for my sweet girl.' I point toward the bag bursting with books, and Lia runs over and begins flipping through them.

'A unicorn book! Oh, this one is a LEGO princess book . . . Vincent!' Lia shouts toward the living room.

'What's this about a LEGO unicorn?' Vincent saunters into the room, his gray joggers low on his hips. A hint of his taut stomach peeks through as he lifts his arms for a hug from Lia.

Lia bolts over, leaps, and he's holding her. With some age-appropriate conversations, she understands Vincent loves her but needs space and likes to be spotless. Naturally, she simply wants Vincent to be happy. After a quick squeeze around his neck, she tells him, 'Okay, you can go wash up now.'

Vincent chuckles, kisses her cheek, sets her down, and heads for the kitchen sink.

'Poppy got books. There's a unicorn one and a LEGO one, but it's not a unicorn LEGO book,' Lia says, following Vincent like a lost puppy.

I thought Vincent's novelty would wear off for Lia after some time, but much like her adoration for anything pink, purple, or sparkly, it hasn't. She stands next to him as he scrubs and stares up at him, wearing a huge grin.

'Oh, got it,' Vincent says, drying his hands on a paper towel. 'Well, which should we read first?'

Lia's face contorts with thought as she studies his face. I know nothing tops unicorns for her, but she also knows how Vincent feels about LEGO.

'How about Poppy reads me the unicorn book first, and then you can read me the LEGO one? It has a princess in it. Are you okay with that?'

'Of course. I love princesses.' He boops her nose.

'I thought you might,' she says, skipping to the couch.

While I read the book about the unicorn who wants to be a horse (and the horse that wants to be a unicorn), Lia snuggles into my side. Her hand rests on my stomach, and she keeps her gaze glued to the pages as we read. When the book ends, she crawls up and kisses my cheek. 'Scratchy.'

'Really?' I ask. 'I thought it was soft.' I tug at my beard, and the silky hairs are smooth on my fingers.

'It's perfect,' Vincent says with a wink, and my heart trips.

'Now, the LEGO book!' Lia scoots over and snuggles into Vincent. She keeps her hands on his sweatshirt, and he appears fine with her so close as he reads about the LEGO princess rescuing her animal friends from the evil LEGO witch.

'That was a good book. LEGO and a princess.' She stares up at him. 'It's like they wrote that book for us.'

Lia bats her eyelashes, and Vincent smiles. She is beyond smitten with him, and watching her weasel her way into his heart warms mine.

'Now, sweetie,' I say, 'I was thinking we could watch a movie in the bedroom and leave Vincent to work on his new LEGO build.'

'What is it?' Lia's over at the table, hands behind her back, investigating.

'It's a big city,' he says, joining her.

'But you built Paris.'

'Yes, this is London.'

'Oh . . .' Lia's eyes bulge at Big Ben, already soaring toward the ceiling.

'But what happened to Paris?'

'I took it apart. Most of these pieces,' Vincent picks up a bowl full of tan bricks, 'are from Paris.'

'So you recycled it?'

'Yeah, I guess you could say that.'

'Lia, let's give Vincent some time alone. We'll check back later, and you can see what he's done.'

'But I want to help.'

Vincent has come a long way since the first time he showed me Paris, but allowing my four-year-old granddaughter to help him build the sweeping London skyline might push things too far.

'Do you know how you could help me?' Vincent kneels, making eye contact.

'How?'

'On construction sites, there's someone called a

foreperson. They don't do any of the building, but they sit and watch and make sure everything goes smoothly.' He pulls out a chair, scooting it away from the table and turning it toward the table. 'Would you like to be my foreperson?'

'Yes!' She plops down, and I fetch a notebook and some crayons for her.

'Why don't you draw what you see?' I suggest. 'It might help Vincent see it from your perspective.'

'Oh, smart.' She adds, 'He might need my drawing to help.'

'I'll make us some sandwiches,' I say.

'No. We need hamburgers and ice cream,' Lia says. 'Vincent and I are okay if you go get them.'

Laughter pours out of me because she truly is precious. I catch Vincent's gaze, and he nods.

'Yes, we'll be fine. I've got my foreperson to supervise me.'

Lia smiles and starts drawing. Comfortable Vincent can handle her in this state, I head to the bedroom to fold some laundry.

When I return, Vincent and Lia are exactly how I left them. He's added to the Tower Bridge, and she's now coloring the sketch she drew.

'Who's hungry?' I shout from the kitchen island. 'Who's ready for hamburgers?'

'Wash up, Vincent,' Lia says.

'Thank you!' he says, heading for the sink. 'My foreperson is keeping me in line.'

After we eat, Lia supervises Vincent for another hour, taking a break for a story from me about a girl learning to ride a bicycle. When we reach the end, her yawning cues me.

'Sweetie, do you want to take a nap? I can lie with you if you like.'

'But how will Vincent work without a foreperson?'

'I'll manage,' he says, picking her up for a hug. 'You're a fantastic helper.'

'You did a good job,' Lia tells him. She kisses his chin, and my chest fills with warmth and tenderness, touched by her sweet gesture.

'Come, sweetheart.' I put my hands out, but she's not budging from Vincent's grasp.

'Poppy, now that Vincent lives here, will you get married? Mommy says you could get married if you want.'

Vincent coughs, but he recovers quickly, saying, 'Lia, we could. And who knows, we might someday.'

'But for now . . .' I put my arm around Vincent, turning the three of us into a little huddle. 'We're happy Vincent moved in. Sometimes, people who love each other get married. But sometimes, they don't. It doesn't mean they don't love each other any less.' I rest my head on Vincent's shoulder, and Lia leans over and snuggles in. 'We're a family. Vincent. Me. You and your mommy and daddy.'

'And Sweetums,' she whispers into my beard.

'Yes, even Sweetums,' Vincent says. 'Where is the monster?'

'Probably under the bed.' I pull Lia over and set her on the floor, and Vincent washes his hands. 'He gets a little overwhelmed with . . .' I nod toward Lia, already heading into the bedroom on a kitty search and rescue mission.

'I totally understand.' Vincent takes a paper towel and dries his hands. 'But I'm doing better and better.'

'You are.' I pull him close. He smells like cucumber and mint, and I'm tempted to nibble his cheek. 'I'm glad you're here. Permanently.'

'Me too.' He kisses my cheek, and with his lips on my skin, all his things here, Lia in the next room, everything feels right.

Lia's scream interrupts the moment. 'Found him!'

'Let's go rescue Sweetums,' Vincent says.

He takes my hand, and we head into the bedroom to join the rest of our family.

Epilogue

Vincent

Six Months Later

'Nice job, builders.'

A swarm of second graders shove the last of the straws into plastic tubs on each table and race for the line by the door. They know better than to push, but they each want to be as close to the front as possible. Kent says there's no award for being first, but they don't seem to understand.

'Next week, we're going to build bridges out of snap cubes that span from one table to another. Be thinking about how that might look,' I explain as their teacher arrives at the door to retrieve them.

I have ten minutes to reset for the next group and my special helper scoots across the floor, retrieving the few rogue pieces, and swiftly returning them to their bins.

'Thank you, Brodie.' I peek at him under one of the tables. He's stretched out, his entire front splayed on the tile floor, but he doesn't seem to mind.

'Got it!' his raspy voice calls and he holds up a dust-covered white straw.

Today's activity, building towers. Using only simple plastic straws, groups of students collaborated to build a structure. To add a little competitiveness to the mix, I asked them to see who could build the tallest tower.

'Brodie, I'm not sure what I'd do without you.' Certainly not lie on the filthy floor and retrieve them myself.

Brodie's an amazing helper. He's quiet, listens, and waits to jump in with any task. He's like one of those ball boys at tennis matches, eagerly standing by to jump into action. Mrs Barton, Brodie's special education teacher, designed a new plan for him. I'm not exactly sure of the details, but he now earns small chunks of time with both Theo and me for staying on task. It's win-win, really.

'Well, buddy, it's almost time for you to go back.' And like clockwork, Theo appears.

'Mr Manda,' Theo says with a nod.

'Mr Berenson.'

With no prompting, Brodie jets over, wraps his arms around my waist, and squeezes. Hard. I'm used to it now and breathe through the pressure.

'Come on,' Theo calls and Brodie releases me from his grip and runs to take Theo's hand.

And they're off. I have seven minutes until the next class arrives, and I quickly head to the staff bathroom to scrub down.

Over the summer, in the span of two weeks, Shreya's video game went live, then viral, and one of the big gaming companies snatched it up. She quickly resigned and moved to Silicon Valley to begin her new role as a video-game mogul.

With a sudden opening for a STEM teacher, Kent suggested I consider. After the Hopscotch fiasco, I was ready for a change and, with Kent's support and conditional certification from the state, I applied and got the job. Kent assured me that the committee's decision had nothing to do with the fact that I'm sleeping with the principal. He actually recused himself, which made me more comfortable taking the job. And as a STEM teacher, I report to the district technology director, not Kent, so there's no conflict of interest.

I open the door after drying my hands, and Kent's face greets me. He looks both ways down the empty hallway and pushes me back inside the bathroom.

His lips gently press against mine, sending a shiver down my spine. The cool spearmint from the toothpaste and toothbrush he now keeps in his office greets me and I immediately grab his waist and pull him close.

'How?' I mutter into his mouth.

'I know everyone's schedules.' He raises his eyebrows mischievously. 'And I had an inkling you'd be washing up.'

I press my lips against his, savoring the way he always knows the perfect moment for a stolen kiss.

'I should go,' I whisper. My body remains frozen, captivated by the warmth and softness of his beard, making it difficult to leave the surprise moment and go back to my classroom.

'I'll see you at home?' he asks.

'Yes. I'll grab takeout.'

'Say hi to Val for me,' he says and with one last kiss, we head back to finish our days.

Later that evening, snuggled on the sofa, Sweetums takes up most of Kent's lap. I lean on his side and the cat's tail gently taps my thigh, making sure I know he's there. Sweetums and I have come to an understanding. He doesn't smother me, and I don't scream in horror at his existence. My cleaning crew migrated here, and they do a pretty good job of keeping the pet hair to a minimum. Kent also bought me one of those robot vacuums to assist in between visits. I came home one day to find Sweetums riding the contraption like a horse around the living room. I took a video and texted Kent and he suggested we buy Sweetums a cowboy hat. Giddyup!

'Ah, my boys,' Kent murmurs, with his feet up on the coffee table. Between the cat and me, we really are blanketing him.

I snuggle in and, somehow sensing my closeness, Sweetums does the same. What a bugger.

'You know, Ruth was asking me about something today,' Kent says.

'Oh lord. What now?'

'She asked if we'd talked about getting married.'

The words make my chest tight. Marriage? Leave it to Ruth to complicate things.

'Married? Um, I, well, what.' The words fumble out, but make little sense.

'Relax. I'm thrilled with this,' he says, leaning down and kissing the top of my head. 'I've been married. And honestly, I don't need it. I want you. Here with me. And I have that.'

I huddle into his chest, kissing his ratty sweatshirt right where his heart beats.

'But if you wanted to get married, I'd do it,' he says. 'Whatever my handsome boy wants.'

'I want you.' My hand squeezes his. I have no desire to experience the wedding planning chaos Marvin and Olan are faced with.

'Well, you've got me.' His beard rests on my head, the familiar tickle of his whiskers comforting my soul as he squeezes me. 'Forever.'

As we cuddle and kiss, I can't help but smile at the way Sweetums adjusts underneath us. As he shifts his enormous furry body, I realize how many people are eager to accommodate me. It only took me allowing them in. Being here with Kent, and yes, even the cat, safe and cozy, I've found my true home – extra napkins included.

Acknowledgments

To the entire Bookstagram and BookTok communities – your support for my stories has buoyed me in ways I'm not sure I can fully express. Every post, meme, gif, comment, reel, etc., means the world to me. Thank you for lifting my stories and my spirits.

Jay Leigh – Your friendship and counsel continue to be a foundation of support for me. Don't ever stop writing on your phone.

Gillian and Zoe – All my love to you both for your insight and guidance. There'd be no shmekel without you.

A.J. Truman – Thanks for reaching out and pestering me. Teasing you brings me such immense pleasure, and that's how I know we're brothers from another mother.

A.M. Johnson – I will never stop telling you Modest is the Hottest. Thank you for your friendship and support.

Ashley Bennet – Somehow, you and your filthy monsters have become a muse. Thank you for always being sassy with me.

Brian Kennedy – Your stories amaze me. Don't let anyone ever tell you tall and handsome aren't a winning combination.

Clio Evans and Max Walker – Giddyup, friends! I love you both.

Kayla Grosse – I adore you, your horse . . . and maybe the bird isn't all that bad.

To all my author friends, you continue to inspire and amaze me.

Mel Saavedra – Your early and continued belief in my work has been nothing short of monumental. I'm not sure I can ever express what your early faith in me did for my self-confidence. You are such a damn boss. I'm in awe of you.

Kirt Graves, Mark Sanderlin, and Evan Parker – I will never stop thanking you all for the voices you've given my guys.

Emily L. – You keep me in line in the best ways possible. Thank you for all you do.

Erika – I always dreamed of having a therapist who 'got me,' and the universe finally brought us together. I'll never stop being grateful for you.

Karen (both of you!), Emily, Jillian, Deedee, Maggie, Nate, Sarah, Susan, Patti, Brandon, Jeremy, Ron, Derek, and all my friends – Your encouragement and faith in me continue to buoy me.

Elise V. – The OG. There are two things I love about you. Your face. (Okay, and your heart.)

Manda Waller – You've given me so much, I had to do it.

Stevie Finnegan – you keep aiming for the stars, and those dang stars don't know who they're up against. You continue to wow me.

Alex Logan and the entire Forever Team – Thank you for helping me bring these stories to a broader audience. You're all the true dream team.

Hannah Smith and the entire Penguin team – Thank you for helping my stories shine worldwide.

Mom – Thank you for always believing in me.

Dave – How does my love for you grow with every passing year? Our love is approaching mighty oak status, and I couldn't be happier about it. Thank you for your support, insight, and the perfect title. I can't wait to dedicate the next book to you.

And last, to you, dear reader, I hope you enjoyed Vincent and Kent's story. I'd be honored if you left a review and shared my guys with the world. Knowing you're enjoying my love stories only multiplies the delight I take in writing them. Stay tuned! There's more love coming soon!

On a station platform, with nothing to read,
and a four-hour train journey stretching ahead of him...

That's where the story began for Penguin founder Allen Lane.
With only 'shabby reprints of shoddy novels' on offer,
he resolved to make better books for readers everywhere.

By the time his train pulled into London, the idea was formed.
He would bring the best writing, in stylish and affordable
formats, to everyone. His books would be sold in bookstores,
stationers and tobacconists, for no more than the price
of a ten-pack of cigarettes.

And on every book would be a Penguin, a bird with a certain
'dignified flippancy', and a friendly invitation to anyone who
wished to spend their time reading.

In 1935, the first ten Penguin paperbacks were published.
Just a year later, three million Penguins had made their
way onto our shelves.

Reading was changed forever.

—

A lot has changed since 1935, including Penguin, but in the
most important ways we're still the same. We still believe that
books and reading are for everyone. And we still believe that
whether you're seeking an afternoon's escape, a vigorous debate
or a soothing bedtime story, all possibilities open with a book.

Whoever you are, whatever you're looking for,
you can find it with Penguin.